"Simone St. James is known for brilliantly mixing thriller elements with supernatural mayhem, and *Murder Road*, her most recent novel, offers readers plenty of both. . . . Fast, chilling, entertaining, unexpectedly touching, and with two broken, memorable characters at its core, this might be St. James's best novel yet."
—*The New York Times Book Review*

"Buckle up for a grisly ride. . . . There's more going on than meets the eye."
—*People*

"St. James's intricate plot skillfully mixes gumshoe detective work with unexpected supernatural chills, not to mention winning characters that easily earn readers' affection. This highly recommended title will thrill fans of St. James's work and earn new ones along the way."
—*Library Journal* (starred review)

"From its nerve-shredding start to its thrilling end, *Murder Road* steers the reader down creepy back roads, past urban legends so vivid you'd swear they were true, and into the marriage of two damaged souls you can't help but root for. Part love story, part campfire tale, it's a trip well worth taking."
—Riley Sager, *New York Times* bestselling author of *Middle of the Night*

ALSO BY SIMONE ST. JAMES

The Haunting of Maddy Clare

An Inquiry Into Love and Death

Silence for the Dead

The Other Side of Midnight

Lost Among the Living

The Broken Girls

The Sun Down Motel

The Book of Cold Cases

Ghost 19

MURDER
ROAD

SIMONE ST. JAMES

BERKLEY | NEW YORK

BERKLEY
An imprint of Penguin Random House LLC
penguinrandomhouse.com

Copyright © 2024 by Simone Seguin
Readers Guide copyright © 2025 by Simone Seguin
Excerpt from *The Sun Down Motel* by Simone St. James copyright © 2020 by
Simone Seguin

BERKLEY and the BERKLEY & B colophon are
registered trademarks of Penguin Random House LLC.

Book design by Elke Sigal

ISBN: 9780593200391

The Library of Congress has cataloged the Berkley hardcover edition of this
book as follows:

Names: St. James, Simone, author.
Title: Murder road / Simone St. James.
Description: New York: Berkley, [2024]
Identifiers: LCCN 2023022573 (print) | LCCN 2023022574 (ebook) |
    ISBN 9780593200384 (hardcover) | ISBN 9780593200407 (ebook)
Subjects: LCGFT: Paranormal fiction. | Thrillers (Fiction) |
    Horror fiction. | Novels.
Classification: LCC PR9199.4.S726 M87 2024 (print) |
    LCC PR9199.4.S726 (ebook) | DDC 813/.6—dc23/eng/20230523
LC record available at https://lccn.loc.gov/2023022573
LC ebook record available at https://lccn.loc.gov/2023022574

Berkley hardcover edition / March 2024
Berkley trade paperback edition / February 2025

Printed in the United States of America
1st Printing

For anyone who was told they're weird because they read too much.
Because you're not, and you don't.

CHAPTER ONE

That July night seemed full of possibility, with the empty highway stretching out before us. I had just woken up from a nap in the passenger seat, my head foggy as I remembered where we were. I took off my flip-flops and pulled my bare legs up, crossing them and running my hands through my hair. The digital clock on the dash said it was two in the morning, and the road didn't look like the same road we'd been on when I fell asleep. I wondered where we were going. There was no way I would fall asleep again.

"We're lost," I said.

Eddie glanced over at me from the driver's seat. "I don't think so. We took a wrong exit, that's all. I'll get us back on the interstate."

I looked out the window at the narrow country road, lined with dark trees, and thought we were definitely lost—but the truth was, I didn't care. I was riding at night in Eddie Carter's Pontiac, which had a front seat like a sofa. It was July of 1995 and I was twenty-six years old. I was here because Eddie and I were on our honeymoon. We had been married just over twenty-four hours.

We were headed for a motel that was a cluster of cabins on the shore of Lake Michigan. We'd budgeted enough money to stay exactly five nights. We planned to swim, play Scrabble, barbecue burger patties on the rusty charcoal grill, drink half-warm beer from a cooler, swim some more, then go to bed.

Repeat five times, and then we'd make our way home to the small apartment we rented together in Ann Arbor, and Eddie would go back to work fixing cars and I'd go to my job at the bowling alley. We'd both go to work every day, then we'd come home and have dinner that was probably one of six kinds of sandwich, and then we'd go to bed. Repeat every day, forever.

I glanced over at Eddie. He was frowning, concentrating on the road. His brown hair had grown out since he left the army, though he still kept it short. He was wearing a light gray T-shirt and worn jeans. He wasn't a huge man, but he was sleekly muscled, and his biceps were hard under the sleeves of his T-shirt, his physical presence at odds with his quiet, studious expression. At twenty-seven he was a year older than me, though he seemed much more mature. As I looked at those biceps, it hit me yet again that I had married a man instead of a boy.

Married. I had to toss the phrases around in my head, trying to get used to them. *I married him. We got married. Eddie married me. I am his wife. We are a married couple.*

The words still felt strange.

"Do you want me to pull the map from the glove box?" I asked him.

"I think I know where we are," Eddie said. "Roughly, at least.

Something about this is familiar. I think we're heading south. There should be a turnoff to get back on the interstate."

"Are you tired?"

The question seemed to amuse him. "No."

Right. He'd slept in all kinds of weird places, at weird times, while he was overseas. I didn't know the details of what he'd done in Iraq—he didn't talk about it much. But I'd seen Eddie say he was going to sleep for exactly one hour, and then do it, as if his brain had a timer. It was one of his mysteries.

I leaned forward and turned on the radio, twisting the dial and watching the needle move along the numbers. Most of the stations around here were off the air at this time of night, and much of the dial was static. I finally found some country music that wavered in and out of existence, like a ghost passing from room to room. "Haunted cowboys," I said as a man's voice warbled patchily into the silence of the car. "Dead a hundred years, and still trying to drink whiskey and find a woman."

Eddie smiled. He was the only person I'd ever met who liked my jokes.

"Don't worry, April," he said, which was a little strange, because I wasn't worried. Or was I?

I looked out the window again. It was pitch-dark out there, not a streetlight or lit window in sight. A three-quarter moon hung low and crisp in the sky. It was the kind of night that wasn't suffocatingly hot, but if you slept with the window open, you'd wake up with clammy skin and damp, chilled sheets. You'd stay tucked in bed until sunrise, when it started to get hot again.

"There's no one out there," I said. "It's like we launched into space."

"Not true." Eddie pointed. "There's someone right there."

Sure enough, through the trees a light glowed. Low at first, then brighter, lighting in a smooth flow. It wasn't the flip of a switch or a flashlight. It took me a moment to place it, but it seemed more like someone turning up a kerosene lamp, making the flame go higher.

Was it inside a house? Or someone outside in the trees? I couldn't tell. I watched the light as we passed it, turning as it shrank behind us. I should have felt comforted, but I wasn't.

"What was that?" I asked as the country music on the radio changed tunes, then wafted out of range again.

"Beats me," Eddie said. "Look, we'll give it another ten minutes. If we don't see a sign, we'll—Oh, Jesus."

I turned back to face front, and I saw what he saw. In the beam of the headlights was a man at the side of the road. A teenager, maybe. He wore a baggy jacket and was walking slowly, his head down. As our headlights hit his back, he didn't turn.

Eddie slowed the car so we didn't pass him, but kept him in our headlight beams. "Drunk, do you think?" he asked me.

I watched the figure take another slow, careful step. He still didn't turn our way, though we must have been the only car to come down this road for a long time. On second look he was small for a man, and I noticed jeans that flared at the bottom.

"I think that's a woman," I said.

"Could be." Eddie kept the car at a crawl, inching behind her. There was something strange about the way she didn't turn, but there was also something pathetic about it. "She could still be drunk," Eddie said.

"Maybe," I said.

4

"She might need help. Should we stop?"

I thought about the light we'd passed behind us, and something cold touched my spine. "I think she needs help."

"All right. Roll down your window."

I cranked the window down as Eddie pulled up beside the figure. He leaned across me as the car slowly rolled, his voice sounding friendly and authoritative. "Hi there. Do you need help?" he called out my window.

For the first time the figure paused and lifted her head. It was a woman with brown hair cut short, exposing her ears and the back of her neck while bangs fell over one eye. Her skin was pale, and I could see a faint spray of freckles across the bridge of her nose.

She stopped walking and turned our way, squaring her shoulders as if she'd just noticed us. She didn't speak.

"Do you need some help?" Eddie asked again. "We can drop you somewhere."

The woman looked at me. I gave her a smile and a wave. I hoped it made her feel better. A lot of people thought I was pretty—they used the word *pretty*, not *beautiful*. I was high school yearbook kind of pretty, not the kind of beautiful that made men crazy. Still, before Eddie I'd been asked out all the time. There's no accounting for taste.

"You can get in," I told the woman. Or girl? It was hard to tell in the dark. "We're nice people, I promise."

The girl had fixed her gaze on me, as if Eddie wasn't there. "I shouldn't," she said. Her voice was soft and low, like she was making an effort.

Of course she was wary. It was the middle of the night. The girl wove in place, and I put my hand on my car door handle, thinking I might get out and help her. Eddie put his hand on my knee, halting me.

I looked at him. He shook his head.

Staying where I was, I turned back to the girl. "We're heading for the Five Pines Resort," I said, giving the name of the cheap motel Eddie and I were going to. "We took a wrong turn off Interstate 75. I'm April and this is Eddie. Eddie Carter. We're married. Just married."

Whether the girl took all of this in or not was anyone's guess. She was still looking at me—as if she'd seen me before, or maybe as if she was memorizing me for later. She was wearing a jacket that was too big for her and fell past her hips, the sleeves too long. It might have been Army green. She pulled it tighter around her and looked down the road behind us.

I followed her gaze, leaning my head out of my window. There was no one else on the road, but I thought I heard a soft sound. Leaves shuffling along the ground. The air was oddly cold. I blinked into the darkness, trying to match a movement to the sound. There were leaves stirring, lifting as if in a breath of wind. And yet there was no wind that I could feel.

"Are you okay?" Eddie asked the girl as I stared at the leaves. "Are you sick?"

The girl kept her gaze fixed on the road. Maybe she was watching the leaves; I couldn't tell. Her voice sounded like it was coming from the other end of a telephone line. "No, I'm not sick."

The leaves settled, and I turned back to her. "What's your name?"

The girl paused again. She still seemed reluctant, but it would be wrong to just drive away and leave her. She was all alone and it was the middle of the night. Where was she going?

I thought I heard the shuffle of leaves again, faint on the road behind us. I was suddenly glad I hadn't gotten out of the car. Stranded girl or not, I felt the urge to leave, to drive as fast as possible. I wanted to get out of here.

The girl's fingers curled into the fabric of her coat, clutching it tighter. She bit her bottom lip briefly, still looking down the road, and then she seemed to come to a decision. "I'll take a ride. Thank you."

She opened the door to the back seat and got in. She moved slowly, like an old lady, and I wondered if she was hurt. She didn't have a bag or even a purse. She leaned into the back seat and briefly closed her eyes, as if she'd been on her feet forever.

"What's your name?" I asked her again as Eddie pulled off the shoulder and onto the road again.

"Rhonda Jean."

"That's a nice name. Where are you going?"

Rhonda Jean seemed to pause, as if thinking about this or changing her first answer. "Coldlake Falls." She closed her eyes again, resting her head against the back of the seat. "It's a few miles ahead."

"I've heard of that place," Eddie said. "I have no idea where, though."

I opened the glove box and pulled out the map, folding and refolding the complicated squares and squinting at it in the darkness. "Is it on the way to the Five Pines Resort?" I asked Eddie.

"No idea, but I'm sure there will be someone there to ask for directions."

"Depends how big a town it is," I said to Eddie, still turning the map in my hands. "It's late. Maybe nothing's open. If we get lucky, we'll find a gas station."

"I don't think it's that small," Eddie said. "There has to be something."

"There's a hospital there," Rhonda Jean said.

Eddie and I both went silent. I felt a trickle of alarm move up my spine.

I looked at the girl in the back seat. She was motionless, her eyes still closed. Her hands clutched her jacket shut.

"Did someone hurt you?" I asked her, my voice low.

Rhonda Jean winced at that, though she didn't open her eyes. "I'm sorry."

In the driver's seat, Eddie's voice was as low and calm as my own. "Do you need a doctor, Rhonda Jean?"

"I don't know." Rhonda Jean's eyes blinked open, and for a second they were unfocused. "I don't think a doctor will help."

I let the map slide from my hands, down to my feet. I kept my gaze on the girl in the back seat. Everything became clear and still in my head. I knew now that this was why she had looked at me at first like she recognized me. It was because she did. We'd never seen each other before, but we recognized each other. Women like us recognized each other all the time.

Two things happened at once. When I thought about it later, I was sure about it. The timing was very clear. Both things happened at the same time, like a switch had been flipped in my life, changing it forever.

The first thing was that I reached into the back seat and touched the edge of Rhonda Jean's jacket. I gently pulled it open. It was unfastened, only wrapped around her like a robe, and her grip was limp now and unresisting.

Inside the jacket, on the front of her shirt, I saw the black wetness of blood.

At the same time, a pair of headlights appeared out the back window, a car on the road a mile behind us, light pinpoints in the dark.

I looked from the back window to Rhonda Jean's face. Her eyes were open, focused now, and she was staring at me.

"I'm sorry," she said again. "He's coming."

CHAPTER TWO

For a second, I just looked at Rhonda Jean's pale face, seeing the pain and exhaustion etched there. Maybe I should have felt surprised. I didn't know. I only knew that I bypassed surprise and felt things I didn't know existed click in my brain at those words.

I'm sorry.

He's coming.

"April?" This was Eddie in the driver's seat. His voice sounded stern, army stern. He knew something was wrong.

"Rhonda Jean is injured," I told him, still turned around in my seat and looking at the girl. "Really bad. Under her coat. She's bleeding everywhere."

Eddie swore, just the one harsh word, and the car sped up. "She said there's a hospital up ahead in Coldlake Falls."

My gaze moved past Rhonda Jean to the back window again.

The headlights were still there. They were getting bigger, as if the car behind us had accelerated. "Eddie, go faster."

"The car behind us?"

"Yes."

We sped up even more, Eddie fast and careful in the pitch dark, looking for the signs for Coldlake Falls. The blood on Rhonda's chest and stomach was moving, soaking thickly into the fabric of her shirt and downward. I could see it staining her jeans.

None of this was real. It shouldn't be real. But I knew it was.

I'd been in the passenger seat of a car once before, begging the driver to go faster. *Please, faster.* A long, long time ago.

"Who is he?" I asked Rhonda Jean.

"I don't know," she said, her voice a rasp.

"How did you get to the side of the road?"

"I walked."

"From where?"

She seemed to fade out a little, then back in again before she answered. "I don't know."

"He found you somewhere?" I asked her. I gestured to her body. "And he did this?"

Rhonda Jean shook her head, but I wasn't sure if that was a response to my question. "It doesn't even hurt," she said. "Is that weird?"

The headlights behind us had receded, then come forward again. As if the car had seen us accelerate and had accelerated to match us. We were already speeding through the black, empty night, but Eddie must have seen what I saw in the rearview mirror, because I heard the Pontiac's engine open more as we went faster.

I reached back and grasped Rhonda Jean's hand. It was ice-cold, slick with blood. "We're taking you to the hospital," I said.

Her expression didn't flicker. "Sure, okay."

"But tell me what happened to you. Stay awake and tell me."

Her hand moved faintly in mine, but I gripped harder and didn't let her go. "He's following us," she whispered, as if someone could overhear. "He knows I'm in this car."

"Who? Who is he?"

"Coldlake Falls," Eddie said from the front seat as a sign flashed past our speeding car. "Five minutes, tops."

Rhonda Jean's hand twitched in mine again, and her chest moved up and down. Breath gasped from her throat, and I realized she was starting to panic. "Calm down, baby," I said to her, the term of endearment springing from my lips out of nowhere. "Just be calm. We're ahead of him. We're getting to the hospital. We're going to win."

She didn't believe me. Part of her wanted to, but she didn't. "I'm not going to make it," she said, gasping.

"You are. It's just a little blood. They'll sew you up, good as new. Hold on and tell me what happened."

But she shook her head. There was something inside her mind, something immense that cast a giant shadow over everything, like a monster in a horror movie.

"Is this real?" she asked.

"It's real, baby," I said. "It's real, and we're going to get through it. Just hold on."

Incredibly, the headlights behind us were gaining on us, their brightness beginning to flood the car. "Jesus, this guy is fast," Eddie said.

The headlights got brighter, brighter. I squinted into them, trying to see the vehicle or the man behind the wheel. All I saw was light and part of a grille—he was in a truck of some kind, high off the ground.

"Eddie," I said.

"I know. The turnoff's up ahead."

Another sign flashed past us—COLDLAKE FALLS—and without dropping speed Eddie took the turn, flying us off the two-lane road. He glanced back at the truck and swore before turning back to the road again. For the first time, he looked shaken, pale. I'd never seen him look like that before.

Still gripping Rhonda Jean's hand, I turned and watched through the back window as the truck—it was some kind of large, dark thing, gleaming like a beetle—sped past the turnoff and into the night. Then it was gone.

Seconds later we were bathed in light again, this time from the streetlights of Coldlake Falls.

He was avoiding the light, I thought. *He let us go because he didn't want to be seen in the light. What did Eddie see?*

I gripped the cold, bloody hand in mine. "We're almost at the hospital, Rhonda Jean. Hang on."

There was no answer. The girl in the back seat had passed out.

The hospital was small, a four-story brown brick building lit with fluorescents beneath a concrete overhang. I ran inside and begged the person at the emergency desk to send someone out as Eddie pulled Rhonda Jean's unconscious body from the car. He picked her up beneath the shoulders and the knees, like Rhett

Butler in *Gone with the Wind*. When the EMTs took Rhonda Jean from him and put her on a stretcher, the front of his T-shirt was smeared with gore.

I was bloody, too. The hand that had gripped Rhonda Jean's was covered in blood, and in my haste I'd smeared it on my olive green shorts and my white tee. The bloody handprints looked like I'd wrestled someone to the ground. I had blood darkening and drying under my fingernails. My flip-flops were still on the floor of the front passenger seat somewhere, and my feet were bare.

Through the glass doors we could see a nurse behind the emergency desk, staring at us. She picked up the large brown handset of her desk phone and started to dial, her gaze never leaving us.

That was when I realized: Eddie and I looked like murderers.

"Shit," Eddie said, looking down at himself. He glanced at the car, which was still running, then looked at me. "April, should we run?"

"What?" The shock must have shown on my face. Not because of what he'd said, but because I was thinking the same thing.

We could get into the Pontiac and drive away as fast as we could. We could floor it. Who would come after us, and how long would it take before they started? How far away could we be by then?

"Forget it," Eddie said, misreading my expression. "Forget I said anything."

"It's fine," I said, but my mind was ticking over. We could drive farther up the peninsula, then double back down to Ann Arbor. We could be home by the time the sun was up. No one here knew our names. We'd have to clean the car, or better yet, get rid of it altogether.

That would be wrong, I told myself. Because someone had killed that girl, Rhonda Jean. The person in the truck had killed her. I was sure of it.

But all my panicked body knew was that the killer wasn't me.

I looked at Eddie again. He was watching me, his gaze intent, and I had no idea what he was thinking. I opened my mouth, but I didn't know what I was going to say.

It didn't matter, because it was already too late. The police were pulling in.

CHAPTER THREE

I never thought I'd get married. My childhood was a 1970s nightmare, filled with dark, garish colors and deep shadows, like *Rosemary's Baby*. Once I got out of that childhood, I never looked back. By twelve, I was basically an adult, looking out for my mother and me. At fifteen I learned to wear the same hairstyles and the same makeup that all the other girls wore. I blended in, except for the fact that I knew how to pack everything I owned in a single bag within forty-five minutes, knew how to get to the bus station in the middle of the night if I had to, knew how to introduce myself under a new name.

At eighteen, I was alone.

Even without Mom, I still moved around, never staying long enough in one place to be too noticeable. South Carolina, Illinois, Michigan. I got jobs waiting tables and answering phones. Restaurant managers had no problem putting me at the hostess stand, because I had the kind of face that was perfect for it. Pretty, pleasant, mostly forgettable. I dated—a pretty girl my age was expected to date or she would attract attention—but I never let anyone get too close. I wasn't the clingy girlfriend, asking whether we were serious, asking whether he wanted me to move in. There were a million of me in America. I doubted even the boys I dated remembered me after a while.

All I wanted was to survive. I certainly never dreamed of finding a husband or children, of settling down in a house somewhere. I wanted to be left alone, expected it.

In Ann Arbor, I got a job at a bowling alley, serving half-cold hamburgers and stale chips at the snack bar. I moved in with roommates I found in the classifieds, in an old house that was renting for next to nothing. The place smelled like pot smoke, Doritos, and beer, and the local pizza place knew our order by heart. Roommates rotated through, accompanied by various boyfriends, girlfriends, and other hangers-on. The TV was almost always on, with someone sitting in front of it. Late-night movies, *Sesame Street*, reruns of *The Rockford Files*, reruns of *Knight Rider*, *Baywatch*, *The X-Files*, and more recently, the O. J. Simpson trial in all of its endless droning—whatever was on, someone was watching, half paying attention. The house had a dissociated lack of caring, a complete ennui, that suited me perfectly. No one ever asked me questions or wanted to hang out.

One Saturday in February, my roommates were gone and I had the house to myself. Dressing in my bedroom, I realized I'd left my favorite T-shirt in the dryer, two stories down in the basement. Wearing only jeans and a navy blue lace bra, I walked out of my bedroom into the hallway.

There was a man standing there—young, muscled, fit enough to tackle me. I was too startled to notice that instead of attacking he stood frozen, staring as I came out in my bra, horrified. I screamed. The strange man cried out: "Sorry!" and ran down the stairs.

That was how I met Eddie Carter.

When I had recovered and put on a sweatshirt, I found him in the kitchen, looking miserable. He was a friend of one of my roommates—Greg, or maybe Gary. Eddie had just come back from Iraq, and Greg or Gary told him to come over, to just walk in, because Greg or Gary would be home. Instead, there was no one home but me in my bra, and Eddie was really, really sorry about it.

We talked for half an hour, standing there in the kitchen. When it was clear he wasn't a creep, he asked me out. I said yes, but I thought: *He's way too nice. There's no way I'll sleep with him.*

That was February. Now it was July, and we were married.

I looked at my husband's face in the lights of the solo police car that pulled into the parking lot, the red and blue flickering over Eddie's features. By Eddie's own admission, he'd never had much luck with women, which amazed me. He had a nice jaw and great cheekbones and gray-blue eyes with dark lashes. His hair was brown and usually tousled, he had to shave every morning or get scruff on his cheeks, and the army had given him a body I never, ever got tired of. He didn't talk much, an attribute I came to realize was because he was painfully shy. The longer I'd dated him, the more I'd realized that Eddie was the world's best-kept secret, manwise. I never had to fight anyone for him. It was inexplicable, refreshing, and terrifying.

His expression had gone carefully blank as a uniformed policeman got out of the car. Eddie glanced down at his T-shirt, then at me.

"April," he said.

"I know," I replied. "What can we do?"

Eddie's gaze moved to the approaching policeman. I couldn't quite read what was behind his eyes—I was still learning all of Eddie's expressions—but he seemed to be turning thoughts in his head. Then he looked at me again, and something seemed to register. "Your feet."

Before I could say anything about my bare feet, he reached past the open passenger door, looking for my flip-flops.

"Hey," came the policeman's voice, alarmed.

"Eddie, be careful," I said.

The muscles of Eddie's back tensed, and then he unfolded himself back out of the car, a flip-flop in each hand. He dropped them on the pavement next to my feet with a slap. He held my hand to help me keep balanced as I slid my feet into them.

"Don't tell him about the truck," he said, his voice low so that only I could hear.

"Why not?" I whispered.

"Just don't."

What did that mean? I hid my confusion by looking down as I scrunched the thong of each flip-flop between my toes. Then I looked up.

The policeman was alone. He was about thirty, with light brown skin and dark brown eyes. Tall and lean, with a gold wedding ring on his left hand. The night shift patrol guy, summoned by the ER nurse.

"Hi there," he said, pausing a few feet from us. His feet were spread slightly, and one hand was on his belt, a pose that was anything but casual. "I hear you brought a young lady to the hospital."

"Yes, we did," I said.

The policeman looked at me with my bloodstains, then Eddie with his bloodstains and army bulk. He looked at our car, parked haphazardly behind us, the engine running, the back door still gaping open where Eddie had dragged out Rhonda Jean. There was blood smeared on the inside of the door.

There was a second in which the policeman obviously didn't know what to do. This close to the lake and all of the vacationers, I imagined his training had mostly to do with drunk kids, summer break-ins, and loud parties that ran too late. It was doubtful he'd come across a stabbed girl and her two bloody rescuers before. Still, the uncertainty lasted only briefly before he said in a calm voice, "You'll excuse me if I take a simple precaution."

He walked to the driver's side of the car, leaned in, and turned off the car, taking the keys and pocketing them. Then he came back around the car to us.

He pulled a notebook from his pocket and flipped it open, taking out a pen. "What are your names?" he asked, still keeping his distance.

"Eddie Carter," Eddie said. "This is my wife, April."

"Delray," I said as the policeman wrote in his notepad. "My name is actually April Delray. I haven't had time to change it yet."

The policeman looked at my wedding ring, then up at me, questioning.

"We're just married," I said into the silence.

"We were on our way to the Five Pines Resort for our honeymoon," Eddie added.

"Your honeymoon, huh?" the policeman said. He made another note, writing carefully. "You said it's called Five Pines?"

"Yes," Eddie said.

The policeman wrote that down. "Okay. My name is Officer Syed. Maybe we can talk inside?" He gestured behind him to the hospital.

He was still nervous. He was hiding it well, but his stance was tense, and the notebook was gripped too hard in his hand. He was a lone patrolman with no partner, faced with two people who might be murderers, and one of those people was very big and strong.

Assert your authority, I wanted to tell him. *Act like you are already in control. That's how you dominate someone bigger than you.*

Instead, I smiled at him and said, "Sure, Officer. Lead the way."

The look he gave me was wary and surprised at the same time. "After you," he said.

Eddie and I walked into the hospital, where Officer Syed directed us down a hallway, away from the ER. We saw no one except the duty nurse and one orderly, both of whom stared at us without bothering to hide it. This was a small hospital in a small town at three in the morning, and except for Rhonda Jean, we were the only ones here.

Officer Syed led us to a room with a sofa, a TV, and two chairs—a staff break room. He directed us to the sofa and sat in one of the chairs.

"Do you have some ID?" he asked politely, pulling out his notebook again.

We handed our driver's licenses over, and then I sat with my hands in my lap. I tried not to look down too often, so I wouldn't keep staring at the blood.

"Ann Arbor," the officer said when he had taken our address down. "That's a ways from here."

"Yes," Eddie said. "I told you, we're on our honeymoon."

"Have you ever been to Coldlake Falls before?"

"No."

"Never picked up hitchhikers around here?"

I snapped my gaze to the officer, but he wasn't looking at me. He was looking at Eddie.

"Hitchhikers?" Eddie asked, bemused. "No, we don't pick up hitchhikers."

"Never?" the officer asked.

"Never."

"If you haven't been to Coldlake Falls before, what brings you here for your honeymoon? As opposed to, say, anywhere else?"

Eddie glanced at me. Officer Syed followed his gaze, as if remembering I was in the room.

"There was an ad in the local paper," I said as both men stared at me. "In the travel section. For the Five Pines Resort. We thought it looked nice."

"Was that girl a hitchhiker?" Eddie asked Officer Syed.

The officer frowned at him. "What?"

"That girl. Rhonda Jean."

"Is that her name?"

"So she said."

Now Officer Syed was staring at Eddie again as if he'd said something wrong. "I don't know if she was a hitchhiker. Was she hitchhiking when you found her?"

"I don't know. She was standing by the side of the road."

"What road?"

"I don't know the name of it. The two-lane road that leads off the interstate."

Officer Syed blinked at Eddie calmly. "She was standing there in the middle of the night as you drove down the road."

"Yes," Eddie said.

"On your way to the Five Pines Resort."

"Yes."

There was a heavy silence as Officer Syed rubbed the side of his nose and looked down at his notebook again. He was not in charge of this situation. It felt like something bad was about to happen. Like something bad was already happening. Which, of course, it was.

"Okay," Officer Syed said at last, picking up his pen. "I think we should start from the beginning."

There was a brief knock on the break room door, and then it opened. Two men came in. One was wearing a brown suit that was grievously rumpled. The other, oddly, was wearing a navy blue warm-up suit with white stripes down the sides. It zipped up to his chin.

The warm-up suit man was obviously in charge, because he spoke first. "Officer Syed, we appreciate your help," he said. "We'll take it from here."

Officer Syed looked startled, but he stayed in his chair. "Excuse me?"

"State police," the one in the rumpled suit said to Eddie and me. He pulled a badge from his pocket and showed it to us, then turned to the officer. "We've been called in to take this over. You're no longer needed."

"I'll have to talk to my supervisor," Officer Syed said, still planted in his seat. "I'm not authorized to leave this scene."

They argued back and forth, but the man in the warm-up suit ignored them. He looked at Eddie as the other two talked past his shoulder. And then he looked at me.

He was fiftyish, maybe. It was hard to tell. His face was unlined but his hair was salt and pepper, cut short to his scalp. His eyes were dark blue. His gaze fixed on me, taking in my bloody clothes, my flip-flops, my messy blond hair. His stare wasn't sexual, but I felt exposed anyway, and my gut gave a familiar squeeze as I felt spiky sweat on the back of my neck.

Fight or flight, they called it. An old, dark human instinct. Mine was particularly honed.

Beware of this one. Get away if you can.

Officer Syed had risen from his chair and was reluctantly moving toward the door. His presence hadn't been particularly comforting, but compared to these two men, I realized he'd been relatively harmless. I risked a glance at Eddie and saw that he was staring at the man in the warm-up suit while the man stared at me. Eddie's eyes were hard.

Finally, Officer Syed was gone, the door closing behind him. The room went quiet. I wondered if I should take Eddie's hand, next to me on the sofa. I wondered if that would be a good move or a bad one.

Neither man had yet given us his name, I realized.

"Is there a problem?" Eddie finally asked, his voice calm.

"Sure, there's a problem," the man in the warm-up suit said. "That girl in the ER just died. She had stab wounds on her chest and stomach. As of now, we have a murder case."

CHAPTER FOUR

My name," the man in the warm-up suit said as he sat in Officer Syed's vacated chair, "is Detective Quentin. This is Detective Beam."

I was making quick calculations. Two detectives had appeared in the backwoods of Michigan at three o'clock in the morning. And fast, too. Rhonda Jean must have died only minutes ago.

"I didn't see your badge, sir," I said to Quentin, my tone polite.

"True, you didn't," Quentin said as Beam, chairless, faded into the background and leaned against the wall. Beam, at least, looked like a man who had been roused from bed in the middle of the night and had put on whatever had been folded over the back of the nearest chair in the dark. Quentin didn't even look tired.

"Do state police have detectives?" I asked, polite again.

Quentin didn't blink. "What would you know, young woman, about the structural and hierarchical nature of the state police?"

I narrowed my eyes, squinting at him. "Nothing, I guess."

"I see. And if I ran your name in my files, miss, what might I find?"

"Stop interrogating my wife," Eddie broke in.

"Nothing," I said, replying to Detective Quentin. It was true—he'd find nothing. My mother had made sure of it, and so had I.

"Hey," Eddie said, leaning forward. He was getting angry. He angled himself so his army bulk was perfectly clear. "If you have a question, Detective, just ask it."

Quentin turned his dark blue eyes to my husband, as if noticing him for the first time. He took in every detail about Eddie in silence, and then he said, "You're obviously military. Which branch?"

"Army," Eddie said.

"You served in Iraq?"

"Yes. Is that your question?"

"No, it is not. There is no knife in your car. Where is it? Did you throw it out the window?"

I could hear my mother's advice in my head. *Don't talk. Get a lawyer.* It didn't matter that we were innocent—in fact, that made it even more important.

But Eddie and I couldn't afford a lawyer, even if we knew one in this town. There was no chance we could get high-quality legal representation at three o'clock in the morning with no money to pay the bill.

"I don't know where the knife is, because my wife and I didn't murder that girl," Eddie said, unfazed by Quentin's question. "We found her at the side of the road and brought her to the hospital. Can we go now?"

Detective Quentin just stared at him with those uncanny eyes.

Behind him, Detective Beam was motionless, watching and listening. He only glanced briefly at Eddie and me. Then his gaze went back to Quentin and stayed there, fixed and blank.

"You cannot leave town," Quentin said slowly, as if he was just now making a decision. "Not yet. We have some things to sort out here. We want to question you in daylight and have you show us where you picked this young girl up. Was it on Atticus Line that you found her?"

"What?" Eddie said.

"Atticus Line. The road."

"I have no idea what road it was. We were lost."

"I see," Quentin said calmly. "These are the things we're going to get to the bottom of, Mr. Carter. I'm going to have officers drive you to a place nearby where you can get a few hours' rest. I'm afraid we're obliged to keep your car for now."

He was polite now, because he wanted us to do something. He wanted minimal argument.

We had no choice. I could see it, and so could Eddie.

"Fine, then," Eddie said, speaking for both of us. "We'll go."

We were driven in a squad car to a neighborhood in the dark center of town. We were told that the house we pulled up to was a local bed-and-breakfast, and that we could have a room. We were given our suitcases from Eddie's car. By then I was too exhausted to ask many questions.

The woman who came to the door was somewhere in her forties, with brownish-blond hair in a short haircut and glasses that took up most of her face.

"This is stupid," she said without preamble to the officers who dropped us off. "You all can't keep them yourself? They could be murderers."

"Detective Quentin's orders, Rose. Right now they're just witnesses," one of the cops replied, as if Eddie and I weren't standing there.

Rose looked at our bloody clothes. "Sure. Witnesses. I get a call from Detective Quentin at three in the morning about witnesses." She pointed behind her to a doorway off her dark, overdecorated living room. "Your bedroom's in there. Bathroom is down the hall. Don't get blood on my linens or I'll bill you for it."

"They'll get picked up at seven," one of the cops said. "In the meantime, there'll be a squad car keeping watch outside." He was saying this for our information as much as for hers. The message: Don't run.

"A squad car with one of you sleeping in it, more like," Rose said dismissively. "Like I wasn't married to a policeman for ten years."

Their bickering was giving me a headache. I picked up my suitcase and walked to the bedroom Rose had directed us to, Eddie following.

The bedroom was lined with shelves filled with decorations: figurines, dolls, pots of fabric flowers, doilies, china rabbits and cats. The curtains on the single window were sky blue and puffy, the bedding sky blue to match. The comforter was quilted with a fringe like the hem of a prom dress, and the throw pillows were covered in white lace. Above the headboard hung a gilt-framed photo of Princess Diana wearing a formal white dress, a crown placed in her hair.

Normally, Eddie and I would make jokes about a room like this, but not tonight. Within ten silent minutes we were changed, our bloody clothes dropped into a heap in the corner of the room. I got into the ridiculous bed and Eddie got in behind me, his chest against my back and his knees drawn up against the backs of mine. I remembered that we fit like this, that he was becoming achingly familiar to me.

"April," he said softly against the back of my neck when we were settled. "We need to talk."

If we hadn't picked up Rhonda Jean, if we'd continued on, we'd be at the Five Pines right now, drifting off after our first round of official honeymoon sex.

But if we hadn't picked up Rhonda Jean, she would have died by the side of the road. She wouldn't have had anyone to hold her hand, even briefly. She'd be lying abandoned and unknown in the dark, alone. Going cold.

"I suppose we do," I said to Eddie.

I wondered what he would bring up first. The fact that we were in trouble, maybe. The fact that a girl we didn't know was dead. The fact that we hadn't told anyone about the truck that followed us down Atticus Line. The fact that the police had said they were coming to pick us up again at seven o'clock, only a few hours away.

"Thank you for not telling them about the truck," Eddie said.

"Okay. But I don't know why."

He was quiet for a long minute, breathing against my skin. "When we made the turnoff and it came up behind us—when it passed us—I saw something."

His muscles were tense against me, hard as granite. He was holding his body perfectly still.

I remembered that he'd looked back as the truck passed, and when he'd turned back to the road he'd appeared shocked. "Did you see the driver?"

He lay tense and silent for another long beat, and then he let out a breath. "No. I don't really know what I saw. Maybe nothing. You know that I see things sometimes."

I put my hand over his on my waist, stroked the backs of his hard knuckles. "You used to. The doctors say that should go away with time."

"Yeah, they said that. And it hasn't happened in a while."

He didn't seem like he was going to continue, so I repeated, "Eddie. What did you see?"

"A girl." His voice was so quiet that if he wasn't right next to me, his breath against my ear, I wouldn't have heard. "A girl with long hair, in the bed of the truck as it drove away."

"In the truck bed?" I blinked in the darkness. "Was she lying down?"

"She was sitting up. Her hands gripping the side. She was a teenager, maybe. It was hard to tell because she was unclear, fading in and out. It's hard to explain. She was . . ." He cleared his throat. "She was staring at us."

Damn it. My mind raced. They'd prescribed medication for Eddie after his discharge, but he'd run out a long time ago. We'd hoped his problems were over. But a girl sitting in that speeding truck bed—was it possible? If she was real, why did Eddie think she was fading in and out?

"You think you really saw her?" I asked him.

"I don't know."

"Okay." I kept my voice calm. I ran my fingers over his knuckles again. "It was just a shadow. There was no need to tell the police about that. But the truck—"

"I don't want to tell them about the truck."

"The truck was real, Eddie. I saw it."

"So what?" His voice was rough. "We didn't see who was driving. We didn't see a make and model. We didn't see a license plate. There's nothing to tell."

"It was chasing us."

"Was it?"

I was quiet. The truck behind us had sped up—I had seen the lights get bigger. Hadn't I? Rhonda Jean had said, *He's coming.*

But I hadn't seen a girl in the truck bed, fading in and out and staring at us.

"Eddie," I said, "they think we did it. If we saw someone else, someone who might have seen something or done something, we have to tell them. They think we're murderers."

He was still tense behind me. "That detective, Quentin. He's going to ask questions if we tell him. He's going to think I'm crazy. Then he's going to dig into my records. And he's going to dig into you, too."

"He won't find anything," I said, though my heart was pounding a hard beat in my temples.

"Are you sure about that? Are you willing to bet everything on it?" When I didn't answer, he continued, "He isn't stupid, and he's some kind of higher-up. I know a commanding officer when I see one. Quentin is a bigwig who comes to a hospital in the middle of nowhere at a moment's notice at three o'clock in the morning. He

31

kicked out the local guy and took over within minutes. *Minutes.* What do you think that means?"

I pressed my fingers into my tired eye sockets. I didn't want to contemplate it, but Eddie was right—I had to. "It means this isn't the first time this has happened."

"That officer, Syed, asked us if we picked up hitchhikers. It was his first question. He asked us about that road. And he wasn't the one who called Quentin and his partner in—he was surprised when they showed up. April, we've walked into a situation here."

I rubbed my eyes, thinking about other dead girls like Rhonda Jean. How many were there? What had happened to them? Eddie was right. When you looked at his past, when you looked at my past—if you looked closely—we weren't as innocent as we seemed. If Detective Quentin was under pressure to find a murderer, he could make a case for pinning it on us if he wanted to. It depended on how determined he was.

"Do you have anything you want to tell me?" I asked Eddie.

"You mean, do I drive several hours out of Ann Arbor and kill hitchhikers in my spare time?"

"Yes."

"No, I don't. Do you?"

"No."

"Okay, we've got that clear. But I keep thinking back. When we picked her up. When you saw she was bleeding."

He paused so long, I had to prompt him. "What?"

"You weren't scared," he said. "You weren't even shocked. You knew exactly what to do."

I'd been horrified when I'd seen the blood on Rhonda Jean. I'd felt grief and dread. And I *had* felt fear. But I'd also felt calm. Prepared, even.

"You weren't scared, either," I whispered.

"I've been in the army. I fought overseas. We got training—months of it. When you said Rhonda Jean was bleeding, my training and my experience kicked in. It was like I was back there." He paused. "April, you work in a bowling alley. You don't get training for that."

His words were laid out the way you lay out plates when you're setting the table. One after the other. Eddie noticed everything when it came to me.

I should have panicked at the time. A normal woman would have, I guessed. I should have screamed. Had I screamed? No, I didn't think so. I hadn't cried, either. Would a normal woman have cried? A woman who hadn't lived through what I had?

Eddie was right. As far as Detective Quentin was concerned, I was April Delray, who would be April Carter as soon as she got the paperwork done when her honeymoon was over. I worked in a bowling alley and lived a quiet life. If there was one thing my mother had taught me, one hard lesson that had stood out among all of the others, it was that the police were never to be trusted—with anything.

I only planned to marry one man in my entire life if possible, and this man was the one. The man whose knees were crooked behind mine right this minute. I wasn't going to let anything threaten that, and neither, I thought, was Eddie.

"Not every war is fought in Iraq," I told him.

I heard the soft hush of his breath. "I know."

Eddie knew me. He knew more of me than anyone else in the world ever had. But even Eddie didn't know everything.

"We'll come up with a plan tomorrow," I said.

Eddie's hand touched my hair, his big fingers letting the wisps of blond slide over them.

"Okay," he said. "Okay."

CHAPTER FIVE

he two uniformed cops who came to pick us up at seven didn't seem too concerned that we might be murderers. They also seemed pleasantly surprised that we were still here, as if they'd thought we'd make a break for it and run away. I wasn't sure how we'd do that, since we had no car and didn't even know exactly where we were. There had supposedly been a police car staked out outside all night. And there was no way in hell I was going to go hitchhiking on Atticus Line.

Rose let the cops in. She was wearing a nightgown that covered her from its high ruffled collar to her feet, a bathrobe, and a pinched look that said she hated all of us. Her hair stuck up on one side, and her eyes were hostile behind her glasses. She'd plunked down some coffee, two pieces of toast, and a couple of hard-boiled eggs on her kitchen table when we came out of our room, and she'd silently dared us to complain.

The kitchen was decorated just as badly as the bedroom: shelves lined with figurines, little china bowls, jars, dusty fabric flowers, wooden carvings, dangling beads. A crocheted piece of fabric in a frame on the wall told us that *Home and hearth are where the heart is.* A clock with a face decorated with roses ticked loudly next to it, and on the shelf below that, a china clown grasped a clutch of balloons in his hand, a sad smile on his face. Princess Diana was in here, too: a framed photo of her smiling hung above the stove, and a painted portrait of Charles and Diana hung in the living room. It looked like Rose was a Diana fanatic. She had copied Diana's haircut, though the rest of her didn't look like Diana at all.

We ate everything Rose gave us, even though my stomach was in knots. I stared at Princess Diana and swallowed. You have to eat, especially when things get bad. Having a full stomach gives you a better chance to think.

"Don't look so put out, Rose," one of the cops said as he helped himself to a cup of her coffee. "These two are your only customers."

"Think I'll get paid?" Rose's voice was unpleasant, like a violin that was badly tuned.

"Sure you will," the other cop said. "Just send a bill to Detective Quentin."

That shut her up. It shut the other cop up, too. I looked at Eddie as I drained my coffee. The look he gave me back said, *Here we go.*

As we stood to leave, Eddie reached into the back pocket of his jeans and pulled out his worn leather wallet. He laid a twenty on the table. "Thank you for breakfast, ma'am," he said.

She gaped at him as we followed the two cops from the room. I didn't watch her do it, but I knew she took the twenty.

Everyone always underestimated my husband. Everyone but me.

They put us in a police cruiser, in the back seat like a pair of criminals. There was a net partition separating us from the two cops in the front. The doors of the back seat had no handles or window rollers. It smelled vaguely sour back here, and Eddie had to crouch with his knees up in the small space.

"You have a good night at Rose's?" This was the cop who had teased Rose and taken some of her coffee. He was in the front passenger seat, and he glanced back at us, grinning.

"Shut up, Kyle," the cop driving the car said. Gravel crunched under our tires as he pulled out of Rose's unpaved driveway.

"What? I'm just asking." Kyle looked back at us again. He had dark hair combed back beneath his policeman's cap and a wide, square face that was hard despite his smirking expression. "You guys have sweet dreams, or what? Are you sure you didn't hear anything going bump in the night?"

"Don't listen to him," the other cop said.

"I'm not saying the place is haunted." Kyle put on a fake-solemn expression. "Not at all. But you might want to think twice before you sleep too deep at Rose's. Someone should have warned her husband before he ended up dead in her backyard. He'd been a cop for twenty years. He was lying there when one of the neighbors saw him from an upstairs window and called the police. Rose was a few feet away, busy digging in the garden, like she was about to bury him."

"Jesus, Kyle," the other cop said, annoyed now. Then, to us: "Ignore him. Rose didn't murder her husband. He died of a heart attack."

"That's what you think," Kyle said. "There's a reason no one ever stays there."

So Rose was a widow. The thought barely flitted through my mind. I was busy looking out the window at the town passing by in the summer-morning light. The shadows were harsh already, as if the day was going to be scorching hot.

It was probably the biggest town in this area, a hub for all of the vacation spots farther out on the shores of the lake. There were big old houses, some of them advertising vacation rooms to rent. A main street featured a canvas banner strung above it, advertising the annual Summer Fun Fair happening in a few weeks. There were swimwear shops and diners, corner pubs and B and Bs that were probably more expensive—and nicer—than Rose's. There was an empty parking lot with a sign that advertised the farmers market every Saturday. More signs advertised boat storage and fishing tackle repair. I wondered how far we were from the Five Pines Resort, from the little cabin Eddie and I were supposed to be staying in right now.

Another police cruiser passed us, going the other way, and the two cops up front lifted their hands to the cops driving it.

"Where are we going?" Eddie asked, ignoring the continued banter about whether Rose was a murderer and her house was haunted.

"You're going to meet the detectives," Kyle said. He seemed to be the talkative one. He gave us a grin that was supposed to be humorous but was hard and mean instead. "Then you're going to take them on a little tour. Show them where you killed that girl."

"We didn't kill anyone." I shouldn't have fallen for it—I knew better. But the words still came out of me.

Kyle shrugged. "If you did it, you can be sure Quentin will get it out of you. He's good at that."

It was supposed to sound sinister, I was sure, as if Detective Quentin in his warm-up suit was the gestapo. All it did was remind me to be on my guard. I fished in my purse for my sunglasses and put them on, wishing I'd had time before breakfast to talk to Eddie about what our plan was. I thought about the girl Eddie thought he'd seen in the truck bed. I thought about the truck's lights in our rear window, growing bigger and brighter as it gained on us.

I'm sorry. He's coming.

Rhonda Jean was dead.

I swallowed hard, glad that my sunglasses covered my eyes. I was supposed to be on my honeymoon, and instead I had a dead girl to deal with. My mother would laugh if she knew.

I looked over at Eddie. He was wearing a navy blue T-shirt and his clean jeans. He looked at me, unperturbed by the sunglasses, and touched his finger to my chin, ran it gently along my jawline.

"Those cops we passed going the other way," he said softly, not caring that the two police up front could hear. "They were going back to Rose's to search our luggage."

The cops went silent. Even Kyle.

I frowned. Eddie was right. Why else would a police car be heading back in the direction of Rose's? It made me angry, even though there would be nothing for them to find. Our bloody clothes from last night. My bathing suit. Eddie's jogging shorts and sneakers. Some sunscreen. My tampons and my birth control pills. Eddie's swim trunks and the pills he took when he couldn't sleep.

We were just two people on our honeymoon, and the police would see that from our luggage. And still, it made me mad.

Eddie dropped his finger from my jaw and took out his own sunglasses, a pair of aviators he'd had since the army. When he put them on, I couldn't see my husband anymore—just the man who had spent fourteen months in Iraq, doing God knew what.

Then the car stopped, and the cops let us out to meet with Detective Quentin.

CHAPTER SIX

For a lot of reasons, one of my most vivid memories was of the summer I was twelve. I remembered bright sunlight glinting off windshields on the highway and the feel of old grit under my bare feet. I remembered the sugary frozen ices I had to eat fast before they melted and rubbery sticks of flavorless chewing gum that sometimes were the only meal I would get. I remembered tying my greasy hair back with my last, precious hair elastic, feeling it tear the strands and pull at my sweaty scalp. And I remembered my mother, wearing faded, tight jeans, her permed blond waves falling past her shoulders, her eyes hidden behind white-rimmed sunglasses. I remembered that no matter how hot it was, her grip on my arm was always cold.

Every year, without fail, when the cicadas started screaming and the pavement got hot beneath the soles of my sandals, I remembered that summer. It had changed my life. It had made me who I was, April Delray, the pretty girl who was an expert in moving through life unnoticed when she wanted to. Until Eddie had noticed me.

I told him about that summer on our fourth date, as we sat on the run-down sofa in his apartment. He'd cooked for me on that date—spaghetti and meatballs, a meal I later learned he considered the best in his repertoire. It was the first time he'd cooked for me, the first time I'd been to his apartment. Normally, the big question of a date like this—to end up in bed or not?—would have hung over us, but with Eddie I didn't obsess about it. Instead, I told him the worst thing that had ever happened to me.

We'd already eaten the spaghetti and washed the dishes. I watched a muscle in Eddie's jaw tick as I spoke, and I watched his handsome eyes darken with shadows.

When I'd finished, he'd taken my hand and kissed the back of it without saying a word. I had felt his breath on my skin. His big hand had encompassed mine.

My heart had cracked when he did that, and my heart never cracked. Not for anyone, ever.

Now the memory of that summer was crossed with the memory of Eddie kissing my hand in his kitchen. I wondered if that was how marriage worked, if the memories you made with the person you married started taking over the ones that had come before, like a radio station that fades out on the dial as another one comes in.

As it happened, we didn't go to bed together that night—that came later. Sitting on his sofa, my stomach full of spaghetti and meatballs, I'd still had the idea that Eddie Carter was too nice for me to sleep with. I was still in the well-worn habit of assuming I'd live my life all alone. I'd had no idea I was already falling.

Now we stepped out of the back of the police cruiser. The sun was blazing hot already, the sky burning blue, the wind nothing but a tired breath. Sweat trickled beneath my shirt between my shoulder blades.

We were in the parking lot of a grocery store that hadn't opened yet, and to my surprise, I realized I knew where I was for the first time since last night. We were next to the turnoff Eddie and I had taken from Atticus Line into town, when we'd been speeding away from the truck behind us.

There were two other cars in the parking lot besides the cruiser we had pulled up in, one of them another police cruiser, one of them an unmarked car. The cars were all parked with their noses together, like the circle of an old wagon train. Kyle and the other cop who had driven us stood by Eddie and me. Two other uniforms had exited the other cruiser, and I realized that one of them was Officer Syed from last night. He looked at Eddie and me, then looked away.

The third car was a Cutlass, and standing alongside it were Detectives Quentin and Beam. Quentin had traded his warm-up suit for a pair of suit pants and a dress shirt unbuttoned at the throat, with no jacket and no tie. Like the warm-up suit, the look was casual, yet it was strangely formal on him. Beam was in a full suit, and he already looked sweaty and a little bit mad.

"Thank you, Officers," Quentin said to Kyle and his partner. "You may go."

Kyle's fake-jovial face went hard, but he didn't argue. His

partner was already turning back toward their car. Kyle looked at Eddie and me; his type could never resist a parting shot. "Have fun, kids," he said. "Don't do anything I wouldn't do."

"You may go," Detective Quentin repeated, and in that moment I could see that Kyle hated him. I could also see that Quentin didn't care.

The two cops got back in their cruiser and left.

Detective Beam, meanwhile, had pulled out a map and unfolded it over the hood of the Cutlass. He smoothed the squares of folds out, pinning the edges as the hot, faint breeze worked under the paper. Detective Quentin gestured for us to come closer.

"Mr. Carter," he said to Eddie. "You were driving last night, correct?"

"Yes," Eddie said.

"Please show me the route you took."

Eddie stood over the map, looking down at it through his sunglasses. "Here," he said, pointing to the paper. "We were on the interstate. I remember passing a sign for Greendale. I must have turned off somewhere around here." He pointed.

"You don't recall exactly where?" Quentin asked.

"It was dark and late. We were lost."

Quentin nodded. "Why did you exit the interstate?"

"I thought I was going the right way."

"There's no sign that says anything about Five Pines Resort, which you say is where you were going." Quentin's expression was blank, impossible to read, even though he wasn't wearing sunglasses. "So why did you exit?"

"I thought I was going the right way," Eddie said again.

"Based on what? Have you been to this area before?"

"No." Eddie stood back from the map. "Have other people died? Is that what this is about?"

Detective Beam said, "What makes you say that?"

Eddie looked pointedly at the police surrounding us. "Just a hunch."

"Mr. Carter." Detective Quentin's voice was calm. "You and your wife are suspects in that young woman's death until I am satisfied and say that you are not. Is that clear?"

I looked over at Officer Syed and the other uniformed officer. The other officer looked to be about twenty, blond-haired and blue-eyed, and he was checking me out without bothering to hide it. I was wearing cutoff jean shorts, sneakers, and a blue-and-white nautical striped T-shirt with a wide boatneck that almost touched my shoulders. I'd packed for a honeymoon on the beach, not a police interrogation. The blond cop was checking out my legs.

I ignored him and looked at Officer Syed. To my surprise, he was also watching me, though his look wasn't lascivious. He gave me the briefest shake of his head, invisible to everyone but me.

What did that mean? Was he telling me to stay quiet? That he didn't believe I'd killed Rhonda Jean? That he did believe it?

"Who was she?" Eddie asked. "Rhonda Jean. Was she a local girl? Did you find her family?"

"I'd appreciate it if you'd get in the car," Detective Quentin said, ignoring the question. "We're going to the place where you exited the interstate, and you and your wife are going to walk me and Detective Beam through what happened last night. The faster I get my answers, Mr. Carter, the faster we can all go home."

Quentin was lying. We weren't going home—at least, not today. The police still had our car, and they were going through our luggage. We'd shown up with a murdered girl in our back seat. We weren't going anywhere.

It wasn't legal and it wasn't fair, but the system wasn't fair. People like Eddie and me didn't get to call up a team of high-priced lawyers and make a dream team. We got to rely on our wits instead. I hoped Eddie would follow my lead, because I had the feeling I had more experience with the police than he did.

At least the back seat of the Cutlass had door handles. The air-conditioning did its best in the hot air. We drove as a two-car convoy, with Detective Beam driving the Cutlass, Detective Quentin in the passenger seat, and the two uniforms in their cruiser behind us.

"Nice weather for a honeymoon," Detective Quentin said. "How long have you two known each other?"

I wasn't answering that, and neither was Eddie. This wasn't a social trip. Eddie took my hand in his silently, grasped it. I opened my hand, feeling the powerful warmth of his grip, running my thumb over one of his big knuckles. We would get through this. We would.

"You should probably answer our questions," Detective Beam said from the driver's seat.

"We don't need to," I said. "I'm sure you already know all about us."

"I couldn't find much information," Detective Quentin admitted mildly. "I didn't have a lot of time. The car is in Mr. Carter's name and registered to your address. Mr. Carter did military service from which he was discharged at the beginning of this year."

Quentin had an oddly formal way of speaking, calm and

without inflection. It should have been soothing, but instead, the more he spoke, the more wary of him I became.

"You, Mrs. Carter," Quentin continued. "Or should I call you Miss Delray?"

"Mrs. Carter," I said, and Eddie squeezed my hand.

"All right, Mrs. Carter. You don't have much of an official record of anything. You have a driver's license and that's about it. You're something of a ghost."

A ghost. He thought I was a ghost. He had no idea. "I live a quiet life," I said. "Not everyone commits crime all the time."

"That makes you very admirable." Quentin's tone was hard to decipher, but I thought perhaps he didn't believe me. "A young lady who lives a simple life and finds a decent man to marry. You don't see that often these days."

If there had been something heavy in the back seat, I would have been tempted to smash the back of his smug head with it. But I curled the fingers of my free hand and took a breath. I knew he was trying to goad me. It was what I would do if I were him.

In this moment, he suspected me of murder. More than one, if my guess was correct. A woman who would stab a hitchhiker—or watch her husband stab her—and then take her to the hospital would have to be what my mother used to call a Prime Bitch. Detective Quentin wanted to know if I was a Prime Bitch or not. The fastest way to find out was to make me mad. It was a game of one-upmanship, pure and simple.

I stared out the window and didn't take the bait, though I wanted to.

"How many other people have been killed?" Eddie asked.

"You're persistent, Mr. Carter," Quentin replied.

"You must have called the Five Pines Resort, at least," Eddie said, ignoring him. "You wouldn't be very good cops if you didn't."

Detective Beam looked at Detective Quentin, but Quentin was staring straight ahead. "Of course we called them," Beam said, annoyed. "They verified you have a reservation."

"Then why don't you believe we were going there?"

"Because I've never heard of the Five Pines Resort, and when we looked it up, we discovered it's miles west of here, on Lake Michigan. You were going in the wrong direction, Mr. Carter."

Eddie scratched his chin. "So let me get this straight. April and I got married in Ann Arbor—which you can also verify—and made reservations for our honeymoon. We did all of this with the purpose of coming to a deserted road in the middle of the night, where we somehow knew a young lady would be, and killed her. Then, instead of driving off and getting away with it—because no one would ever know it was us—we drove her to the hospital. That was our plan?"

"We're close to the interstate now," was Quentin's only reply.

I was looking out the window, trying to recognize the landscape. I thought it looked familiar in daylight, but I couldn't be sure. It had all been so strange last night—the light we'd seen in the trees, the dark road. The scratchy country music. The leaves stirring behind Rhonda Jean when I'd rolled down the window to talk to her. The fact that Eddie hadn't wanted me to get out of the car. Had we really been going the wrong way?

Detective Beam made a turn, and then we were on the interstate, which was nearly deserted at this time of morning on a weekday. The sun was all the way up now, heating the blacktop. Beam picked up speed.

The detectives were silent, the tension thick in the car. Eddie and I had stopped for a hamburger, I remembered. But that must have been much earlier. Wasn't it?

"Up here," Eddie said, his voice calm, his expression flat behind his sunglasses. "We made the turnoff up here."

"There's no sign," Detective Beam pointed out.

"We didn't have the map out. I thought this was the right direction."

"And yet," Quentin said, "we found an unfolded map on the floor of your car."

"That was after we realized we were lost," Eddie said. "April took out the map."

Beam made the turnoff, and the noise of the interstate vanished quickly behind us. We were on a two-lane road lined with trees, and everything clicked into place. I remembered this.

Detective Beam slowed the car as Detective Quentin said, "Please point out where you found the young woman last night."

Eddie was silent. We cruised slowly down the road, the harsh sunlight dappling between the leaves overhead. I remembered how dark it had been, except for that one strange light that we couldn't explain. It should have been a less frightening place in daylight, but it wasn't. There were no other cars, no wind, no houses, no sign of life. I had the sudden urge to tell Beam to go faster.

Eddie squeezed my hand briefly—a signal. I looked out the window and saw the stand of trees where we'd seen the light last night.

"It was somewhere up here," Eddie said. "Right, April?"

My voice was rough from being silent so long. "Yes, I think so. Right along here."

Beam slowed the car. "Was she on the right shoulder or the left?"

"Right," Eddie said.

"Did she have her thumb out?"

"No. She was just walking, real slow and not very steady. We thought she might be drunk. We also thought she was a boy at first."

Beam pulled over, and we all got out of the car. The cruiser pulled up behind us, and Officer Syed and his partner got out. "Were there any landmarks that you recall?" Quentin asked.

My sneakers crunched on the gravel of the shoulder as I turned in place, looking around. "It was so dark," I said, answering Quentin.

They asked more questions—did we get out of the car? What exactly did Rhonda Jean say?—as we walked along the shoulder of the road. Quentin made a brief gesture to the uniformed cops, and they spread out ahead of us, scanning the ground for blood or any other clues.

The emptiness on Atticus Line was so complete it was like a deafening noise. I'd never seen a road like this—so empty of people, so empty of anything, that it felt like a void. What was this place? Where had Rhonda Jean come from, standing here in the middle of the night in the silence? How far had she walked? Where had she been going?

Who was she? Where was home?

And who had been out on this road last night, trying to run us down?

CHAPTER SEVEN

Beam, sweating in his suit, spread his map on the hood of the Cutlass again, making marks with a ballpoint pen. The young, blond, uniformed cop crossed to the other side of Atticus Line, scanning the other shoulder. Eddie stood with his hands in his jeans pockets, staring down the empty road, lost in thought. I kept picturing Rhonda Jean in that oversize coat, holding it closed over the blood covering her body. I left the road and started walking into the trees.

"Mrs. Carter," I heard Quentin call behind me. Then I heard footsteps jogging through the grass, and Officer Syed was walking next to me.

"Best not to piss him off," he said in a low voice, though we were too far away for Quentin to hear.

"I don't know if this is the right place," I said, frustrated. "There are no landmarks on this stupid road, no lights. It was dark. There's no sign Rhonda Jean was even here. How does a girl get stabbed and start walking and not leave any trace behind?"

"There isn't much traffic on this road," Syed said. "To be honest, most people avoid it."

"No kidding. Why?"

He shrugged. He must be hot in that uniform, but except for a small trickle of sweat on one temple, he showed no sign of it. "Rumors."

I stopped walking. We were in the trees now, the heat breathing the smell of pine on us, mosquitoes flitting in the shadows. The others were out of sight and earshot, Quentin trusting that Syed would bring me back. "Not rumors," I said, facing Syed. "Other murders. Am I right?"

He scratched the back of his neck, looking behind him before answering. "We get hitchhikers on this road."

"Right. And why does this part of Michigan get so many hitchhikers?"

"Up that way, past the turnoff to town, is Hunter Beach," Syed said, pointing down the road in the direction we'd gone last night. "It's over an hour down the road, but it's there."

"What's Hunter Beach?"

He mopped the sweat beading on his forehead beneath his cap. "It's a place where the kids go. It's kind of a known spot, where they can camp on the beach, stay as long as they like. There's an old house that's used as a hostel, places to pitch tents. It draws hitchhikers and backpackers, that sort of crowd."

"You let them camp on the beach?" I asked.

"It's private property. The man who owns it doesn't live there, and he lets anyone use it. He's owned it since the sixties, and he owns a good section of the beach, so no one can really complain. We've talked to him a dozen times over the years, but he always says that he believes the kids should be free to use the beach however they want. You can see why they like to go there."

I started walking again, looking for something—I didn't know what. "So Rhonda Jean was trying to get to Hunter Beach."

"Probably. She wasn't a local girl. Her ID was from Baltimore."

"How old was she?"

"Eighteen."

I pressed my fingertips to my eye sockets behind my sunglasses. Eighteen. "How many others have died around here? That's why we're suspects, right?"

Officer Syed seemed to remember where we were, who we were. "Mrs. Carter, I'm supposed to ask you the questions, not the other way around."

"Sure," I said. I slapped a mosquito from my arm and changed direction to come out of the trees and onto the road.

"Mrs. Carter," Officer Syed said as he followed me, "I have to be honest. Even though this is a murder, you seem to be pretty casual about it."

I could see the two detectives on Atticus Line, as well as the blond policeman. Eddie was talking to Detective Beam, pointing in one direction, then the other. As I watched, Quentin lowered to a crouch on the shoulder of the road, looking at something on the ground.

"I'm the opposite of casual," I told Officer Syed. "Very much the opposite. What should I do, according to you? Scream and cry?"

"Maybe." He didn't seem very convinced.

"I don't have time for that." The heat hit me as I walked onto the baking road. A few far-off birds called, but other than that, Atticus Line was silent. "I haven't seen a single car since we came here."

"I told you, there isn't much traffic. Mrs. Carter—"

"Do you think she came all the way from Baltimore just to go to Hunter Beach?" I stared down the road in the pulsing heat, thinking about Rhonda Jean in her oversize coat, the freckles on the bridge of her nose.

"Who knows?" Officer Syed sounded exasperated. "Hunter Beach has been around for decades. It's one of the places these kids today, these backpackers, would know about."

Eddie and Detective Beam were having an animated discussion. Beam held the map, folded into a half-manageable shape, and Eddie was pointing as he talked. Beam shook his head.

Detective Quentin stood a few feet away from them, not taking part in the discussion. He was standing still, seemingly unbothered by the heat beating down on him. His gaze was fixed on me.

Officer Syed followed my gaze. "We should go join them, or I'll be in trouble," he said.

"Sure," I said. *It's so hot out*, I thought. *Why was Rhonda Jean wearing that jacket? And why didn't she have any luggage?*

And suddenly, I was cold. The summer heat evaporated and a chill blasted through me, so real and so heavy I let out a surprised breath. It felt like a bubble of icy air had ripped straight through my body, freezing my throat. As the July sun beat mercilessly above me, I shivered hard.

Officer Syed didn't seem to notice. He was walking away, wiping his forehead again.

The cold dissipated, and then I was dizzy. My stomach roiled and my head ached as if I had the flu. I blinked and bent, putting my hands on my knees and trying not to throw up as the feeling passed.

Sweat popped on my skin, coating my face and making my sunglasses slide down my nose. I could feel Detective Quentin still looking at me. Maybe they were all looking at me now.

Before I straightened, my gaze caught on something next to my feet. A corner of faded pink visible from under the dirt and dead leaves on the side of the road. Getting myself together, I leaned down and tugged at it.

It was a cloth flower. It was old and weathered, the cheap silk faded and dirty. The plastic stem was snapped, as if the flower had been part of a bouquet at some point. The rest of the bouquet was long gone.

Attached to the flower was a small card with faded writing on it, the letters inked in calligraphy. Through the dirt, I could still read the words.

In memory of Katharine O'Connor. March 2, 1993.

CHAPTER EIGHT

The police kept us until noon. When we finished pointing out what we remembered on Atticus Line, they brought us to the Coldlake Falls police station to take a formal statement.

They questioned us separately. My interview took an hour and a half, during which I was asked over and over to repeat my version of last night's events. I left out the truck and the girl Eddie thought he'd seen in the truck bed. I left out the flower I'd seen by the side of the road. And, of course, I left out everything about both Eddie's past and mine. Other than that, I was honest.

It was as good as they were going to get from me.

When they finished with us, they drove us in another squad car back to Rose's. The sun was at its merciless zenith, pulsing high in the cloudless sky. The window air conditioners at the B and B were humming loudly and the lights were off, the living room lit by bright sunlight coming through the lacy curtains. Rose was nowhere to be seen, but there were two tuna sandwiches in plastic wrap on the kitchen table with a handwritten note: *Eat it if you want it.*

We ate the sandwiches in silence. Exhaustion was creeping up on me, mixing with the heat and lack of sleep and pulsing behind my eyes. Eddie was restless, deep in thought. When we adjourned to our bedroom, he changed into his shorts and sneakers.

"I'm going for a run," he said.

I knew better than to point out how hot it was outside. Eddie was used to it, and he didn't care. He was a dedicated runner. "Wear sunscreen," I said, pushing my sneakers off and getting on the bed. "Drink water."

He grinned at me, the first smile I'd seen from him all day, and I remembered it yet again: We were married. Actually married. For a second I ached for the honeymoon we could have had, lazily swimming and then making love. Despite everything, I had the urge to pull him into bed with me right now, but this room was creepy, and Rose could listen outside the door at any minute. I sighed. It was going to have to wait.

"I'm bad luck," I told him.

"It's me who's bad luck," he replied. "It's followed me all my life."

"That's not true. Your parents are nice. You had a nice childhood."

"I had a nice childhood after my parents adopted me," he corrected me.

He'd been six when his mother gave him up, old enough to have memories of her. Old enough to be aware that she didn't want him anymore.

But he'd been adopted almost immediately, and his adopted parents were good, kind people. His adopted family had aunts and uncles and cousins in Ann Arbor. I'd met some of them, and their kindness was alien to me, their commitment to chatting about chili recipes and watching football games almost unnerving. These were people who had led decent, stable lives, and if they were a little boring, it was a small price to pay. I had started to wonder if I could let myself have a life like that.

It had almost seemed possible until Eddie and I ended up in Coldlake Falls, covered in blood.

"Maybe both of us are bad luck," I said. I leaned over the bed and scrutinized the shelf under the bedside table. "What are the odds that Rose has a subscription to *Glamour* so I have something to read?"

"Not good," Eddie said.

I found a paperback novel and picked it up. It was *Flowers in the Attic*. "There is something very wrong with that woman," I said.

"Shh. She might be listening." Eddie walked to the door. "I'll do my best not to get murdered while I'm on my run. I'll be back in a little while."

I watched him go, because he was Eddie and I was allowed to appreciate the back of him as he left a room. Then I turned on the fan in the corner to bolster the whiff of cold air coming from the air conditioner, propped myself on pillows on the fussy bed, and started reading *Flowers in the Attic* for the first time since I was fifteen, while Princess Diana watched silently above my head, judging. I fell asleep after the first ten pages.

When I woke up, it was still hazily bright outside. The book was under my hand. The fan creaked as it oscillated in the corner. And Rose was sitting in the chair next to the bed, staring at me.

I blinked. For a sleepy second I thought she was a ghost, she was sitting so still. Then I realized she was real.

Rose frowned at me, as if annoyed. Her hands were in her lap, her nails painted pink against her light-blue jeans. She seemed in no hurry to say anything.

I was too groggy to feel particularly alarmed. "What are you doing here, Rose?" I asked.

"What did they say?" It was the same grating voice I remembered from this morning.

"This is my room," I said, scrubbing a hand over my face. "You need to leave."

"They said I murdered Robbie, didn't they?"

"What?" The nap had been a powerful one, and the fussy, lacy room was soporific. I couldn't summon any outrage, just the weird feeling you get when you first leave a dream. "Who?"

"Kyle Petersen." Rose's voice was truly angry, though it wasn't directed at me. She lifted her hostile gaze away from me and aimed it at the opposite wall. "That little turd thinks he can pass judgment on me. On anyone. He's as useful as an itch in the pants. Robbie said he was one of the worst recruits he'd ever seen."

I tried to follow. She was talking about the cop, Kyle. The one who had joked about Rose killing her husband, then digging his grave in the garden.

"And Chad Chipwell?" Rose said this slightly unbelievable name with spitting disdain. "When did he ever have a thought of his own in his head? He's so gullible you could tell him Jimi

Hendrix is still alive and he'd scratch his head and ask when he's putting a new record out."

This must be the cop who drove with Kyle. Rose's rant was creepy and completely inappropriate. I had no idea why I was entertained by it.

"Yeah," I said, propping my shoulders up on my pillow and running a hand through my sleep-rumpled hair. "Kyle told us you killed your husband and that he haunts this place. The other one, Chad, told us not to listen."

Rose snorted. "They're just jealous because Robbie was a good cop. The best one they had in this stupid town. He could have moved to the state police and been a detective, but they wouldn't promote him because of the color of his skin. So instead of making Robbie detective, we got Quentin." She rolled her eyes behind her huge glasses. "The almighty Quentin, praise the Lord."

That made me smile. I sat up straighter in bed.

"And Beam," Rose went on, not needing any cues from me. "He's only good at pushing paperwork, if that. Robbie caught him sleeping in his car on a stakeout once. Beam threatened to have him fired. Did you eat the tuna?"

"Um, yes," I said, wondering for the first time where Eddie was. "It was delicious, thank you." I glanced at the clock radio on the bedside table, sitting on a lace doily beneath a frilly lavender lamp. It was three o'clock.

"Good. I got frozen hamburger patties for dinner. I fry them up. I got buns, ketchup, mustard. You can have some if you like."

I cleared my throat. "Sure, that sounds good." I was fully awake now, and I looked Rose in the eyes. "So, you don't think my husband and I are murderers?"

Rose looked straight back at me without blinking. Her gaze was flat, but there was something there, flickering in the depths. Intelligence, maybe. Anger, perhaps. Or it could have been the determination of a woman who has survived bad things. Who had maybe done bad things. Like me.

"I don't know you," Rose said in her blunt, unpleasant way. "I could see you going either way. But your husband?" She shook her head. "That man has never killed anyone in his life."

"He served in Iraq," I told her.

"Sure he did. And why did he come home? He didn't like it much, did he? If he was the killing type, he'd still be there."

I stared at her, my lips parted in surprise.

"It doesn't matter what I think," Rose went on. "Quentin thinks he has you pegged, and he's not going to take his eyes off you. If you really are a murderer, you can try it on me, but you'll have a fight on your hands. Robbie taught me plenty while we were married." She pursed her lips and looked down at her hand, where she picked at the arm of her chair. She was quiet a moment before she said, "What really happened last night? When you picked up that girl? What did you see?"

So Rose wanted something, then. That, I understood. "I'll tell you," I said slowly. "But I have questions of my own."

Rose looked up at me. "You want information? About what?"

"This town."

She smiled. "If you want gossip, this town has plenty, and I know all of it. Just tell me what you want to know."

CHAPTER NINE

I've lived here all my life," Rose said as she walked ahead of me into the kitchen. "I know everyone here. Robbie, he was from Grosse Pointe. He moved here in '79. He was police down there, so he was experienced by the time he came to Coldlake Falls. His parents still live down in Detroit. Both of my parents are dead— my mother died five years ago, my father the year after that. Throat cancer, both of them. You ever heard of two married people dying of throat cancer?"

Now that I had her talking, it seemed like she wasn't planning to stop. She reached into a cupboard and pulled out a bag of chips, then a bowl. She opened the chips and poured them into the bowl, then took a container of creamy onion dip out of the fridge. Still talking, she grabbed a chip and dipped it.

"People in this town hate me," she said. "You want some chips and dip?"

I pulled out a chair from the kitchen table and sat down, rubbing the last of the grogginess from my face. "I'm fine, thanks."

"You're too pretty for this place." Rose ate another chip as she imparted this information. "That isn't a compliment. You have nice hair and a nice face, that body. People aren't going to like you. You should get ready to deal with that up front."

I frowned. I was still wearing the cutoff jean shorts and navy-and-white striped shirt I'd put on this morning, and I had no makeup on. "This is just how I look."

"Too bad for you, then." Rose sounded like she was sorry for me. "People think pretty girls get the best of everything, but in my opinion they get the worst of it." She motioned to the large picture of Princess Diana on the living room wall, the portrait of her standing next to her husband. "People think Princess Diana has it easy because she's beautiful, but she doesn't. She doesn't. She has it harder than anyone."

I didn't know what to say to that. I honestly was nothing like Princess Diana. Still, Rose was looking so reverently at the photo that I gave her a moment of silence, like you do when someone is praying. "You really are a big fan of hers," I said at last, when Rose was quiet for too long.

Rose blinked at me. "She's the greatest person in the world," she said sincerely. "Robbie never liked that photo because he doesn't like Charles—he says Charles is a stuck-up prig. But he let me put it up because he knew it's important to me. I'm not stupid. I know I'm not like Diana, that I'm not beautiful like her. Like you. At least no one really notices me. You have a job back home?"

I looked away from the photo on the wall. "I work at a bowling alley."

"Huh." Rose thought this over as she ate more chips, the gooey white dip dripping off the edges as she lifted them to her mouth. "That's not too bad, I guess. At least you're not a ball-busting career woman."

I laughed at that, thinking about the desultory way I'd criss-crossed the country since I was twelve, how I'd ended up in Ann Arbor with nowhere else to go. "I am definitely not a career woman."

"People wouldn't like it, that's all. I'm a career woman myself, of sorts, running this place. But like I said, people already don't like me. If you were a lawyer or something, Quentin would hate you even more than he does already."

If I were a lawyer, Eddie and I would be home by now. Which only made what Rose said more true. I didn't want to talk about Quentin, his cold eyes, or his warm-up suit. "Did you know a girl named Katharine O'Connor?" I asked.

Rose's jaw paused in her chewing, then started again. "What do you know about Katharine O'Connor?"

"I saw part of a silk flower with her name on it. An old one. By the side of the road on Atticus Line when the police took us there this morning."

Rose nodded. "She wasn't from around here. The cops think she got picked up hitchhiking. She was strangled and left at the side of the road. That was a few years ago, when Robbie was still alive. They never found who killed her."

"Someone picked her up, then strangled her, and never got caught?"

"Yes." Rose swirled a chip into the onion dip. "It happens on that road. Maybe you heard. Hitchhikers aren't safe there. The kids at Hunter Beach know that, but sometimes one of them comes along who doesn't know, maybe, or thinks the danger doesn't apply to them."

"If Katharine wasn't from around here, then who left the flowers?" I asked.

"The Hunter Beach kids, probably. She was one of them. Now, tell me what happened last night."

I told her. I'd already told the police the same thing, over and over. I told her about Rhonda Jean, the blood, the stab wounds. I paused, thinking about the truck. Eddie wouldn't want me to talk about the truck and the girl he'd seen in the back.

But I must have given something away in my expression, because Rose peered at me from behind her huge glasses. "There's something you're not telling the police," she said.

I shook my head. I was tempted to grab a chip and dip it, just to keep myself from talking, but the sight of the gooey dip, now with crumbs in it, turned my stomach.

"Robbie said that no one ever tells the police the truth," Rose said. "Even innocent people. You could have Mother Teresa, or even Princess Diana, and you put a cop in front of her and she'll tell a lie. Robbie said that the key to police work was making people tell you all of the things they don't want you to know."

I licked my dry lips—talking to Rose was a lot like being questioned by the police, but weirder—and hedged. The truck bothered me. The girl Eddie had seen bothered me. I'd been keeping it in for too long. "We think someone may have been following us, that's all."

"On the road?"

"We aren't sure, so we didn't say anything." It was just enough of a lie. I couldn't tell on Eddie, that he wasn't sure what he'd seen. That he saw things sometimes. Rose kept staring at me, probably waiting for me to say more, but I stayed quiet.

Still, Rose waited. The clock ticked on the wall over the mantel in the living room. Charles and Diana gazed down on both of us, unseeing.

The front door opened and Eddie walked in. He was soaked in sweat from his run, his hair wet and his shirt sticking to his chest and back. He closed the door behind him and paused, looking from me to Rose and back again.

"What's going on?" he said into the silence.

Rose turned and put an elbow on the kitchen table, looking at him. "You two have a problem," she said. "I'll help you, I suppose."

"A problem?" I said as Eddie came toward us across the living room.

Rose gave me a look like I was stupid. "Well, let's see. You got Rhonda Jean dead in your car, Detective Quentin thinks you're a murderer, and whoever killed that girl knows you picked her up. I'd call that a problem, wouldn't you?" She leaned back in her chair. "I seem to remember the police took your car away. Right?"

Eddie was standing next to my chair now. He put his hand on the back of it. *You told her*, that gesture said.

"Yeah," he said to Rose. "They took our car."

"I thought so. You need to figure your way out of this." She picked up the bowl and held it out to Eddie. "Want a chip? I'm going to lend you Robbie's car."

CHAPTER TEN

When he was alive, Robbie drove a gray Honda Accord, boring and boxy. The interior smelled like old cigarette smoke and something that resembled musty cardboard. The car was kept in the garage beside the breezeway, where the heat tried to penetrate curls of chilled damp air and almost succeeded.

Eddie had showered and changed, and now he wore his jeans and a faded Tigers T-shirt. As usual with any vehicle, when he got into Robbie's car he had to push the seat all the way back to fit his legs in.

"I guess it's because you're a military guy," Rose said in surprise as she watched Eddie try to get comfortable. "I thought Robbie was tall. Looks like I was wrong."

"This sure is nice of you, Rose," Eddie said as we buckled ourselves in. Eddie had rolled down the driver's side window, and he leaned an elbow on it and gave her a smile where she stood by the rack of dusty gardening tools. It was a sincere smile, the only kind Eddie had, and it made Rose visibly melt a little. "April and I appreciate it."

"They won't know you're gone," Rose said. "The Coldlake PD doesn't have enough manpower to follow you around all day and night. They'll probably do a drive-by to make sure you're still here, but I'll just say you two are sleeping. You have a few hours at least."

"What happens in a few hours?" I asked her.

Rose shrugged. "More questions, maybe. They won't want to leave you alone too long. Until you're cleared, they want to keep you on your toes. That's what Robbie would do." She pointed. "When you leave the driveway, go left, then left again at the stop sign. A mile down you'll see the signs for Atticus Line and Hunter Beach. I'd start there if I were you. Rhonda Jean was probably headed there when she was killed. Someone there might know her."

"The police will probably already have been there," Eddie said.

Rose gave a snort that was the purest sound of derision I'd ever heard. "Maybe, maybe not, but if any of those kids told the truth to a cop, I'm my aunt Fanny. You should have better luck than they do."

Eddie followed her directions, and we drove in silence for a few minutes. It was the first time we had been completely alone, without the possibility of someone listening in, since we'd pulled up at the hospital with Rhonda Jean last night.

Finally, Eddie spoke, his voice soft. "You told her."

"Not much," I said. "Just that someone might have been

following us." I glanced at him, at the tight clench of his jaw as he drove. It wasn't anger; it was embarrassment. Eddie hated the idea of anyone knowing about his problem with seeing things. "We can't just ignore it," I said. "Rose is right. I saw the truck, too. Whoever killed Rhonda Jean knows who we are. We have to do something."

"I know." He looked tormented for a moment. "The sight of that girl keeps going around and around in my head. Clinging to the side of the truck bed as it drove. And I don't know if I even saw her. Just now, on my run, when I was on my way back—" He shook his head.

"Tell me," I said.

He hesitated, but I was the only person in the world that Eddie told these things to. So he said, "I came around the corner and was jogging up the sidewalk toward Rose's house. I thought I saw a man go around the side of the house toward the backyard. So I followed him. But when I got to the backyard, there was no one there."

"Maybe it was a neighbor," I said.

"If it was a neighbor, I would have seen him in the yard. But I'm telling you, the yard was empty, and there was nowhere to hide. The man was wearing jeans and rubber boots, a gray sweatshirt. I saw all of it as clear as I can see you now. April, I'm going crazy."

"That's not true." I shook my head. "I know you, and you're not crazy."

"Then explain what I saw."

I blew out a breath. "Didn't those cops say Rose's house was haunted? Maybe that's what it was."

"Haunted by a dead gardener?"

We both laughed at that, the sound of it diffusing the tension. "He was pulling his celestial weeds," I said.

"Watering his heavenly grass."

"Telling ghostly kids to get off his lawn." I looked over at him, and I couldn't help it. I leaned across the divide between the passenger seat and the driver's seat and put my arms around his neck, kissing the warm, rough skin of his jaw where the stubble came in.

"April, I'm driving," he said.

I didn't answer. I kissed along his jaw and the skin of his cheek, then back toward his ear. I could feel the reassuring muscles of his shoulders under my arms, and I ran my fingers up the back of his neck, where the hair was growing in longer than the military would allow.

"I'll get pulled over," he protested, but he didn't shrug me off.

I kissed beneath his ear and felt a small tremor go through him. The tension in his body, brought on by the conversation, fizzled gently away. His skin smelled like soap and the sweat he'd washed off from his run, like hot sunshine, and I breathed it in. "You have summer skin," I said.

"Yeah, well, it's summer." He sounded resigned, but he liked it. He still hadn't shrugged me off.

"Let's pull over somewhere and park."

"In Robbie's old car?"

"Why not? He won't care."

"I'm not a back seat type of guy."

I smiled against his skin. "Never?"

"Never."

That was news to me, but I immediately knew it was true.

Eddie really wasn't a back seat type of guy. "I guess I have to wait, then."

He lifted a hand from the wheel and circled my wrist with his fingers, halfway between a protest and a caress. "You do, because Hunter Beach is just up ahead." He pointed to a sign that went by out the window.

I kissed him once more, feeling that tremor again, and then I reluctantly dropped my arms and slid back into my seat. The paved highway ended and the road turned to gravel, the Accord bumping like an amusement park ride. The trees pressed close to the narrow road, but up ahead I could see a blue stripe of water— the lake. We had arrived.

CHAPTER ELEVEN

The entrance to Hunter Beach was marked by a hand-painted sign posted next to a set of steps leading down to the beach. There was only one other car here, a white van that looked like it had been driven through a bank of mud and had been in at least one accident. There was nothing else in this gravel clearing except the sound of gulls over the lake and the wind in the trees behind us.

I walked to the top of the steps and looked down. They were homemade steps, built into the slope with rough stones and old pieces of wood. At the bottom was the beach itself, the sand dark and rocky, the waves of Lake Huron cold and lively in the wind. The sun baked down hot here, but the wind lifted the hair from my neck and blew the mosquitoes down the shore.

I glanced at Eddie, who shrugged. Then he started down the steps. As I descended after him, I could see past the last of the trees farther down the beach. There was a cabin there, made of dark wood. Laundry flapped from long clotheslines behind it. Surrounding it were tents pitched in the sand, dark blue and brown and Army green. Closer to the water was a firepit lined with stones and surrounded by folding chairs. There was no fire in the pit, but I could see three people in the folding chairs, sitting and maybe talking. One of them turned my way as I came to the bottom of the stairs, and the other two followed suit.

I kept pace at Eddie's shoulder as we walked toward the people at the firepit. I put my sunglasses on.

The people around the firepit were young—teenagers, or early twenties at most. There was a girl with long, straight brown hair, and another with a sandy brown braid. The third was a boy with long, dark blond hair in a tangle of natural curls past his shoulders. He was wearing a T-shirt and a pair of worn cargo pants. As we got closer, I saw the T-shirt had a graphic of Che Guevara's face on the front.

"Hi," the boy said as we approached. He was very relaxed in his old lawn chair, his knees sprawled open. The two girls didn't speak. "Do you guys need directions or something?"

Eddie's tone was polite. "Does one of you own this place?"

The three of them exchanged glances, and then they all laughed.

Beside me, Eddie didn't stiffen. His body stayed completely relaxed. The stupid question had been intentional so that he wouldn't seem like a threat.

Everyone underestimated my husband. Everyone but me.

"Do we look like we own this place, man?" the boy said. He held his arms out from his sides. "Okay, sure, this is my domain."

"Honey," I said in a soft voice, touching Eddie's wrist. Playing the square right alongside him. I turned back to the three kids—kids who weren't much younger than me. "Um, hi. We're looking for some information? We're not really sure where to start."

"What do you want to know?" This was the girl with brown hair. She was wearing a spaghetti strap lace camisole under a pair of denim overalls. Her feet were bare.

I adjusted my sunglasses. My sandals were digging into the warm sand. "Do any of you know a girl named Rhonda Jean? I think she was on her way here a few nights ago."

The three of them went quiet and exchanged another look, their laughter gone. Finally, the boy spoke again. "What do you know about Rhonda Jean?"

"We're just looking for some information," I said, shrugging. "Like, where she's from or where she lives. Anything you might know."

"Is she okay?" This was the girl with the braid, who was wearing cutoff jean shorts and a red-and-black flannel shirt. The sleeves of the shirt were rolled down and it was fully buttoned, as if it wasn't ninety degrees out. Her expression was alarmed. "How do you know Rhonda? What happened to her?"

"She's a friend of yours?" Eddie asked the girl. "You're expecting her?"

The girl looked back and forth between Eddie and me. "You're not police?" Her tone phrased it as a question.

"Do we look like police?" I asked her, mirroring what the boy had said a few minutes ago.

"Does one of you know Rhonda Jean?" Eddie asked again.

The girl with the braid looked at the other girl. "Kay, did something happen to Rhonda Jean?"

"How would I know?" Kay asked.

I glanced at Eddie. "Let's go in the house," Eddie said to me.

I nodded and followed him.

This was a simple power play. The three kids at the firepit wanted information from us, so by walking away we made them follow. Besides, I really wanted to know what was inside that house.

We climbed the wooden steps to the porch. The front door was a few inches ajar. Eddie knocked on it politely. "Hello?" he called. "Anyone home?"

There was no answer, so we pushed the door open and walked in.

It was a cottage with a large main room. The shades on most of the windows were down, and several fans ran in the corners, so the place was dark and almost cool. There was a basic kitchen along one wall, the sink filled with used frying pans and plates. There was a small, spare dining table with two wooden chairs. The rest of the room was taken up with sofas and soft chairs arranged around a large TV that wasn't on. The furniture was strewn with articles of clothing and battered pillows. Pinned to the walls, their edges curling, were posters: *Alien*, Smashing Pumpkins, Pearl Jam's *Ten* with the silhouette of raised arms. And most prominently, right above the TV and also on the kitchen wall, Kurt Cobain.

Officer Syed had told me that the man who owned this place let the backpackers and hitchhikers use it however they wanted, and I could see that here. How many places had I been to that looked just like this? How many hostels, how many apartments shared by the roommates of the guy I was on a date with? That exact poster of Kurt Cobain in *Unplugged*, wearing his secondhand cardigan, had hung in the house I'd lived in the day I met Eddie.

Tension crawled up my shoulders to my neck as I pushed my sunglasses to the top of my head. I'd never been to this place, but I still knew it. The hostel in Phoenix. The apartment I'd shared for two months in South Carolina. I'd sat on those sofas and listened to whatever guys were hanging around talk about whether Soundgarden was better than Nirvana, pretending to care. Pretending I was just like the rest of them, while feeling like I was no one at all.

"April?" Eddie's voice was soft.

I swallowed. "There's no one here." I pushed the tense words out.

"Just give it a second. They'll come to us."

He sounded so sure, and he was right. Behind us, the door opened, letting in some of the summer sunlight. The three kids from the firepit came in, along with another boy, this one closer to a man, dark-haired, with a beard and a ratty jean jacket.

"Hey," the long-haired kid said. "This is Todd. I guess he's the closest to being the one in charge around here."

Todd didn't offer to shake our hands. He put his fingers into his jeans pockets and gave us a narrow-eyed look. "What can I help you with?"

Eddie said, "We're looking for information on a young woman named Rhonda Jean. We think she was headed here. Do you know her?"

Todd looked between us again. "Is something wrong?"

It clicked in my mind, the reason none of these people knew

what we were talking about. I looked at Eddie. "The police haven't been here."

His eyebrows rose a fraction in surprise as he realized it, too. A young woman hitchhiking, presumably headed for Hunter Beach, had been murdered, and Detective Quentin hadn't come here yet to ask these kids what they knew. What did that mean?

"The police?" Kay asked. "Why would the police come?"

We had to tell them; we'd come too far now. If they weren't going to hear it from the police, then they would have to hear it from us.

Eddie took a step forward. "We're not from here," he said. "We were passing through town. We picked up a girl named Rhonda Jean, who maybe was hitchhiking. She'd been stabbed."

"Stabbed?" The braid girl's voice was a high near-shriek, slicing through the empty room. Todd went pale. The long-haired kid looked like he wanted to turn and run.

Eddie nodded. "She died. We feel bad about what happened. We'd like to know more about her. We don't even know if the police told her family."

A high-pitched keening came from the girl with the braid, and Kay took her arm. "Gretchen," she said softly. "Sit down."

The girls moved to one of the sofas, and the rest of us followed. I took a seat on an old La-Z-Boy, kicking aside an empty chip bag. Gretchen was still making the keening sound, as if she was trying not to cry. Kay patted her back a little awkwardly, as if the two girls didn't know each other very well. I caught the long-haired kid looking at my legs and gave him a glare that would melt ice. He looked away.

"We didn't know Rhonda Jean all that well," Todd said,

running a hand through his messy, dark hair. He'd sat on another sofa, with Eddie on the other end. "She was here, what? Two weeks? Maybe three?"

We'd had it wrong. Rhonda Jean wasn't heading for Hunter Beach when she was killed; she was leaving. "Where did she stay?" Eddie asked.

"She roomed in Gretchen's tent," Todd said.

"She didn't have a tent." Gretchen wiped her face with her palms. "She said she came from Baltimore. Her dad was a big businessman or something. But he hit her, and he hit her mother, and Rhonda Jean couldn't stay anymore. She wanted out."

The back of my neck went cold. It shouldn't have; these were old scars, healed over.

"She was backpacking around the country," Gretchen went on. "Looking for work for cash under the table. She'd heard it was free here, so she came. The bus only stops in Coldlake Falls. If you want to get to Hunter Beach from there, you have to walk or hitch."

I didn't ask about taxis, and neither did Eddie. We knew better. A taxi from Coldlake Falls to Hunter Beach might be twenty dollars or more. Twenty dollars was food for three days, longer if you stretched it. There was no one here who would pay that kind of money when walking and hitching were free.

I'd lived that life, and I was still living it now. Eddie and I had enough to get by, and that was all. I didn't think I'd ever taken a taxi in my life, and if I asked Eddie, he'd probably say the same.

"I let her sleep in my tent," Gretchen was saying. "She was quiet, friendly, got along with people. She put money into the communal grocery tin. She had a couple of old paperback books she liked to read on the beach. I think she just wanted to be left alone."

"What was her last name?" Eddie asked softly.

"Breckwith." Gretchen seemed to be the only one in the group who had known Rhonda Jean. If she'd stayed here for three weeks, then she'd definitely kept to herself. I looked at the two men, trying to read their expressions. Could one of them have done this?

"Did she tell anyone she was leaving?" I asked.

Gretchen shook her head. "She packed her things last night and she was just gone." She started to keen again.

"She left at night?" Eddie asked. "That seems strange, doesn't it? Why would she go to the Coldlake bus station at night? Buses don't leave then."

Gretchen was crying too hard to answer, so Kay said sullenly, "Who knows? She probably thought she'd walk to the bus station, then sleep there until the first bus left. They start at six."

Maybe, but it didn't sit right. Walking hours to a bus station at night wasn't something I would have done—not unless I had a very pressing reason to leave. Sleeping alone on a bus station bench, waiting for the first bus to leave, wasn't the action of a girl who was having a good time at Hunter Beach.

"No one saw her leave?" I asked.

"We let people come and go here," Todd said. "You're not an-swerable to anyone. That's why people come." His words had an edge to them, and I realized that to him, I represented some kind of establishment type. It would have been funny if it weren't so sad. I was probably the same age as him, and I'd lived exactly the same kind of wandering life. It was weird, how being married made you seem like a grown-up. Until I landed in Ann Arbor, I hadn't been a middle-class girl looking for adventure and a place with no rules. Like some of these kids, I'd been traveling to survive.

I glanced up at Kurt Cobain on the wall. The sadness in his eyes had always unsettled me. I was pretty sure he'd despise the fact that his face was up on the wall. As for his music, I was a Guns N' Roses girl. I'd begged Eddie to let me play "Paradise City" while we walked down the aisle, but he'd had to say no because it would upset his parents.

Two days ago. We were married *two days ago*. I'd worn a pearl-colored satin sheath I bought at a thrift store for seven dollars, and Eddie had borrowed his father's suit. We'd stood in front of a justice of the peace while his mother sobbed and his father held back manly tears. My secondhand heels had pinched my feet, and I'd done my own hair and makeup. I'd felt like I was finally starting a life.

"Rhonda Jean probably walked," the long-haired kid was saying. "Cars don't come this way very often. If you want to get to the bus station, you walk and hope that one of the locals drives by."

"There are locals around here?"

"Sure," Todd said. "Up the beach a ways. There are a few houses. They're set back from the road, so you can't see them if you took the main road in. Sometimes you'll have luck hitching at the Dollar Mart parking lot, which is half a mile that way." He pointed past the kitchen.

Eddie nodded, like he'd been interrogating people all his life. "Who owns the van parked at the entrance to the beach?"

"I do," Todd said. "We use it for grocery and supply runs."

"You didn't offer to take Rhonda Jean to the bus station?"

"She didn't ask me." Todd's voice rose, defensive. Eddie had struck a nerve. "She just packed and left. Like Gretchen said."

"You could have driven her!" Gretchen's voice was high and

wobbly, near tears. "She's just a girl alone! You know what happens on that road, especially at night! We all know!"

"Those are just stories," the long-haired kid said, though he looked like he was about to throw up.

Gretchen whirled on him. "Rhonda Jean is dead!" she screamed. "Are they just stories now? Someone stabbed her, and we all know what happened! The Lost Girl got her!"

"Gretchen, shut up," Kay said, angry.

"What's the matter with all of you?" Gretchen looked around the room. Her cheeks were splotched with red. Todd shifted in his chair, the long-haired kid looked down at the floor, and Kay still looked angry. "Don't you *care*?" Gretchen shouted. "She was our friend!" When the room still rang with silence, she got up and left, banging the front door behind her.

Into the silence she left behind, I said, "Who is the Lost Girl?"

"It's a stupid legend," Kay said, her voice thick with disgust. "It's been around forever. Like there's some girl haunting Atticus Line, killing hitchhikers. It's idiotic."

I looked at her angry face and realized she was afraid. I remembered the blast of cold I'd felt on Atticus Line, the memorial to Katharine O'Connor.

"Listen," Todd said, his voice still defensive. "The point is that we can't help you. We don't believe in ghosts. We didn't know Rhonda Jean very well. She was just passing through, like the rest of us. No one even saw her leave."

The long-haired kid looked up and took a breath.

"I did," he said. "I saw her leave."

CHAPTER TWELVE

That's bullshit," Todd said.

The long-haired kid looked uncomfortable. "It's true. I saw her."

"Mitchell, be quiet," Kay snapped. "We don't even know who these people are."

"My name is Eddie Carter, and this is my wife, April," Eddie said. "We're just passing through, like you are."

"What did you see when Rhonda Jean left?" I asked Mitchell.

Mitchell glanced at Todd, who was glaring at him. Then he looked at Eddie. When he spoke, he directed his words at Eddie, as if there was no one else in the room. "She didn't say goodbye to any of us, like Gretchen said. I was up in the parking lot, having a smoke last night. I was sitting on the back bumper of the van. I just needed to be alone for a few minutes, you know?"

"I know," Eddie said.

Mitchell nodded, his shoulders relaxing an inch. "Rhonda Jean came up the steps. She had her backpack on. She didn't see me. She just walked right past, headed out to Atticus Line."

"What time was this?" I asked.

He shrugged. "Midnight, maybe. I don't know."

"What was she wearing?"

"Jeans and a T-shirt, I guess." Mitchell still directed his words at Eddie, as if he'd asked the question. "It was a hot night. She started walking up the road. I thought maybe I should call out to her, ask where she was going. You know, say goodbye or something. But her head was down and she was just walking, like she was deep in her head. And I barely knew her. By the time I'd thought about whether to say goodbye, she was already too far away."

Silence hung in the room for a minute as we all took this in. He'd sat and watched Rhonda Jean walk off to her death. If he'd said something, would she have turned back? If he'd called to her, was it possible this wouldn't have happened?

"Is that all?" Eddie asked.

Mitchell shook his head. "A truck came down the road. Rhonda Jean put her thumb out to hitch, and it stopped."

I felt my fingers dig into the fabric arm of the La-Z-Boy chair, and I tried to breathe. "What kind of truck?" I asked.

"A pickup truck. It was black." Mitchell squinted into the distance, remembering. "I couldn't see who was driving. Just taillights. But it stopped for Rhonda Jean. She opened the passenger door and said something, and the person driving responded. I think it was a man." He shook his head. "I don't know, really.

I don't remember hearing a woman. But it was a ways up the road, and I couldn't hear very well. They were too far away. I don't know what they said."

"And then what?" Eddie asked.

Mitchell looked like he was going to be sick again. "And then Rhonda Jean got in," he said. "I remember thinking, okay, that's okay. She's got a ride to the bus station. Because, you know, I was worried about her walking in the dark."

There was another beat of silence. Then Todd said, "It's not your fault, man."

But it was. It was everyone's fault. It was Todd's for not offering a ride when he was the only one with a vehicle. It was Kay's because she had never bothered to care. If there was one thing I knew, it was the feeling of carrying someone's death on your hands. The knowledge that if you could rewind time, you could do something differently and that person would still be alive.

Sometimes you regret it, and sometimes you don't. But you carry it either way.

There were more questions to be asked, but I let Eddie ask them. I got up and walked out of the cabin.

Gretchen was outside one of the tents, rolling up a sleeping bag and tucking it into its cloth sleeve. She had angry tears on her face. A couple of other kids milled about, watching us curiously, but I paid no attention to them.

"Hey," I said, approaching her. "Are you leaving?"

"Leave me alone," she snapped, leaning into the tent and pulling out an empty backpack.

I ignored that. "I'm sorry about Rhonda Jean. I liked her. She seemed like a sweet girl."

"Whatever," Gretchen said.

I glanced at the beach, where a boy and a girl were kicking a hacky sack back and forth with almost no skill whatsoever. "I want to know about the Lost Girl," I said.

Gretchen put her backpack down and straightened. Her expression was a painful map of grief, fear, and raw pain. Adulthood, she was learning, completely sucked. I knew how she felt. "Forget it," she said. "It's just a stupid story, like Kay said."

"Who was she?"

"I don't know."

"Have you seen her?"

"No." Gretchen looked away, her fingers unconsciously touching the end of her braid. "I mean, I don't think so."

"What does that mean?"

She watched the kids on the beach and didn't seem to hear my question. "There was a girl in the seventies, I think," she said. "She was found by the side of the road on Atticus Line. They never figured out who she was or who had killed her. She was just a hitchhiker. She was—she'd been dead a long time when she was found. No one cared. She's still on Atticus Line, or at least that's how the story goes. You can feel her. You can hear her sometimes, calling to you. Or you see a light in the trees."

I felt cold sweat on my neck. I'd seen that light in the trees, right before we picked up Rhonda Jean.

"That's how the story goes, anyway." Gretchen hadn't noticed my reaction. "It's one thing to see the lights, or to hear her. But if you actually see her, walking by the side of the road . . ." She trailed off.

"Then what?" I tried to keep my voice calm. I wanted to shake the answers out of her. I clenched my fists at my sides.

"People die sometimes." Gretchen wiped at her face. "If you see her, you'll be the next one found at the side of the road."

"Do you know the name Katharine O'Connor?" I asked.

The girl shook her head. "Was she one of them? I've only been here since May."

Of course. Everyone here was transient. No one would have been here long enough to know Katharine. "Someone left a memorial to her on the side of the road. Fake flowers with her name on them."

"She was probably traveling with friends."

We were both silent for a second, picturing it. Katharine's friends, leaving a bouquet where her body had been found as they made their last trip to the Coldlake bus station. Whoever they were, they'd been scattered for years now, probably gone back to their lives.

"I never believed it," Gretchen said. "I always thought it was a stupid campfire story. Something the guys made up to scare the girls. I never thought I'd know—" Her expression twisted and she bent, putting her hands on her knees. "Rhonda Jean," she said, her voice hoarse with grief, and then she started to sob.

You let her go, I thought, staring at her bent back. *All of you let her go, and now she's dead.* But she was so young, practically a child. I had to remember that. I hadn't been a child for a long time.

I reached out and touched her between her shoulder blades, rubbing up and down. Through the flannel shirt, her skin was so hot I could feel it. I patted her awkwardly.

"Why did she leave?" I asked.

"She liked Mitchell," Gretchen said without pausing, her hands still on her knees. "Mitchell didn't like her back. He didn't even notice her. She felt like she didn't fit in here. She'd heard of a camp in Nevada that was hiring summer staff. She said she was going to get a bus down there and apply. She was hoping to see the Grand Canyon."

So Rhonda Jean hadn't just left, then. She'd told at least one person about her plans, though when she walked away in the middle of the night, she had probably done it on impulse. Maybe she'd decided she'd had enough of being overlooked by the guy she liked. Then, as she'd walked away to her death, the guy she liked had sat there, smoking a cigarette and watching her leave, oblivious to her feelings. Life wasn't fair.

"Tell me honestly," I said as Gretchen straightened up and wiped her eyes again. "Forget the Lost Girl for a minute. Is there anyone here that could have done this?"

"You mean, followed her and killed her?" Gretchen's brows furrowed. "No—I mean, not that I can think of. I don't know most of the people here very well."

"Does anyone here have a car besides Todd?"

"No." She shook her head. "These murders started in the seventies, before a lot of us were born. It doesn't make sense that it was one of us." She looked at me, alarm starting in her face. "Wait a minute. Will the police come here?"

"Yes, they will," I said.

"When?"

I shrugged. *Whenever they get it through their heads that Eddie and I didn't kill Rhonda Jean.* "Probably soon."

"My parents will kill me." She turned back to the belongings she was packing. "I'm getting out of here." She pulled something from the pocket of her bag. "You can have this. Give it to her parents, maybe. I don't want it."

I took it. It was a photo, taken on the beach. Todd was standing there, making a goofy face. Gretchen was standing next to him, smiling. And next to Gretchen was Rhonda Jean, with her freckles and her shy smile. The sight of her hit me like a blow.

The photo was slightly blurry and overexposed, but each face was clear. "You're sure you don't want this?" I asked.

"I don't want anything to do with any of this," Gretchen said, her voice thick with misery and fear. "I can't look at it. Take it."

I slid the photo into my pocket. "Do you want a ride somewhere?"

Her glance was brief, but I read it clearly. "I'll get Todd to take me. There's probably more than one of us leaving. We'll take his van. I think he owes us."

She was right; he did. But she also didn't trust Eddie and me.

Maybe Todd had killed Rhonda Jean. Maybe she had gotten in his van instead of a mysterious truck, and Mitchell was just covering for his friend. It was certainly possible. Or maybe Eddie and I were lying, and we had killed Rhonda Jean ourselves.

Either way, Gretchen had to take a risk to get to the bus station. She was picking the devil she knew, at least a little bit.

I'd been this girl. For years and years, I'd been her. She'd never believe me if I told her the truth.

"Be careful," I said to her. "Please."

But Gretchen had turned away, and she already wasn't listening to me.

CHAPTER THIRTEEN

Robbie's car was blistering hot by the time we got back inside, and Eddie had to roll the windows down while he started the engine. I winced as the backs of my thighs hit the hot vinyl seat.

"You okay?" Eddie asked me, and I knew he didn't mean my scorched skin.

"I'm fine," I said.

He let the feeble air-conditioning start to blow as the car cooled down, but he didn't put it in gear. He just waited.

"I'm really fine," I said.

"No, you're not. You got up and walked out. I've never seen you do that before. And now you're upset. I can tell."

Oh, hell. I felt a twist of panic start up in my chest, somewhere behind my rib cage. "Can we just go? I have nothing to say."

Eddie sighed and pushed his sunglasses up on his head. He reached to Robbie's cassette player and pressed the EJECT button.

A cassette popped out of the player like a piece of toast. "Okay. I can listen to some"—he peered at the cassette—"Waylon Jennings while I wait." He pushed the cassette back in and hit PLAY. The notes of "I've Always Been Crazy" wafted through the car.

I clapped my hands over my ears. "Jesus Christ."

Eddie said nothing. As the air-conditioning cooled us off, he cranked his window closed. That made the music louder.

I gritted my teeth. "Eddie."

"April."

We were in a standoff. I could make the music stop, but we weren't going anywhere until Eddie decided to drive the car. I was strong for a woman, but he outweighed me. We were stuck.

Was this what marriage was going to be like? The two of us in a standoff when we didn't agree? When I'd dated before, I'd never let a man get this deep. When a man pushed me somewhere I didn't want to go, I had simply walked away.

The urge to do that now was strong. I could get out of the car and get away from this, from him, from how I was feeling. I could just start walking, like Rhonda Jean had.

But suddenly, that didn't feel like I would be walking away—it felt like I would be running. This was my life now, this car, this man, this Waylon Jennings music. I'd run for survival before, but this wasn't survival, and I wasn't a coward.

"You know what happened when I was twelve," I said finally, forcing the words out.

Immediately, Eddie reached to the tape deck and turned it off. "You and your mother escaped your father," he said.

It was the story I'd told him on our fourth date, when he'd cooked me spaghetti and meatballs. The story of the summer I was twelve. I'd told him of the night my mother had awoken me, her cold hand gripping my shoulder as I lay in bed. She'd told me to put my most valued belongings in a bag and get in the car. She'd told me to be quiet.

I'd packed a teddy bear, a copy of *My Friend Flicka* stolen from the library, underpants, two T-shirts, my favorite bead necklace, a toothbrush, a hairbrush, and the pink wallet I kept hidden under the mattress, which had eighteen dollars in it. Maybe I had predicted this night would come, or maybe I was just the type of girl who was ready to run. I hadn't bothered to think about the distinction.

I'd forgotten shoes, so I'd gotten into the car barefoot. My mother had coasted slowly down the street with the lights off at first, sneaking away like a thief in the night. Then she'd turned the lights on and started to speed, and I'd begged her, *Faster, drive faster. Drive faster.*

My name hadn't been April Delray that night. That girl's name was long gone, as was my mother's name. We'd driven away in the stifling California summer night to become other people. It was wildfire season, and when I dreamed about that night, I could smell smoke as we drove away, leaving our old life behind in ashes.

We'd wandered for years, my mother and me. She took waitressing jobs, and I was tall and pretty enough that if I put on makeup and did my hair, I could appear older and work behind the counter at Dairy Queen, using a new ID. We'd stay in one place for a while, and then we'd move. We had to stay safe, she said.

After the first few years, I started taking care of her. Of us. I paid bills and made sure there was gas in the car. I got a driver's license—I used an identity that was two years older than my real age for a while—and drove my mother to and from her shifts. I got us through one move, then another.

Then, when I was eighteen, my mother was gone and I was on my own. I told Eddie my mother was dead.

"Those kids back there," I said to Eddie now. "Those girls. They remind me of me. I lived like that for a long time."

Eddie nodded. "Not exactly like that," he said reasonably.

"No. I wasn't on a journey to find myself. I was trying to survive. But those kids are running, just like I was. Rhonda Jean was running. I've hitched before. I've stayed with strangers. Rhonda Jean could have been me."

Eddie didn't answer that. He just took my hand and held it in his. My hand was chilled and clammy, but he didn't seem to mind.

"This place," Eddie said, after we'd sat for a moment in silence. "It's strange, don't you think? There's something wrong about it. Something I can't put my finger on."

He was right. We were sitting in our borrowed car, looking over the lake, but behind us was Atticus Line, the place where Rhonda Jean had started walking, according to Mitchell. It bothered me that the road was behind us. It was so uncannily quiet. Unless I looked in the rearview mirror, I wasn't sure if there was something coming our way.

"I don't want to go back to Rose's yet," I said.

Eddie's voice was calm. "Quentin will be looking for us."

"I don't care."

"Neither do I." He looked at me. "They could end up pinning this on us if we're not careful. Do you understand that? They need someone, and we're right here, being cooperative little bees. She was in our car, bleeding to death. They can forget about all the other details if they want to. That's all they need."

Eddie was right, and yet I didn't feel fear. I'd faced worse things than Detective Quentin, as intimidating as he was. "Then we'll be careful," I said, "and maybe we won't be as cooperative as they want us to. Starting now."

He nodded. "I've been thinking about our next move. Todd said there was a Dollar Mart nearby. Maybe the people who work there have seen Rhonda Jean or know her, if she'd been there before."

I looked out the window at the water. "Rhonda Jean didn't just leave without telling anyone. She told Gretchen she was going to Nevada. She liked Mitchell, and he didn't like her back, so she was leaving."

"Mitchell, who was the last one here to see her," Eddie said. "According to his story, it was right here."

Maybe it was the air-conditioning, but despite the heat of the day I felt cold travel up my spine. Like the cold I'd felt earlier as I'd stood on Atticus Line.

If you see her, you'll be the next one found at the side of the road.

A ghost? Or an urban legend, created to cover up for a murderer?

If you were the one left by the side of the road, did it matter which one it was?

I pulled the photo Gretchen had given me out of my pocket and handed it to Eddie. He studied it in silence for a long moment.

"Quentin hasn't been here yet," I said. "He doesn't know what we know."

Eddie's eyes stayed on the photo. "He's busy looking at us. Our backgrounds. Trying to figure out if we're lying."

"That's true. But right now we're a step ahead of him. I don't think that will last."

"He'll probably be here in a few hours at most," Eddie agreed, putting the car in gear. "We don't have much lead time. Let's go shopping at Dollar Mart."

CHAPTER FOURTEEN

Dollar Mart was a yellow-and-red box in a vast square of parking lot, baking in the July sun. An outdated sign with removable letters, placed at the road next to the entrance, said CLOSED JULY 4. SPARKLER, as though someone had removed the final "S." There were barely half a dozen cars in the huge lot.

I got out of Robbie's car and looked around. From Hunter Beach, this place would be about a half-hour walk—worth it, maybe, if you could pick up a ride from one of the locals in the parking lot. Eddie and I hadn't passed a single car on the way here, so this would be a better bet than standing on the road.

Rhonda Jean hadn't gotten her final ride here, but it sounded like the kids from Hunter Beach came here. Eddie and I crossed the parking lot to the store, my flip-flops slapping against the hot pavement.

I shivered again as we stepped inside, the bell over the door ringing above our heads. The air-conditioning in here wasn't strong, but I still had chills. Eddie was right; there was something off about this whole place. Coldlake Falls, Hunter Beach—all of it. How had we ended up here? I didn't exactly remember Eddie taking that wrong turn. Had I been sleeping? Why couldn't I remember it?

Eddie and I walked through the store, past aisles of canned goods, an aisle of plastic cutlery and folded paper tablecloths. Elevator music tinkled out of the sound system. We glimpsed a few lonely people in the aisles, and that was all. The entire place seemed half-asleep, wilting in the summer sun.

A girl with greasy hair stood behind the counter. Eddie approached. "Hi," he said to her. "Is it okay if I ask you a question?"

Her eyes darted to me, then somewhere over her shoulder, then back to Eddie. "What?"

Eddie slid the photograph of the Hunter Beach kids over the counter. "Do you know any of these people? Have you seen them in here?"

The girl looked at the photo, then shrugged. "Maybe. I guess."

Eddie's voice was patient. "Take another look."

He could have been a cop, I thought. I watched the calm expression on his face, the way his gaze held hers, firm but not intimidating. The girl was staring at the photo, biting her lip, unaware that she was instantly doing as he asked. I knew I was good, but I also knew that my husband of two days just might be smarter than me.

"They've been here," the girl said. "They're Hunter Beach kids. They were with a few others. The owner doesn't like the Hunter

Beach kids to come in here, because sometimes they hang around outside and ask for rides. But he wasn't here that day, so I let them stay. They bought cigarettes and food. I don't think they stole anything."

"When was this?" Eddie asked.

"Two, three days ago?" the girl asked no one. "Um, three."

The bell above the front door jangled, and I peered around the nearest shelf to look. I didn't see anyone. The door wasn't moving.

I shifted to look back at Eddie, who was still talking to the girl. "What do you remember?" he asked her. "What were they doing? Did they say anything you recall?"

"They were talking about a beach party that night." There was definitely a note of envy in the girl's voice. She was around the same age as the Hunter Beach kids. "Um, they only had twenty dollars in cash. And her." She pointed to Rhonda Jean. "I remember her."

The bell over the door jangled again. Again I looked and saw nothing. Was it possible for a bell to malfunction? That didn't make any sense.

"Why do you remember her?" Eddie asked.

"Because she was crying."

A waft of cold air touched my back, like a fingertip.

The bell over the door jangled a third time, and this time I stepped all the way around the shelf and looked at the glass door, peering up at it. It wasn't moving. There was no one outside who had just left. No one had just come in. I looked out at the parking lot. There was no one out there, either, except—

"Oh my God," I murmured. Then I said, loudly: "Eddie."

"Excuse me," Eddie said to the girl. He must have noticed the tone in my voice, because in a second he was at my shoulder, the photo in his hand.

"Look," I said.

His body tensed next to mine.

In the parking lot was a large, black pickup truck, its engine running. It crouched near the lot's entrance to the street, unmoving, the sun glinting off it. Exhaust furled behind it, and I could hear the faint rumble of its engine. It seemed to be waiting. I couldn't see the driver through the sun reflecting from the window.

Eddie strode forward, pushing open the door. The bell jangled overhead yet again, the sound slicing through the store. I followed, trying to keep up with his long strides.

The heat hit me again as we stepped outside. Eddie kept walking, fast, making a beeline for the truck, his gaze fixed on the driver's window. The truck still idled, unmoving.

"Hey!" Eddie shouted.

The driver of the truck gave no response.

This was, I realized, a moment that could go either way. We could stop and watch, waiting for the truck to do whatever it was going to do. We could wonder if we were right, if this was the truck we'd seen last night, if we would ever know the truth or if it would always be a mystery. We could let it go.

But that wasn't Eddie. And that wasn't me.

You weren't scared, Eddie had said to me last night. *You weren't even shocked. You knew exactly what to do.*

And I'd replied: *You weren't scared, either.*

"Hey!" Eddie shouted again, not slowing his pace. It was a big parking lot, shimmering in the heat, and the truck was still idling at the entrance. It was going to drive off. I suddenly knew it as surely as if a voice had said so in my ear.

I opened my mouth, but before I could say anything Eddie pulled the keys to Robbie's car from his pocket, turned in one swift motion, and tossed them to me. "Get the car."

I caught the keys in midair and turned to run to the car, my flip-flops making noise on the pavement. Eddie kept walking.

"Get out, coward!" I heard Eddie say. My heart jumped into my throat—he was going to get himself killed—but my head stayed cool. I unlocked the Accord, jumped into its oven-hot interior, and started the car.

My gaze went to the truck again, and I froze.

Behind the cab of the truck, a hand appeared. It was white, thin, a woman's hand. The fingers curled over the side of the truck bed, as if the woman had been lying down and was pulling herself up. A second hand joined it. I stared in shock as cold waves pulsed through me in the hot car.

As I watched, the girl in the truck bed pulled herself up. Her head appeared over the side now, her face pale in the bright sun. Her hair was ditchwater brown, long and straight, parted in the middle. Nothing about her was worldly—not her skin, not her hands, not her eyes. She was staring at us.

For the first time, Eddie's step faltered. He stopped and stared, his face going ashen as he looked at the girl's unearthly face.

She stared back, unmoving. The truck idled.

Then the truck's engine roared, and the truck moved. It reversed on a wild trajectory that would have thrown anyone out of the bed. But the girl simply stayed where she was, her hands on the side of the bed, not even swaying. Her hair didn't lift in the wind.

The truck's engine gunned again, and it made a turn toward the exit. I put the Accord into gear and hit the accelerator, heading for Eddie. I braked next to him just long enough for him to get into the passenger seat. Then, as he slammed the door, I took off after the truck with the girl in it, heading for Atticus Line.

CHAPTER FIFTEEN

ell me you saw that," my husband said.

The truck had made the turn off the side road toward Atticus Line, and I tried to keep it in my sights as I chased it. "I saw it."

"Say it." He sounded shaken, the only time I'd ever heard him sound like that. "I need to hear it."

"A girl in the truck bed," I said, hitting Atticus Line and accelerating. "Brown hair. Hands on the side of the truck bed. Staring at us."

I'd seen a lot of bad things in my life—maybe more than my share. But I had never seen anything as terrible as that girl, as her face, as her undead hands. She was a dark, cold hole in the fabric of reality, punched through with a naked fist. The word that came to mind was *unholy*, though I had never been religious a day in my life. I had never imagined something could be as vibrantly, furiously dead as she was, and I never wanted to see her again. And yet I was chasing her down Atticus Line.

Eddie's hand gripped the door handle next to him, his knuckles white. Over the sound of the engine, I heard him breathing. He'd thought he was seeing things, that his problem had come back. He was trying to understand that the girl in the truck bed wasn't a hallucination.

And if she wasn't a hallucination, she hadn't been last night, either.

"Which is worse?" I asked him, my eyes still on the road and the truck in front of us. "That she isn't real, or that she is?"

"I don't know." His voice was torn. He took a breath and gathered himself. "He's making a turn up here."

In a wink of sunlight off chrome, the truck disappeared from the road ahead. There must be either a driveway or a side road up there. I couldn't go too fast, or I'd miss it and waste valuable seconds having to reverse. I couldn't go too slow, or I'd lose the truck.

"Steady," Eddie coached me as I approached where the truck had vanished. "Here. On the right."

There was a narrow dirt road leaving Atticus Line. Was it a road or a driveway? I couldn't tell. I swerved onto it, hearing the Accord's tires grind in the dirt and gravel as we headed into the relative dimness of the trees. Unless someone had a driveway several miles long, this was a road. There was no truck in sight.

Eddie cursed. "There has to be a driveway ahead," he said. "It can't be far. Keep an eye out."

I couldn't speed too fast on the dirt road, not without spinning my wheels in the gravel. I had to ease off the gas to keep control. The truck would be better on this road, surer and faster.

We cruised down the dirt road, farther and farther away from Atticus Line, the harsh light dappling through the trees overhead. Where the hell had the truck gone? It was too big to easily hide.

"There." Eddie pointed to a dirt driveway that branched from the road. An old mailbox at the foot of the driveway had a hand-carved sign: SHANDLER.

I turned onto the driveway, and we bumped along its rough surface. The trees opened up and we could see we were on a piece of farmland. There was a farmhouse, its white paint dusty and peeling, and a barn behind it. A lone horse was in the field beyond, drowsing and twitching its tail in the shade of an old tree.

The black truck was parked in front of the farmhouse, its front tires on the worn-out grass. The engine ticked in the silence. There was no movement.

I parked, and Eddie and I got out of the car. There was a second in which we both paused, looking at the truck. Now that the engine wasn't running it had lost some of its menace, but though it wasn't growling it crouched in silence, as if waiting. The sun beat down on my head and sweat started to bead between my shoulder blades.

Eddie moved first. He strode toward the truck, his gaze fixed on it. He wasn't shaken anymore.

I followed, my flip-flops shuffling in the dirt and gravel of the drive. I didn't feel cold, the way I had at the Dollar Mart; instead I felt hot, my chest tight. I made myself go round to the back of the truck. If the woman was still here, I'd be able to see her.

Eddie had gone to the truck's cab to look in the windows. "No one here," he called to me. There was no sound from the driveway behind us or from the house. Whoever had driven the truck had disappeared.

Trying not to flinch, I moved closer to the tailgate and rose onto my toes to look into the bed. There was no woman. But there was something else.

"Eddie," I said. "Look."

He came around the side of the truck and looked into the bed. He didn't have to lift to his toes to do it. "Oh, shit," he said.

It was a backpack, made of dark blue weather-stained canvas, a pack that had been well used and had traveled a lot of miles. I could see patches sewn onto it, also faded: an American flag, another patch that said *Lollapalooza*. The backpack was stuffed full and zipped shut, as if whoever had been carrying it had simply dropped it in the truck bed and disappeared.

Whose pack was it? The truck owner's? The woman's?

Was it Rhonda Jean's? Mitchell had seen her with a backpack. She hadn't had a backpack on her when we picked her up.

"Don't touch it," Eddie said.

Inside the farmhouse, a phone rang, loud and shrill. We heard it clearly in the summer air. It rang and rang. Ten times. Twelve. Fifteen. Then it stopped.

I glanced around. The driver of the truck had to be somewhere. The nearest stand of trees was over twenty feet away, on the other side of the driveway. Had he run there? Or was he in the house, ignoring the telephone?

Then I felt the cold. It crawled up my belly and my chest. Inside the house, the phone started to ring again.

I turned back to Eddie and there she was, past his shoulder, standing outside the barn. The girl with brown hair parted in the middle. She was so still, and something about her was so cold it made me want to scream. I could see the frayed cuffs of her jeans and the crew neck of her T-shirt. She was staring at us with those eyes. Those eyes—

"April?" Eddie said, looking at my face.

I made my mouth move. "She's behind you," I whispered, as if the girl could hear.

Eddie didn't turn. Instead he closed his eyes, as if some kind of sensation moved through him. "I can feel her staring."

I was frozen, no more words in my throat.

Finally, Eddie turned. "Hey!" he shouted, as if she was a trespasser on his lawn. "Hey there!" He started walking toward her, and I rounded the truck and followed, my head pounding with fear. I didn't know who the girl was, but I knew that I didn't want to get any closer to her. My stomach curdled.

"Hey!" Eddie shouted again, but the girl didn't answer and she didn't move. She simply stood there. "What do you want?" he called to her.

If you see her, you'll be the next one found at the side of the road, Gretchen had said.

"What's your name?" Eddie said. "Who are you? Maybe you should—"

A man came from the open barn door, sprinting. He ran past the girl, almost as if he didn't see her, and straight for Eddie. He hit Eddie in a football tackle at top speed, and both men went down.

Eddie didn't even shout. He bucked and shoved at the man, forcing himself out from under him. The man scrabbled at Eddie, trying to land a punch on his face, trying to get his hands around Eddie's throat. The girl standing by the barn had vanished.

I looked around for a weapon I could use or could hand to Eddie, but there was nothing. I considered running into the barn and finding something there, but it looked like I wouldn't have to. Eddie was powerfully strong, and it was becoming clear that the man who was attacking him was much weaker. He was thrashing and fighting, but Eddie was beginning to overpower him.

Eddie pinned the man's wrists into the dirt. "What the hell do you want?" he roared in the man's face, enraged. Sweat and dust covered his cheekbones.

The man's chest was heaving and I could hear the rasp of his breath. It was loud and pained in the silent air, as if he was having an asthma attack. Still he fought Eddie, trying to kick him and pull his wrists free.

He wasn't much older than Eddie and me, with thinning brown hair and a scraggly beard. He was wearing navy blue work pants and a buttoned flannel shirt. He was taller than Eddie, thinner, not as muscled. His labored breathing made him weak, but he was a vicious fighter. Eddie winced as one of the man's bony knees hit him in the meat of his thigh.

"Answer me!" Eddie shouted at the man.

In response, the man pulled one of his hands free and latched it to Eddie's throat, squeezing as hard as he could.

One of Eddie's fists hit the man's temple hard. The man's eyes rolled back in his head.

That's when I raced up the front steps of the farmhouse, pushed open the unlocked door, and ran for the telephone.

CHAPTER SIXTEEN

Detective Beam was smoking a cigarette. I'd watched him pat his pockets, then set the pack of cigarettes on the table between us. I'd watched him produce a plastic lighter from a different pocket. Finally, I'd watched him light the cigarette and smoke it.

They'd split us up this time. Detective Quentin had taken Eddie, while Detective Beam took me. He had thinning brown hair and a belly that mildly strained the front of his shirt. He was decent enough, and he was probably a good detective, but he didn't interest me. The cigarettes interested me.

He'd left the lid of the pack flipped open, so I could see the ends of the cigarettes. I could see the edge of the ripped foil. I stared at that foil, knowing exactly how it would feel against my fingers, the way it crumpled so easily and softly that it was a little creepy. There was nothing else in the world, I realized, that felt quite like cigarette pack foil.

"Mrs. Carter, are you listening to me?" Detective Beam asked.

I shook my head. My mother had smoked cigarettes nonstop on that first long drive out of California, that frantic escape. She'd lit one after another. The stench had made my eyes water, but I'd sat in the passenger seat in silence, trying not to cry as the car's air-conditioning blew an imprecise and unpredictable stream of air somewhere near my face. I'd had my first cigarette at thirteen.

Eddie didn't smoke, and I'd quit long before I met him. I both loved and hated cigarettes in equal measure. I loved them because of the primitive hit they gave my brain. I hated them because they made me just like my mother.

A headache was pounding softly, almost lovingly, behind my eyes.

"Let's go over it again," Beam said.

My mouth was dry as I said, "We saw a truck we recognized from last night. We followed the truck. There was a backpack in the back of the truck. A man attacked Eddie and Eddie fought him off."

Beam ground his cigarette out in the ashtray next to his elbow. How long had we been here? There were no windows. It must be night by now. There had been waiting—so much waiting. For the paramedics to check Eddie out. For the police to bring us here. For the questioning to start. And now, more waiting. My eyes felt like they had been rubbed with sandpaper, and my stomach folded in on itself with hunger.

"Neither of you mentioned a truck in your original statement," Detective Beam said.

I was silent.

He waited for a minute, and then he said, "Okay. So you didn't mention a truck to us, which would have been important information. But you saw the truck today, and you followed it."

"Yes," I said, my gaze dropping to the cigarettes again.

"Do you want a cigarette?" he asked, following my gaze.

"No, but thank you for asking."

"Okay, then. So there was a backpack. And a man attacked your husband. And that's the end of the story."

"Yes, that's it."

"We're not being recorded in here, Mrs. Carter. No one can hear what you tell me."

I decoded that. It meant *no one will know what you say, but no one will know what I say, either.* I braced myself.

"You know what I think?" Detective Beam asked.

I didn't answer. Hungry or not, did he think I couldn't sit here all day? I had nowhere else to be.

"I think that between you and your husband, he's the nice one."

I snapped my gaze up to his.

He had my attention now, and he leaned back in his chair, making it creak softly. "It's possible that what you say is true," he said. "It's also possible that after attacking Rhonda Jean Breckwith, the two of you stashed her backpack somewhere along Atticus Line. You went back today to pick it up so you could dispose of it. You saw Max Shandler's truck, maybe, and you followed him home. Or maybe you just picked his driveway at random. It doesn't really matter. What matters is that you planted the backpack in his truck bed, but he caught you, and he and your husband got in a scuffle. It didn't go quite as you planned." He leaned forward again, his eyes on mine. "It didn't go quite as *you* planned."

I kept my expression blank as I revised my opinion of

Detective Beam. Quentin was the star detective, the one that everyone was terrified of, while Beam was middle-aged, a little puffy, the workmanlike second fiddle. But Beam was better at this than he let on.

He was wrong. But he was so, so close. Closer than he knew. Because if it meant my own survival, or mine and Eddie's, I *would* plant a backpack of evidence in someone's truck. And Eddie would rather die than do that.

"Your husband is an open book," Beam said. "We know everything about him—his parents, his military record, everything. But you?" He shook his head. "You, April Carter, formerly April Delray, are something of a mystery. There isn't much paperwork on you at all. We can't even find a birth record. Where were you born?"

"California." When telling lies, stay as close to the truth as you can so they're easier to remember. I was better at this part than he was.

"Where are your parents?"

"Dead."

"What were their names?"

"None of your business."

"How did they die?"

"It doesn't matter."

"Doesn't it?"

"Not to me."

He sighed and rubbed a hand over his jaw. I heard the familiar rasp of a man who needed to shave. "You got your first driver's license when you were twenty."

That was true, and it wasn't. My first driver's license had been under a different name, because I'd needed to be older than I was. But I'd decided to make April Delray permanent—at least I hoped to—so I'd had to get one in that name as well. It was a lot of work. "Not everyone can afford a car," I told the detective.

"Something isn't right about you," Beam said. "You look like a pretty, unassuming newlywed, but it doesn't quite fit. Everything about you is murky. I think that the best case is that you're scamming your husband somehow."

That made me mad. "I am *not* scamming Eddie."

"No? Does he know your parents' names and how they died? Should I ask him?"

I didn't answer. They could ask Eddie all they wanted. I'd told him enough, and he would keep my secrets. The ones he knew, anyway.

"The worst case," Beam went on, "is that you killed Rhonda Jean Breckwith and made your husband, who is smitten with you, help cover it up."

I shook my head. "I don't know how else to get it through to you. You're looking at the wrong people. We ended up here because we took a wrong turn. It was just bad luck."

"I've seen bad luck, and this isn't it," he replied. "Something brought you here. Why don't you tell me what it was?"

I was about to say something—I didn't know what—when the door opened. Detective Quentin stepped in. His shark's eyes looked at me for a minute, speculating. Then he turned to Beam. "Detective, can I speak to you outside for a moment?"

Beam complied, but I caught the surprise and frustration in his expression before he covered it up. This wasn't a bit of police theater; Quentin was truly interrupting him. Without a word, he pushed his chair back and stood, following Quentin from the room.

They were gone for a long time. I was so hungry all I could think about was hot dogs. I had a craving for one. I wondered where to get a hot dog in Coldlake Falls. And an ice-cold Pepsi.

The door opened again. Quentin stood outside, and he didn't come into the room. "Mrs. Carter, you're free to go," he said in that dead voice of his. "We're sorry to have taken up so much of your time."

I stood and walked past him into the corridor. I turned the corner to the front room of the Coldlake police station, where there were a few police milling about or talking on telephones. Eddie was already there, waiting for me. He looked sweaty and tired and handsome. He still had dirt smeared on his shirt and his face. He took one of my hands in his. "Are you all right?" he asked me.

"I'm fine," I said, confused. "I'm hungry."

"Same here. Apparently, we're free to leave."

And go where? How? They had driven us here in police cars. Robbie's car was still parked next to the black truck, I assumed. We were stranded yet again.

The front door of the station opened and Rose walked in. "There you are," she said to us. "I came to get you. Let's go."

I glanced around. A minute ago, I'd been a murder suspect. None of this made any sense. But I didn't want to question it. I just wanted out.

"Nice to see you, Rose," Detective Beam said, his tone sarcastic.

Her glance at him was dismissive. "You shush, Beam. I want Robbie's car back in my driveway in an hour."

"Yes, ma'am."

"Don't *yes, ma'am* me like I don't know disrespect when I hear it. That car is my property. I know my rights."

Quentin gave her one of his laser looks. "We have to discuss the fact that you lent the car to two murder suspects, Rose. I'll be in touch."

"You don't scare me, Quentin. Robbie told me plenty about you. About all of you. And they aren't murder suspects, are they? I could have told you that." She looked at Eddie and me. "Let's go."

Before I followed her, I looked at Detective Beam. He looked back, straight into my eyes.

He was right. I wasn't the nice one.

Eddie squeezed my hand, and we headed for the door.

CHAPTER SEVENTEEN

Rose didn't have many answers, and she didn't seem to need them. "They thought it was you," was her explanation as she drove us back to her B and B in her Volvo. "Then they found out it wasn't you. That's all you need to know. If you were in real trouble, they would have arrested you back there."

"Is it a trap?" Eddie asked. "Like they're pretending not to suspect us, but they think we'll slip up?"

Rose snorted. "That's an idea just dumb enough for them to try, but no. Quentin doesn't work that way. He narrows in on his suspect, then goes in for the kill. That's how Robbie always put it. Everyone in the Coldlake Falls PD has heard stories about Quentin. The Coldlake PD is too small to handle the bigger cases, so anything bigger than drunk kids or a domestic dispute got handed to the state police." She shook her head. "Robbie was stuck writing traffic tickets and finding wandering grandmas for his whole career, but when the bigger cases came along, he'd pitch in by knocking on doors. They all did. But it was always the detectives' show."

"How long has Quentin been a detective?" I asked.

"Ten years or so." Rose was in a talkative mood, probably because the topic orbited around Robbie. "He didn't come up in uniform, at least not around here. He just showed up one day as the new detective at state. Came from nowhere, like a spook, Robbie said. No one knows much about his personal life, and he never goes to the Fourth of July barbecue. Robbie said he closed cases, even though he treated Robbie like trash. If he really believed you killed that girl, you'd still be at the police station, and you'd be calling a lawyer while they booked you."

I turned to Eddie. "What did Quentin say to you?"

He rubbed a hand over his face. He looked as exhausted and hungry as I felt. There was still gravel in his hair. "I met plenty of bullies in the army. He's a little like that, but he's smarter. He kept asking me about the trip to Atticus Line this morning. He made me go over again how I took the turnoff last night. What made me decide. Whether I had ever been here before." He was quiet for a moment, and I studied his face. He looked stricken. "I kept telling him it was a mistake, but after a while I wasn't sure I believed myself. Then the door opened and someone told him he had a phone call. And that was it."

We pulled into Rose's driveway. I thought I saw a silhouette in a dark upstairs window, but then the wind blew branches of a nearby tree across my line of sight and the silhouette was gone. "It has to be the backpack," I said, staring at the window for another second before getting out of the car. "There's something in there that points to the guy who attacked you. Or to someone else. Something that leads away from us."

"Whatever it is, it isn't our problem," Eddie said as we followed Rose to the door. It was dark, and the air was heavy, the breeze sporadic and soft. Crickets chirped at a fever pitch. A beautiful July night on my honeymoon.

"I guess not," I said.

"I cooked those burgers," Rose said as she snapped the overhead light on and walked to the kitchen. "They're cold now, but I got buns and ketchup and mustard."

"Thank you, Mrs. Jones," Eddie said. I realized I didn't know Rose's last name, but Eddie did. Rose pushed her glasses up the bridge of her nose, flustered.

"So that's it?" I asked as I pulled out a kitchen chair and sat. "That guy, Max Shandler, picked up Rhonda Jean at random, stabbed her, and left her? Then he waited, saw us pick her up, and followed us? It was just something he decided to do?"

Eddie put his burger patty on a bun and picked up the ketchup. The burgers weren't hot, but we were starving. "Mrs. Jones, what do you know about Max Shandler? He's a local."

Rose looked briefly flustered at the use of her last name again, and then she said, "I don't know the Shandlers too well. They've owned that farm for generations. I don't remember Max being in any particular kind of trouble. They keep to themselves." She sat down in the chair across from me. "Maybe he just snapped."

"What about the others?" I asked. "The other hitchhikers? What about Katharine O'Connor, and the ones before her? The kids at Hunter Beach said the murders go back to the seventies. Is Max Shandler a serial killer?"

"Like Ted Bundy?" Rose looked outraged. "We don't have low-lifes like that in this town. Except for the idiots, we're decent people. If Max Shandler killed that girl, he probably knew her. If she was staying at Hunter Beach, they could have met. Maybe he was jealous. Besides, Max can't have been killing people since the seventies. He's only in his twenties."

The man who attacked Eddie hadn't looked much older than us. Katharine O'Connor had been killed just a few years ago, right in Max Shandler's territory. He could have killed her. But even if he had, what about the others that went back decades?

I wasn't going to get answers tonight, and tomorrow—if we got our car back—we were leaving town.

We ate our lukewarm hamburgers, and then Eddie and I took turns in the shower. I was in bed when Eddie came back from the bathroom, wrapped in a large white bathrobe that—of course—had been Robbie's. I was lying on my back, propped on the pillows in the light of the lamp on the bedside table next to me. I had pulled the frilly coverlet up to my collarbones and was trying not to think about Princess Diana hanging above my head.

Eddie closed the door behind him and looked at me. His hair was damp and I could see a drop of water on his temple, about to roll down into his late-night scruff. He had a red mark on one cheek and scrapes on his forearms from scuffing on the gravel. We were both so incredibly tired, but still our gazes locked and something arced between us.

"April Carter," my husband said gently, his gaze taking me in.

I sat up, biting my lip. "That door doesn't lock."

With perfect gallantry, Eddie slid the delicate, white-painted dresser along the wall and in front of the bedroom door. Then he rounded to the window and double-checked that the blinds were closed all the way.

He undid the bathrobe, and I turned out the lamp, pulling my nightgown off over my head.

I slid down onto my back, feeling the lick of anticipation in my veins. The bed sagged gently as Eddie's big body got in next to mine. Princess Diana was about to get a show, but there was nothing that could be done about it.

Eddie's warm body rolled onto mine, skin to skin, and he pressed his face into my neck. "April Carter," he said again.

"Eddie Carter," I said.

His hands moved down my body, over my waist, my hips. Until Eddie, I had always found the sensation of a man's hands on my skin to be invasive, even when part of me liked it. Too much of a man's touch was like sandpaper, because I was always waiting for the next thing—the dig of thumbs into my soft flesh, the heart-lessness, the letdown. My father had hated me, and the men since had used me. Those two things were what I knew. I didn't expect better.

My first time with Eddie, six whole weeks into dating, had been surprisingly fumbling on both our parts. We'd touched each other tentatively in the dark like neither of us had done this before, and in a way, neither of us had. Eddie had had girlfriends, but with me he was obviously nervous, as if he was afraid I'd scream and run. I'd been locked in my own head, overwhelmed with feelings that hit me like a freight train, too distracted and un-willing to put on a show and pretend I was in ecstasy. By all mea-sures, it hadn't been an auspicious beginning.

And yet.

That first time with Eddie, I was someone I'd never been before. I was April Delray, not the woman who was a lie but the one who was real. Eddie—who hadn't been with anyone since he came home from Iraq, since he'd seen and done whatever he'd seen and done over there—was real, too. And to be honest, it wasn't all bad. Parts of it were very good.

So we'd practiced. And now, newly married with his hands on me, we were getting good. So good that I stopped caring about dead girls or trucks or cops or the predicament we were in. I pulled Eddie onto me and kissed him, wrapping my legs around his hips in just the way he liked. I felt his scruff on my skin and his breath against me. I let my hands wander over the muscles and planes I had memorized like a map, and I felt my hips rise under his, my back arch from the bed. Everything went away, as if it didn't matter. Because it didn't.

We tried to be quiet. But deep down, I didn't care.

CHAPTER EIGHTEEN

I awoke to a gentle tap on the bedroom window. Faint gray light was coming through the blinds, the first light of dawn.

The tap came again. I grabbed Eddie's shoulder, but he was already awake, his body tense beside me. "Stay here," he whispered.

He got out of bed in the near-dark and crouched next to the nightstand. Then, still low to the ground, he angled his head so he could see past the edge of the blind without moving it.

I watched his tense expression turn to a bemused frown. "It's that cop," he whispered.

"What cop?"

"Syed. But he isn't in uniform."

We exchanged a look. Then we reached for our clothes.

Officer Syed was waiting for us in Rose's backyard. He was wearing jeans and a gray tee with a brown leather jacket over it, and the sight of him out of uniform was jarring, as if it made him a different person. The clock radio in the bedroom said it was just after five o'clock in the morning.

"I'm sorry to disturb you," he said as we came out the back door and crossed the grass. "I wanted to talk to you, but not in an official capacity. And not where anyone would see."

I glanced back at the house, which was silent. Rose must be a heavy sleeper. The houses on either side were dark. Rose's neatly fenced yard backed onto shrubby green space and, beyond that, trees.

"What's going on?" Eddie asked.

Officer Syed shifted on his feet. "I guess they didn't fill you in on too much when they let you go."

"They didn't fill us in on anything," Eddie said.

Officer Syed nodded. He was in his early thirties, clean-shaven, handsome, a little tired at this early hour, his dark hair brushed back from his forehead. His wedding ring looked new, like mine. I wondered what his wife was like and if they had any kids. His eyes were troubled, as if he'd heard something upsetting.

"Max Shandler has been officially charged with murder," he said.

Eddie and I were silent. Somewhere far off, a starling called in the trees.

Officer Syed took a deep breath. "I grew up here," he said. "Max is only a few years younger than me. I can't say we were friends, but we were acquainted. Everyone is acquainted in a town this size." He turned to us, his brown eyes pained. "If you're gonna ask if I ever thought Max could do this, the answer is no. He wasn't one of those guys you know is headed for trouble. So no, I never thought he could."

"Did he confess?" I asked.

"No. At first he told us that he was home alone when Rhonda Jean was killed, but then he admitted he had no memory of that night. None at all. He remembers getting in his truck to pick up some beer, and nothing else." He shook his head. "Maybe that's a lie, too—I don't know. Max has a lawyer now, so he isn't talking."

Eddie crossed his arms as an early-morning breeze ruffled the grass. "Was it the backpack? That was the evidence that proved it?"

"Rhonda Jean Breckwith's backpack was in his truck, yes," Officer Syed said. "There's blood on the backpack. There's also blood in the cab of the truck. We're testing all of that. A neighbor passed Max's truck as it left his driveway that night, so we know he left home. And the jacket Rhonda Jean was wearing when you found her, when she died—that jacket belonged to Max Shandler."

We were quiet. I remembered Rhonda Jean in the army-style jacket that seemed too big for her, that she'd pulled closed as she stood at the side of the road. Mitchell hadn't said she was wearing a jacket when she left Hunter Beach and got into the truck.

"After we left Atticus Line with you two yesterday morning, we sent two uniforms to keep searching the roadside," Officer Syed continued. His expression was stark. "They found the knife in the grass. It had blood on it. We're processing it for fingerprints. Max probably kept a knife in his truck because if you get in an accident, a knife is handy for cutting your seat belt. A lot of us keep a knife in our car for that."

I spoke up. "Officer Syed—"

"Call me Kal," he said to me with an attempt at a smile. "It's short for Khalid. It's what you can call me before my shift starts."

"Kal," I said. "You're saying that this man picked up Rhonda Jean, stabbed her, then put his jacket on her and left her at the side of the road? Why would he do that?"

Kal shook his head. "I wish I could tell you. Max doesn't have a criminal record. He's twenty-eight. He works on his parents' farm. He had a fiancée for a while, but it didn't work out. She never called the cops on him that we know of." He lifted both hands and scrubbed them through his hair, his frustration and confusion evident. "I keep thinking, I'm a cop in this town and I had no idea Max could do something like this. No idea at all. And then I think about the other hitchhiker a few years ago."

"Katharine," I said.

"Could he have done that?" Kal asked, tormented. "We're looking into the timeline, but it looks like Max was in town when that happened. Katharine was strangled and left dead—not stabbed, put into a jacket, and left alive. But she was a hitchhiker on that road. Which means it could be—Jesus, I can't even think the words. In my town, right under my nose, while I was dealing with drunks and teenagers and car accidents and beach parties. It can't be."

Eddie supplied the words for him. "A serial killer."

Kal nodded. "Yeah. That."

"Quentin has thought about it, though," Eddie said. "That's why he and Beam showed up so fast that night."

"It's been going on for twenty years," Kal said. "Hitchhikers getting killed on Atticus Line. But it isn't all the time, you know? There's a stretch of years between each one. The victim before Katharine was in 1991, and he was a nineteen-year-old boy. The force is pretty divided about it. Some cops think it's just bad luck— something that happens when you get a lot of hitchhikers on a back road like that, where there's no one to see. People are partying, drinking hard, doing drugs. Sooner or later someone gets killed, and how will you ever solve it when everyone who was there has already left? Most of them don't even give their last names. So maybe it's just a numbers game."

"That isn't what Quentin thinks," Eddie supplied. "That's why he kept asking me if I'd been here before, why we were on that road. Like it couldn't have been a mistake." He shook his head. "He wanted to know if I was hunting."

Or me, I thought, remembering my conversation with Beam. *Maybe it was me that was hunting.*

"Katharine O'Connor was only two years ago," Kal said. "Max could have killed her. So could you. The kid in 1991, too." He and Eddie exchanged a glance, and Kal looked away. "Katharine was an upper-middle-class girl who was taking a year to travel while she decided what she wanted to do with her life. She wasn't a runaway. She was meeting people and having fun. She called her parents collect every other day from wherever she was, until the day that she didn't. Her family was beside themselves. They made a lot of noise. Quentin and Beam worked the case hard, but they never got anywhere. The case went cold."

"And then we showed up," I said. It made sense now, why we'd been leaned on so hard, why we were suspected. The police had nothing to show for Katharine, no results after all of that pressure. They had been looking for someone to blame.

"I haven't been on the force all that long," Kal said. "There's a class system between the local PD and the state police, and with my name and the color of my skin, you'd better believe I'm at the bottom of it. Guys like Quentin and Beam don't sit down with me to talk about their murder cases."

Exactly what Rose had said about Robbie. "Still, you're involved," I said.

"Of course I am. This is my town. I suspect that Quentin has talked to experts to give advice on whether this is one killer. Maybe some of the deaths were linked and others weren't, you know? Maybe one serial killer started in the seventies, and when Atticus Line got a reputation, it drew another psychopath to keep it going. Maybe there's just one person, hunting along that road, starting in his twenties and still going. He wouldn't be that old." He shook his head. "If so, that person couldn't be Max. But Quentin doesn't think any of it is bad luck or a numbers game. He doesn't think those murders happen just because it's a dark, remote road. He thinks there's a killer. There have never been any witnesses— just bodies on the side of the road. No one has ever seen anything. Until you two."

The sun was rising now, the light orange tinged with yellow, like a bruise. The sky was hazy and the wind was hot. Eddie and I had been the break in Quentin's case, until the evidence had pointed to Max Shandler instead. If Max was convicted—if the blood and fingerprint evidence connected him, along with the fact that Rhonda Jean was wearing his jacket and her backpack was in his truck—then it blew up the theory of a single serial killer on

Atticus Line. It also blew up the theory that Eddie and I killed Katharine O'Connor—or anyone else. It sent Detective Quentin back to square one for the earlier murders, which would stay unsolved.

I almost felt sorry for him. Almost.

"One of the kids at Hunter Beach saw Rhonda Jean get into a black truck that night," I said. "She was hitching. She wasn't heading for Hunter Beach; she was leaving."

"You two went to Hunter Beach?" Kal looked shocked. "Who said they saw her?"

"A kid named Mitchell," Eddie said. "Age twenty or so, long, curly hair. Dark blond. Five-six, five-seven maybe, a hundred and eighty pounds. If you're lucky, he might still be there."

Kal looked flustered. "Jesus. I—I'll need you both to come to the station and make an official statement."

"No," Eddie said. "You have your killer. You're done with us. Do your own murder investigation. We're getting our car back and leaving town."

"Mr. Carter, this is important."

Eddie crossed his arms over his chest. In the old tee he'd yanked on to come out here, the pose made his biceps rise. He wasn't posing like that on purpose, but it still had an intimidating effect. "My wife and I are leaving town," he said again. "There's nothing you folks can do to stop us. We'd like our car back, but we'll walk if we have to. No more interrogations. No more drives on Atticus Line. We're done."

CHAPTER NINETEEN

The sky didn't clear as the sun rose. Coldlake Falls was breathless. Sweat clung to your skin and mosquitoes whined in your ears when you stepped outside. My cold shower only cooled me off for a few minutes, and then I was wilting again.

Still, we packed our bags after having breakfast with Rose and telling her our plans. Eddie wanted to pay her for our stay, but she said she was going to send a bill to the Coldlake Falls PD. "I won't give them a discount, either," she said.

"I guess we'll go home," I said as I stuffed my bag of toiletries in my suitcase and dashed a sweaty lock of hair from my face. "Some honeymoon that was. I'll see if the bowling alley can give me some extra shifts."

Eddie put his arm around my waist, and despite how hot we

both were, I felt some of my grumpiness evaporate. "I could call the Five Pines Resort," he said. "Maybe they can still squeeze us in for a few days."

I made a displeased sound. I imagined us pulling up to the Five Pines Resort in our bloody car, looking to unpack our bloody clothes. If the police would give any of it back, that was.

I told myself that bloody or not, we could drive out of here, put this episode behind us, and go on with our lives. Maybe, after enough time had passed, we'd tell it as a hilarious story at parties. *Hey, did we tell you about the time we almost got accused of murder? The time an eighteen-year-old girl died of stab wounds in our back seat? That was really something.*

I wanted out of here. I did.

I also wanted to know who the Lost Girl was. I wanted to know who had killed Katharine, who had left the wreath I'd found at the side of the road. I wanted to know if Max Shandler would be convicted of murder or if he'd somehow get off. I wanted to know if Gretchen got home—or wherever she was going—okay and if the other kids at Hunter Beach were still there. I wanted to know what the Coldlake Falls PD would learn when they went to Hunter Beach to do their own interviews, whether Mitchell would tell them what he'd told us, whether any of the other kids there had information that we'd missed.

The story hadn't ended. But it didn't matter—Eddie and I weren't going to be here for the last chapters. We wouldn't get to read it. And on that long-ago summer night, my mother had taught me that in order to survive, you sometimes have to cut and run. Leave people behind. Just go.

We didn't hear from Detectives Quentin or Beam. Presumably, they were off doing the legitimate police work of a murder investigation instead of spending time harassing Eddie and me. We didn't hear from Kal, and I hoped he was out getting the answers he seemed to need so desperately. I wouldn't get to know the end of his story, either.

Rose made a phone call, and someone at the Coldlake Falls PD told her that our car was being returned to us. Robbie's car had already been returned, parked in Rose's driveway as she had demanded. For a woman who was so lonely and disliked, she had a lot of sway. I wondered if she would ever get over Robbie, or if she would just sit in this house forever, looking at pictures of Princess Diana. I wouldn't get to know.

Eddie and I took Robbie's car and picked up lunch, bringing it back for the three of us. We ate in the kitchen as the air conditioners whirred helplessly.

The afternoon was hot and somnolent. It looked like it was going to storm, and I hoped it would happen, that the sky would just get it over with. There was nothing to do but wait.

Eddie, restless despite our exhaustion and lack of sleep, asked Rose if she had any chores around the house she needed him to do. Rose tried very hard not to look pleased at the offer, though she obviously was. I left them dealing with trash bags that needed to be hefted out of the garage and went into our bedroom, where Rose had made up the bed while we were out. I picked up *Flowers in the Attic* and sat on top of the fussy bedspread, underneath the Princess Diana portrait, my legs stretched out in front of me. I aimed the fan directly at myself and started to read.

W ake up.

A hand touched my shoulder.

Wake up.

I was cold. My throat was dry. I rolled over onto my side, trying to get warmer, and something slid off my chest and off the bed. It thumped to the floor.

I opened my eyes.

I was looking at the chair I'd found Rose sitting in a few days ago. It was empty. The room was silent except for the sound of the fan, still blowing softly. My skin was freezing, as if someone had dragged ice cubes over it. Why was I so cold?

I leaned over the edge of the bed and saw *Flowers in the Attic* on the floor. I'd been reading. I must have fallen asleep, the book on my chest. For how long? Why had I awoken?

There had been a hand on my shoulder. I looked around the room. There was no one here.

The sun slanted through the window—it was late afternoon. The cold seeped from my skin and sweat broke out on my back. I sat up on the bed, feeling the damp of my T-shirt where I'd sweated through it. Despite the fan, it was hot in here.

I listened for a second. There was only silence in the house. Where was everyone?

I swung my feet over the edge of the bed and got up, moving to the bedroom doorway. In the main room there was only silence, broken by the ticking of the clock on the wall. The kitchen was dim and clean, untouched since lunch. The mismatched chairs in the sitting room were empty.

There was no one here, and yet it felt like someone had just been here. Like someone had only now walked out of the room, and if I touched one of the kitchen chairs or one of the chairs in the sitting room, I'd find it warm.

My thoughts were fuzzy as my brain slowly woke. Someone had touched me while I was sleeping. Someone had *touched* me.

There was a faint sound from behind the house, and I walked through the kitchen to the laundry room and the door to the backyard. The door was open, and through the screen I saw Rose and Eddie. There was a pile of dead branches in the middle of the yard, which Eddie had likely cut. Rose was cutting lengths of twine, and Eddie was using them to tie the branches into bundles. Both the front and the back of his T-shirt were soaked in sweat.

At the back of the yard, along the fence that separated Rose's property from the woods beyond, was a garden—a long, dark row of turned earth. There was not a single plant growing in it, not a single weed. I remembered the cop, Kyle, telling us that Rose's husband, Robbie, had died in the backyard while she'd dug that garden with a shovel.

I stared at that garden and a shiver went down my spine. How long had Robbie been dead now, I wondered? A year? Two? More? Why was nothing growing in July? Did Rose go out and dig it fresh every day all summer, so nothing grew in it? Had Robbie really died of a heart attack? I pictured a body lying there, where Eddie and Rose were standing now. What had happened that day?

There was a sharp knock on the house's front door.

I jumped at the sound, biting back a surprised scream. I was completely awake now. I put my hand to my stomach, which was churning, and walked across the empty rooms to open the front door.

A uniformed cop stood there. It was Kyle, the cop I'd just been thinking about a minute ago. Kyle Petersen was his name, according to Rose. He gave me the same smirk I recognized from before.

"Mrs. Carter," he said. "Your husband around?"

"What do you want?" I asked him.

He let his gaze move down and up my body. I was wearing my jean shorts and a cream tee that was probably wrinkled. My hair was likely mussed from sleep. Still, he didn't scare me. I kept my chin up and didn't move from the narrow slot I'd made when I opened the door.

"Well?" I said.

"We're returning your car." He gestured with his chin. Behind his shoulder, I saw Eddie's Pontiac parked at the foot of Rose's driveway. Sitting in the street, the motor running, was a police cruiser with Chad Chipwell, the other uniformed cop, in the driver's seat. When he saw me looking, he gave me a small wave.

"Fine," I said, holding out my hand. "Give me the keys."

Kyle held the keys to the Pontiac up as if he was going to give them to me, but at the last minute he snatched them away, as if I were a toddler and we were playing a game.

"You know," he said, "I had you pegged for killing that girl. Still would, if it wasn't for Max."

"Is he a friend of yours? Congratulations on being friends with a murderer."

His eyes went dark with anger. I never did know when to keep my mouth shut. Then again, I wasn't afraid of him. It was almost fun to watch rage in men like Kyle. They always thought it was so frightening. They had no idea how well I knew real fear.

"You really are a bitch," he said.

"I really am," I agreed. "Give me my keys."

"Get out of town and don't come back."

"Believe me, I will. I'd love nothing more than to get out of your shitty, murdering little town. Now *give me my keys.*"

For a second, I thought he'd say something else. Something worse. Then Chad Chipwell tapped the horn of the cruiser, sending a cheery beep.

Kyle dropped the keys onto the porch next to his feet. Then he turned and walked back to the car.

I waited until the cruiser drove away, and then I stooped to pick up the keys. I looked at the Pontiac, parked on the street, and took a breath. There was nothing for it.

I retrieved my flip-flops and walked to the car. I turned the key in the passenger door and opened it.

It was awful.

The smell blasted out first—the metallic smell of blood, left to fester in the heat. I gasped for air and forced myself to look inside.

The police had done a thorough job. Black fingerprint dust—smeared where Kyle had touched it—was all over the wheel, as well as on the inside door handles and the glove box. Strips of fabric had been cut from the back seat, leaving the foam to spring out. More strips had been neatly cut from the fabric on the floor, and the rubber mats to put your feet on were gone. The former contents of the glove box—a map, the car manual, the ownership papers, one of my hair ties, a few quarters, an old receipt—had been placed into a large Ziploc bag on the front passenger seat. Mixed with the blood stench was the smell of some kind of chemical, or maybe alcohol. It was incredibly strong.

I blew out a breath. *Just get me out of this town.*

I rolled down the window on the passenger side—the roller was covered in fingerprint dust—to let the blood smell out. I slammed the door. I didn't bother to lock it. I didn't think anyone would steal this particular car.

Then I went back to the house to let Eddie know we needed to do some cleaning.

CHAPTER TWENTY

The storm hit as we left Rose's. The lowering skies opened and huge raindrops pelted the windshield, washing away the old road dust. I had the passenger window cranked down, trying to keep the blood smell to a minimum, and my arm and shoulder immediately got wet.

Our bags were in the trunk of the Pontiac, Eddie was driving, and I was sitting cross-legged, my bare feet tucked under my thighs. The scene was almost exactly as it had been the night we arrived—except for the rain, the ripped upholstery, and the smell of blood. We had wiped up as much of the fingerprint dust as we could. The back of Eddie's neck had a pink sunburn from his hour doing yard work.

Eddie flipped on the wipers as we stopped at the light turning onto Atticus Line.

"There's probably another route out of town," I said.

He didn't answer. The light changed, and still he didn't move. "Eddie?" I asked.

He stared straight ahead, motionless as the rain spattered on the roof of the car. There was no car behind us, no other car visible. There was only us, sitting in the intersection at a green light, the wipers moving back and forth in the silence. Eddie's gaze was unfocused, suddenly strange. I felt a chill deep in my stomach.

Then, as the light changed again, Eddie pushed the gas and we drove through the empty intersection onto Atticus Line.

I watched him warily as he accelerated on the slickening pavement. I didn't like the way his body was too still, the way he wouldn't look at me. "Eddie," I said again.

He frowned and looked at me. "Yeah?"

It was just him, my husband. There was nothing wrong with him at all.

I shook my head. "Nothing." I turned away, not caring that the rain was blasting into my window. I needed the fresh air.

The sky got darker, and lightning flashed high up in the clouds, followed a few minutes later by thunder. Eddie turned the headlights on.

"Hold on," he said. "We're going through a storm."

The road was a tunnel in the increasing darkness, the trees flecked with yellowy-gray shadows. The wet smell from the hot pavement was electric. I could nearly taste it. I parted my lips and took a deep breath of it as Atticus Line flew by beneath our tires. *This road*, I thought. *Why are we on this road?*

Eddie eased off the accelerator a little as the wipers worked hard. Wind gusted, blowing fat, warm drops of rain into the car, wetting my hair and the side of my face. I felt water running down my neck, soaking my shirt, and I couldn't bring myself to care. I felt detached, like I was leaving not only Coldlake Falls behind, but a part of me as well.

I didn't believe in happy endings—far from it. I didn't believe that Eddie and I would drive off into the stormy sunset in our bloody car and never have a problem again. My guard was incapable of truly going down. I had wanted so badly to get out of Coldlake Falls, as if that meant Eddie and I could go back to normal, whatever that was. But something wasn't right. I had the familiar feeling that whatever we were driving into, it was going to be bad.

If Eddie felt the same, he gave no indication. He stayed focused on the road, which was harder and harder to see. His jaw was set firmly, as if he was determined.

"Jesus, it's dark," he said.

I tilted my head toward the window and looked up. The sky was uncanny. The sickly lemon tinge was fading, blotted out as if with ink. With every second that passed, it felt more like night. Like the night we had driven into town, except for the rain.

"I don't know what's going on," I said as rain ran down my forehead and my face. "It's barely dinnertime. It shouldn't be this dark."

"The rain is getting worse."

I licked water from my lip and made myself say the words. "Should we turn around?"

Eddie's voice was hoarse. "No. We just need to get through this."

So he felt something, too, then. Something very, very wrong. Suddenly, I agreed with him. We'd come to town on Atticus

Line—we'd leave the same way. If the road wanted to issue us a challenge, we were up for it. All we had to do was drive. What could a road do to us, after all?

I wiped rain from my cheek. And then I saw the light in the trees.

A dim glow, as if from a lantern. It grew stronger, then waned again.

"Did you see that?" I asked Eddie.

"We're not turning around."

"No," I said. "We're not."

Lightning flashed overhead again, illuminating the rain-slicked road. This horrible, dead, empty road where no one ever drove. How many people had died here, trying to hitchhike in or out of Hunter Beach? Rhonda Jean, Katharine before her, more. The thought slid into my mind like a whisper: *Those are just the ones they found.*

Were there bodies on this road still? There were no hikers here, no dog walkers or neighbors. How many hitchhikers had gone missing over the years, never to be seen again? How many of them were just past the weeds at the side of the road? They would be scattered bones by now, a jawbone, a scrap of jeans. Would anyone ever find them?

As if he was reading my thoughts, Eddie drove faster.

The hiss of the tires on the pavement was loud. I was starting to get chilled from the rain, goose bumps rising on the skin of my neck. I put my hand on my neck to warm it, and my hand was cold. But I didn't roll the window up.

The wipers whirred loudly as they sloshed rain from the windshield. Ahead rose a glowing light, white like the light in the trees. But this glow was much bigger.

"What the hell is that?" Eddie asked.

It wasn't headlights; there were no beams. It was just a glow, the edges fading into the darkness. My skin got icy; there was nothing natural about that light. I put my hand over Eddie's on the steering wheel. "Drive through it," I told him. "Fast."

He swore, and I saw his throat work as he swallowed. He didn't take his foot off the gas, but he said, "April, what if it's a person?"

"It isn't," I said.

"It could be. Last time, it was Rhonda Jean."

"It isn't Rhonda Jean. It isn't anyone. *Keep going.*"

Eddie's knuckles were white, the tendons in his arms tight as violin strings. I kept my hand over his, as if I could steer the car for him. If I could have pressed his foot harder, I would have.

Ahead, the glow got closer, brighter. It reminded me of *Close Encounters of the Third Kind*, a movie I had thought a little ridiculous when I saw it. If there were aliens, they wouldn't bother sending signals to Richard Dreyfuss. They would annihilate us, and it would be over in a flash. Simple.

But this wasn't an alien spaceship. This light was *cold*. It was a void in the darkness, even though it was technically light. Somehow, it wasn't light at all.

Eddie didn't brake, and the car flew into the cold light. We were blinded for a second, and all sound stopped except the rain pounding the roof. Then the glow was behind us, the darkness closing in again. Lightning streaked the sky, and in its flash we saw a woman in the middle of the road ahead of us, her back to us as she ran down Atticus Line in the rain.

"Jesus!" Eddie swerved and braked to avoid hitting her. The car skidded on the wet road, the tires skating. Eddie spun the wheel, trying to right us. I was thrown against the passenger door, and I twisted to put my back to it, my hands reaching fruitlessly to grasp at nothing.

The Pontiac kept skidding over the road. Through the rain I could see the girl in the light from the headlights. She was soaked, her brown hair wet down her back. Her T-shirt stuck to her skin. She was barefoot below the frayed hem of her jeans, and her legs pumped as she ran down the middle of the road, right along the faded yellow line.

There was a screech of tires on gravel, and the car spun to a stop on the shoulder of the road. The rain pounded on the roof. Lightning flashed again, but we were out of sight of the running girl.

Eddie lifted his hands from the wheel and pressed them over his eyes. "My God," he said softly, as if to himself. "What's happening?"

I was leaning against the passenger door, where I'd landed when the car stopped. The motor was still running. My hand was gripping the edge of the open window so hard my nails were about to break. I took a breath and forced my hand to unclench.

Eddie still had his hands over his eyes. I'd seen him like this before, when he woke up from the worst nightmares in the middle of the night. I swallowed in my dry throat, unbuckled my seat belt, and sat up.

"Eddie," I said. He didn't answer.

I leaned over and unbuckled his seat belt, too. A gust of wind blew and rain washed into the window, waking me up, reminding me where I was. I was on a deserted road, I had just seen something that couldn't be real, and I had to help my husband.

"Eddie," I said again. I used the only tactic I knew, the one I used when he woke up from nightmares about whatever had happened in Iraq. I crawled across the console between us and wrapped my arms around him, curling against his body.

He wasn't weeping. He wasn't even shaking. He was just still, his hands over his eyes. As if he'd left his own body for a minute, made it shut down until he wasn't dangerous anymore. I felt him take a shallow breath.

I ran a hand up the back of his neck, into his hair. "Eddie," I said again, repeating his name, over and over. I touched him wherever I could, letting my chilled hands run over his forehead, his neck, his tense arms. I rubbed him gently, repeating his name, until he finally lowered his hands.

The words he said then broke my heart. "April. Did that really happen?"

"Yes," I said, stroking my hand over his cheek. He was looking straight ahead; he hadn't turned toward me yet. He couldn't. I knew he needed me to say it. "That happened. There was a bright light, then a girl running down the middle of the road in the rain. I saw it. If you're crazy, then I am, too."

"It was her, wasn't it?"

"Yes."

"What does she want, April?"

I let my palm run over the tight tendons of his neck. "I don't know. Take a breath, honey."

Eddie took a shaky breath deep into his lungs. Some of his muscles loosened a little. "April," he said. "Do we—"

The Lost Girl came running toward us from the dark road, through the veil of rain. Her face was pale and terrifying in the headlights, her eyes black. Her mouth was open. She was screaming.

I could *hear* her. She was screaming.

She ran toward my side of the car, and—too late—I remembered that my window was open. I tried to grasp the roller, but it was slick with rain, and the Lost Girl was already there. Her long, white fingers grabbed my windowsill, and for an awful second I just stared at them in horror, so close to my face.

"Help me!"

Her voice was high and reedy, mixing with the rush of rain. *That wasn't real. She isn't real*, I told myself, and then she screamed again.

"Help me! Please!"

I raised my gaze from her hands—everything was too fast and too slow at once—and I saw the livid purple bruises on her pale neck, the thick trickle of blood from one ear. The blood was smeared in her hair and across her cheek, and it was still pulsing slowly out of her, dark and viscous. Then Eddie's big, powerful hands gripped my shoulders and pulled me away from the window.

I fell back across the console, scrambling away from the window in fear as Eddie lunged across me for the window roller. He gripped it and cranked it around once, making the window squeal as it pushed against the Lost Girl's hands.

"Please," she begged. Her dark eyes were huge, her lips painfully cracked. *"Please."*

Eddie cranked the window roller again. And the Lost Girl reached into the car, gripped his wrist, and pulled him toward her.

He gave a surprised grunt, and I felt his entire body slide partway out of the driver's seat and across the console. I hadn't known that anyone could be strong enough to drag Eddie. His foot left the brake, and the car lurched, trying to drift forward but held back by something. Was the Lost Girl doing this? Was she pulling my six-feet-four husband with one hand and holding back the car at the same time?

She pulled again, and Eddie's grunt was more of a growl. He was trying to free himself from her grip. The car lurched again.

I scrambled over him, into the driver's seat. It was messy, with his legs in my lap, but I slid beneath his weight and put my feet down. I felt the brake against my bare foot.

"Hold on," I said, and stomped on the gas.

The car gave a deep, frustrated roar. The back end had gone into the weeds, and I felt the wheels skid. Pieces of gravel pinged against the car's body. The rain pounded down, and another flash of lightning lit up the sky. I spun the wheel and stomped on the gas again.

This time, something gave. The back of the car fishtailed left, then right. I spun the wheel and gassed it again, and it gave more.

In the passenger seat, the Lost Girl still had a grip on Eddie's arm. She was screaming again, begging us to help her, to get her out of there. Her hand was the white of death against Eddie's tanned arm.

The car loosened from whatever had trapped it and lurched forward. I looked at Eddie, who was still struggling.

"Go!" he shouted at me. "Go!"

I didn't need to hear anything else. I floored the gas and the car came out of the weeds, off the shoulder and onto the blacktop.

Eddie shouted, but he didn't tell me to stop. I couldn't look at him; I was too busy righting the car on Atticus Line, trying to orient myself through the sheets of rain. The Lost Girl was still screaming.

Then she was gone, and Eddie jerked himself away from the window. I got us out of there as fast as I could.

The glowing light was gone, too, and there was only blackness and rain. I had been completely turned around, and I had no idea which direction I was driving; I only knew I was getting away from the Lost Girl. The rain was a solid mass on the windshield, the wipers groaning as I struggled to see the road.

Gradually, I realized I could see more easily. The light was turning grayish orange, tinged with purple, a stormy sky with the sun setting. The rain let up a little. I made sure I was on the right side of the yellow line, and I eased off the gas. I risked a look at Eddie.

He had pulled his legs from my lap and was sitting in the passenger seat. The window beside him was rolled up. He was soaked, his expression grim.

"Are you okay?" I asked him.

"I'm fine."

"Did she hurt you?"

He lifted his hand, shook it. In the dim light, I couldn't see any sign of a mark on his arm. "I don't think so. I don't feel any pain."

I ran a shaking hand through my soaked hair, pushing the messy strands off my face. The hand that still held the wheel ached because I was gripping so hard. "What the hell do we do now?"

Eddie was silent in the passenger seat, watching the road.

"That was insane," I said, because I had to hear the words out loud.

"Yes." Eddie's voice was calm as he agreed with me. "That was insane."

"So?" I asked him. "What now? Where do we go?"

He shook his head. "We don't have much choice about where we go right now, April."

"What do you mean? Why not?"

He pointed to a sign that flew by out the window. "Because apparently, we're driving back to Coldlake Falls."

CHAPTER TWENTY-ONE

By two o'clock in the morning, the rain had tapered off. It pattered gently against the window of our bedroom in Rose's B and B.

We'd come back to Rose's, exhausted and confused, because we couldn't think of anywhere else to go. She had answered the door with a frown, given us an inhospitable grunt in greeting, and said, "You may as well come in." Then she'd gone to her own room and hadn't asked any questions.

So we were back on the bed with the blue bedspread. After we undressed, Eddie fell asleep almost immediately, which was surprising. He was curled up next to me as I lay on my back, his arm around me. Even in sleep, his body was tense. He'd barely spoken since we came back to Rose's. He'd gone deep inside himself to somewhere I couldn't follow.

I stroked his hair gently as he slept. I stared at the ceiling.

I was past the point of questioning what we'd seen. We *had* seen it. The question was, why?

I was sure that everyone who drove on that road didn't see what we had. Maybe no one had ever seen it, and Eddie and I were the first.

The Lost Girl, according to the legend, had haunted the road for years, even decades. And yet no one else had seen the bright light and the girl running down the road. No one else had seen and heard her screaming and begging for help. Gretchen had said something about feeling the Lost Girl's presence, seeing a light in the trees, and hearing her calling. There was nothing in the legend about a girl screaming for help as she ran.

So Eddie and I had been chosen, perhaps. I'd never believed in ghosts before, but that didn't matter. I believed in the lights I'd seen. I believed in the girl who had gripped Eddie's hand and tried to pull him from the car. I had gotten this far in life by being practical, by dealing with what was right in front of my face without dithering. So now I believed in ghosts. Or at least I believed in *this* ghost.

What do you want? I asked her in my head. Everyone had a scheme, something they were trying to get. Ghosts didn't have to be any different. If a ghost stopped your car in the road, then she wanted something. It was the only logic that made sense.

Maybe she had wanted to kill us.

Maybe she had wanted to tell us something.

Maybe she had wanted us not to leave town.

Maybe there was something here for Eddie and me. Something we hadn't found yet or couldn't see.

We hadn't made any plans before Eddie fell asleep. The

smartest thing to do was get up in the morning and try to leave town again. Take another route. She couldn't stop us every time, could she?

I tried to picture the Lost Girl's face. I had seen her so clearly, but now that I tried to recall her in my memory, I couldn't put the details together. I remembered the dark eyes that seemed to encompass everything and her long hair parted in the middle. Everything else was like a photo that had been damaged while it was being developed—it was there, but it wasn't.

Gretchen had said that the Lost Girl was found by the side of the road, and she'd never been identified. *She'd been dead a long time*, Gretchen had said. Left in a ditch to rot. The ultimate indignity.

If I were her, I would be angry, too.

Eddie shifted, but he didn't wake. I stroked my fingers along the warm skin of his temple. Eddie never slept deeply, the relaxed sleep of the untroubled. I had known him a long time before I truly understood how much he suffered in silence, how much he kept tamped down every day.

He had told me a few details of his experience in Iraq. He'd been shot at. He'd said there were homemade bombs that could tear a man to pieces. There were long, dull periods of waiting and routine. Lots of what happened, he said, didn't make the news. He'd been very clear about that. *Don't believe the news, April. The news is only what they want you to see.*

Whatever he saw behind his eyelids at night rarely left him alone. Tonight had only made it worse.

I saw a lot of things, too, when I closed my eyes, that I would rather not see. Maybe everyone did. But Eddie and I had seen more than most.

We were going to see more bad things before this was over. But even so, I didn't think we were going to leave town tomorrow.

If we do this, I thought into the darkness, *we do it on my terms. And if we do it, you owe me. Do you hear me? I don't care if you're dead. This was supposed to be my honeymoon. You owe me.*

The Lost Girl didn't answer.

Reluctantly, I closed my eyes.

CHAPTER TWENTY-TWO

Rose had a part-time job at a grocery store as a checkout clerk. Eddie and I followed her to work the next morning. We filled a cart full of groceries: frozen hamburgers, tuna, canned peaches. SnackWell's cookies and SlimFast bars for Rose and me. Hot dogs and soft white buns. Cans of Diet Pepsi. Bologna, bags of frozen peas and corn, Raisin Bran, Frosted Flakes, ice cream bars, packets of Kool-Aid, bricks of bacon. Rose checked us out, using her employee discount. Her glasses reflected in the fluorescent light, and the green apron made her skin look yellow.

"This is nice of you, I guess," she said, the words coming out reluctantly.

"It's the least we can do." I gave her one of my big smiles. "I think we'll be staying for a few days. We may as well finish our honeymoon."

Rose gave me a narrow-eyed look. We hadn't told her why

we'd come back last night, or why we'd decided to stay in Coldlake Falls instead of going home. We weren't sure ourselves why we were here. Eddie and I needed to regroup.

We drove the groceries back to Rose's and put them away. Then, unable to look at her knickknacks or Princess Diana any longer, we drove to downtown Coldlake Falls, in search of somewhere to eat. Eddie didn't talk much, but I was used to that. Still, I knew he was tense, and both of us were tired after a restless sleep.

Now that I wasn't in the back of a police car, I took a better look at the town. Coldlake Falls was busy on a weekday in July, the pharmacies and grocery stores bustling, sweaty parents and sun-burned kids roaming the sidewalks. It was a town big enough for exactly one Blockbuster—the parking lot full—and a movie theater with *Apollo 13* and *First Knight* on the marquee. It was the place you went to stock up on cold beer or buy sunscreen before you moved on to your campsite or motel. The people here were just passing through. There were a couple of teenagers with backpacks at the bus station, waiting for a bus, but we didn't recognize them. They were likely coming from Hunter Beach.

We found a diner and slid into a booth, the skin on the backs of my thighs sticking to the vinyl seat. It was a small place, packed with people coming and going, smelling of coffee and french fries. A TV on the wall above the front cash register was showing a news story about Tonya Harding. I ordered a Coke and a salad. Eddie ordered a turkey sandwich and made no comment when I stole fries from his plate.

"So," he said after a minute. "We're going to find her, right?"

I paused with a fry halfway to my mouth. Eddie's face had its usual serious expression, but something in the way he looked at me was careful, as if he wasn't sure I'd agree.

"I suppose we are," I replied, keeping my voice light and neutral. Like it didn't matter to me.

I was trying to relax him, but instead he got even more serious. "April, do you want to go home?"

I raised my gaze to his. Though most people couldn't read Eddie's stoic expressions, I could. I'd studied him in depth; he was my favorite topic. So I knew that right now, Eddie didn't want to go back to our apartment in Ann Arbor. But if I asked him to, he would do it.

There was something deeper in his expression, something troubled. Something that hadn't been there before last night. But I couldn't worry about that right now.

"I don't want to go home," I said. There was nothing for me at home. My job was pointless and our apartment was the cheapest one we could afford. I only wanted to be where Eddie was. "I want to find her."

His brow smoothed a little, but he shook his head. "So do I, but I'm not sure why."

"Because it would be meaningful," I said. "We'd be doing something that matters, at least a little. More meaningful than our jobs. More meaningful than playing Yahtzee and taking naps."

"It's a terrible idea."

"We've had terrible ideas before. At least, I have."

"Like marrying me?"

The question was a surprise. I'd never given him an inkling that I didn't want to marry him. Had he wondered about this without telling me? "No," I said. "Like the time I drank vodka

152

before going to the fall fair and eating a funnel cake. I'll never eat a funnel cake again."

His shoulders relaxed. This was how it worked: I eased him down, and in return I got to watch some of the pain leave his body and his face. He'd never met a girl who was willing to put the work in. Well, he'd met her now.

"I guess we need a plan," he said, his voice easier now.

"A ghost plan," I said.

"I don't know how to make one of those."

"It will be hauntingly difficult."

Eddie paused with the ketchup bottle in his hand and smiled a little.

"One would even say vanishingly hard," I tried again.

"April, your puns are terrible." He paused. "It will be fine as long as we don't get spooked."

I shook my head. "I can't believe I married you. How did I ever find you?"

Eddie squished his sandwich flat, making the lettuce crunch. He was smiling now. "You came out of your room with no shirt on, as I remember."

"And it was a done deal."

He shrugged, his eyes on his sandwich, but his cheeks went just a little bit red.

"I wish I'd known how to find the right man earlier," I teased him. "I wouldn't have worn a shirt for all of 1994."

"Too bad," he said decisively. "I found you first."

It was my turn to feel warm. Would this feeling wear off, I wondered? In twenty years, would I be sitting across from Eddie, thinking he was nothing but a nuisance and a pain in the ass?

Maybe, but right now it was hard to picture it. I wondered if he knew that his compliments made me go gooey inside. I didn't think he did.

"It can't have just been the bra," I said, sipping my Coke. "I mean, you'd seen a topless woman before."

"We're not talking about that," he said, his voice firm, his previous tension gone now. Aside from the fact that he'd had a couple of girlfriends, Eddie never gave salacious details. *I didn't marry them*, was his explanation. *I married you.*

"So it *was* the bra," I said.

Eddie paused, as if he wanted to say something else, and then he said, "It was blue. I'd never seen a blue one before. You know what? You've never told me why you said yes to me that day, considering I was basically a Peeping Tom and I had my shirt on."

Why had I said yes to him? I hadn't been on the hunt for a boyfriend, or even a date. I had never let anyone get close to me. I'd just been on my way to get laundry. I should have forgotten about Eddie Carter in minutes, the way I forgot about most of the boys I met. But I hadn't.

"It's because I'm not stupid," I said, spearing a forkful of salad. "Any woman who turns you down is stupid. But it's too bad for the rest of them, because I found you first."

"And here we are," he said. I knew in that moment that he found it as unlikely as I did, that we were married. That we'd been married for nearly five days.

"Here we are," I replied. "And I guess we just agreed to try and find the Lost Girl."

Eddie sighed. "What do we know?"

"Not a lot. Gretchen said she was murdered in the seventies

and her body was left by the side of the road. They never solved it or found out who she was."

We were quiet for a moment. It really wasn't much to go on, and neither of us was an investigator. We didn't know where to start.

"We know what she looked like," Eddie said, his voice soft. "No one else knows that."

I closed my eyes. I could picture the girl we'd seen, with long hair parted in the middle. I could picture the clothes she was wearing. But her face—would I recognize her face if I saw it in a picture?

"We could look at newspapers," I suggested. "This is a small town. A murdered girl would be in the papers, especially if they didn't know who she was."

"We'd have to read a whole decade's worth if we don't know the year," Eddie said. "Do you think Officer Syed would help us?"

I nodded. "The police will have a file, right? He probably won't let us read it, but he can give us something to go on so we don't have to spend a week in the library."

"Someone missed her," Eddie said. "Someone knew she was gone, wondered where she went, maybe filed a report. But she could be from anywhere." His gaze flicked past my shoulder to something, and he frowned before looking back to me.

"What is it?" I asked him.

"That girl in the next booth is looking at us."

"A lot of people are looking at us in here." It was true. Some of the people coming in and out of the diner paid us no mind, but others gave us intent stares, as if they didn't care if we noticed. I knew right away what the difference was between a local and a tourist. The locals had heard that a girl was murdered; the tourists hadn't.

"I know, but that girl is really staring," Eddie said. "She barely looks old enough to drive. Why is she staring at us?"

I craned my neck and twisted around. Sure enough, in the booth behind us was a teenage girl, sitting alone. Her brown permed hair was tied in a ponytail, and she had sunglasses perched on the top of her head, like me. She had a glass of Coke in front of her and was wearing an oversize tee. She caught me looking, and I narrowed my eyes, giving her a warning signal. She blinked back at me slowly and sipped Coke through her straw.

I turned back to Eddie, affronted. "What is her problem?"

"Ignore her," he said. "She's just some local kid. Do you think we should go back to Hunter Beach?"

"We can try, but I doubt they'll talk to us. We need to start with Kal. He won't talk to us if we walk into the Coldlake Falls police station, and I never want to go back there anyway. We need to meet him in private. I bet Rose knows how to get a message to him."

We were interrupted when the girl from the next booth approached our table. "Hi," she said, in a tone that was bold and not shy in the least.

I looked up at her. Now that she was up close, I could see that her T-shirt had Gwen Stefani on it and she was wearing cutoff jean shorts. Black eyeliner lined her eyes, a little smudged, belying the roundness of a face that had only recently emerged from childhood.

"Hi," I said.

The girl had a newspaper in her hand. She put it on the table between us, slapping it down dramatically. "This is you guys, right?"

It was a local paper, the *Coldlake Falls Free Press.* The headline on the front page read: ARREST IN LOCAL HITCHHIKER MURDER. The photo was of Rhonda Jean. It was a school photo, and Rhonda Jean was giving a shy smile that was a little sad, her freckles sprinkled across her nose.

"What do you mean?" I asked the girl, tearing my gaze from Rhonda Jean's face.

"Here." The girl planted her index finger on the article, pointing out a paragraph. *Breckwith was apparently discovered injured on the side of Atticus Line by a couple passing through town, who claimed they were on their way to their honeymoon. Coldlake Falls PD will not comment on whether the couple are persons of interest in the investigation.*

"No comment," Eddie said.

I stared at the line, livid. Which jerk on the Coldlake Falls PD had refused to say we weren't suspects anymore? Quentin? Or Beam?

"It *is* you," the girl said. "I saw you at the grocery store with Rose. You're staying with her, right? Rose doesn't have any friends, and she never has guests."

"Who are you?" I asked her.

"I was curious," the girl said, as if I hadn't spoken. "I figured you might be this couple, so when I saw you get out of your car and come in here, I looked in your car windows. Half the fabric in the back seat is cut out. That means you're these people." She tapped the newspaper again. Her nail was smooth and manicured, painted with opalescent polish. "Rhonda Jean Breckwith was in your back seat, right?"

I glared at her. "You're annoying me."

"How do you know Rose?" Eddie asked.

"I used to work at the grocery store until I got fired. She hates me, but that's cool." The girl looked at me again, unafraid of my murderous expression. "What did Rhonda Jean say to you when you picked her up? Did she say Max Shandler had killed her? I want to know everything."

For God's sake. "Why is it any of your business?"

"I *live* here." The girl sat in the booth next to Eddie. He slid down politely, because he was a gentleman, and she settled in, leaning forward. "This is my town. I've met Max Shandler. If he's been killing girls like me, I want to know about it."

She had a point. Eddie and I exchanged a look. He seemed puzzled and almost amused. We should probably get rid of this girl, but Eddie was in no hurry to do it. I let myself think through the angles for a minute. This girl knew Max Shandler. Maybe she could answer some of our questions.

"What's your name?" I asked her.

"Beatrice Snell. What's yours?"

"April Carter." I nodded toward Eddie. "That's Eddie Carter, my husband."

"Hi," Eddie said.

"Hi," Beatrice said. "Do you think Max Shandler killed Katharine O'Connor, too? What about Carter Friesen?"

The back of my neck tightened, and I saw Eddie straighten a little. "Carter Friesen?" he asked.

"August 27, 1991," Beatrice said. "Stabbed on Atticus Line after getting picked up hitchhiking. He barely made it from the bus station. He was found on the stretch just past the turnoff to town. He was eighteen."

There was a second of silence at the table as we stared at her.

"There are more," Beatrice said. "Rhonda Jean was stabbed, right? So was Carter. But not all of them were. Max couldn't have killed all of them, but if he did the last three, why do you think he changed his method of killing?"

"Jesus," I said. "How old are you, fifteen?"

"Sixteen."

"These hitchhiker cases on Atticus Line," Eddie said, his voice gentle. "You know about them?"

"I know everything." Beatrice pulled the newspaper toward her. "I collect all the information I can find. My sister does, too. You could say it's a hobby, except it's about dead people so we're not allowed to talk about it. I know it's weird, but I don't care. I want to know the truth. I want to know everything about these murders. I want them solved. And now another one has happened, and you two practically witnessed it." She looked back and forth between Eddie and me, her look assessing in a way that was cold for a girl of only sixteen. "Either that, or you did it yourselves. But of course you didn't. Max did. Right?"

I tried to read her. Was she telling the truth? What did she actually believe?

"What do you want from us?" I asked her.

"I want to know what you know, and you want to know what I know," Beatrice said. "Why don't you come to my house and we'll talk?"

CHAPTER TWENTY-THREE

Beatrice had her own car, a shiny blue four-door that gleamed so hard in the summer sun it made me squint. When she opened the driver's door, I could see the interior was immaculate. New-car smell wafted out and hit my nose.

"Want to get in?" she asked us.

"We'll take our own car, thanks," Eddie said.

The girl shifted her weight, thinking. She pulled the pair of silver-rimmed mirror sunglasses from the top of her head and put them on. "That's probably smart," she said as I stared at my own reflection in the glasses. "But park down the street from my house so no one sees you, okay? Follow me."

We got into the Pontiac, parked a few feet away. When Beatrice started her car, "You Oughta Know" blared from the sound system at top volume. She reversed from her spot with a squeal of tires and drove off.

"What are we doing?" Eddie asked as he pulled out and followed her. "She's a child."

"I feel old," I agreed. "But she can't hurt us, right?"

Eddie thought it over as we crossed through town. "Either she knows something or she doesn't. Maybe she's just a lonely girl looking for some attention. We'll find out pretty soon either way."

Beatrice led us out of downtown as the sound of Alanis wafted back at us from her open windows. In a few minutes we were on a suburban street, immaculate and sleepy in the midday heat. Except for a few lazy sprinklers, the drops of water gleaming like diamonds, nothing moved.

She parked in the driveway of a house with white siding and blue shutters. It was less than ten years old, the home of an up-and-coming family. The lawn was perfect green, the garden lining the front of the house bright with pink geraniums. A pot with more pink flowers in it was artfully placed on the porch, a bumblebee hovering over it. Beatrice's brand-new car started to make more sense.

As instructed, Eddie and I drove past her driveway and parked farther down the street. Beatrice had gone into the house, and as we approached, she opened a side door and waved at us. The secrecy was a little excessive, but we rounded the side of the house and went inside, avoiding the front.

"Where are your parents?" Eddie asked.

"At work," Beatrice replied as the door banged shut behind us.

The blast of air-conditioning hit me as we walked in. I exhaled a breath, feeling goose bumps rise on my skin. I was so used to the low-grade air-conditioning at Rose's, and at most of the places we'd been in town, that it felt freezing.

Beatrice didn't seem to notice. "My stuff is all in my bedroom where my parents can't see it," she said, taking off her sunglasses, "but it's, like, weird if we go there, right? Sit down in the kitchen and I'll go get it. Help yourself to a drink from the fridge." She thudded up the carpeted stairs. Eddie and I walked down the cool-tiled hall to the kitchen, where there was a country-style wooden table and chairs and an antique clock hanging on the wallpapered wall. I took a seat on a chair that had a seat cushion tied to the rungs of the back, and Eddie sat opposite me.

The window looked to the backyard, as green and perfect as the front yard was. A chaise longue was placed in the middle of the grass, and another teenage girl lay on it, a towel over her face as she suntanned.

"Who's that?" I asked Eddie.

"She mentioned a sister," he said. "Maybe that's her."

Beatrice came back downstairs with a small stack of file folders, their edges bent with frequent use. She also had a spiral notebook and a pen that was larger in diameter than a thumb. I wondered how she wrote with that thing.

"Okay, I'll start," she said, pulling up a chair as if we were all about to work on a school project. She took out one of the files and opened it. "These are all of the cases I could find of hitchhikers who died on Atticus Line. There are six."

I stared at her in shock. "*Six?*"

"It's a lot, right?" Beatrice said. "The first one was in 1976."

"The Lost Girl," Eddie said. I felt a chill on the back of my neck, and it wasn't just the air-conditioning.

Beatrice looked from Eddie to me, missing nothing. "You know about her?"

"We heard the legend. What is this?" I deflected by reaching to her stack of papers and pulling off the top one. It was a photocopy of a story from a newspaper—a few paragraphs in a single column with no photo, a piece that had been buried on an interior page. The headline read: NO LEADS ON UNIDENTIFIED REMAINS FOUND.

"That's the Lost Girl," Beatrice said. "That's what they wrote about her in the papers."

"They didn't write much." I scanned the short paragraph. It only said that the remains of a woman, between twenty and thirty years of age, had been found on the side of Atticus Line. The coroner's examination concluded that she had suffered several blows to the head, and that she had been there at least a month. The girl had no identification on her, and no one had come forward to identify her. Anyone with information was asked to call police. The article was dated April 30, 1976.

Several blows to the head. The girl we'd seen in that horrible visitation—had it only been last night?—had had bruises, a trickle of blood coming from her ear. She'd still been bleeding, her hair and neck wet with it. *Help me*, she'd screamed.

I felt hopelessness threaten my mood. What did we think we were doing? The Lost Girl could be anyone, from anywhere. We were never going to find her. The police hadn't been able to do it in nineteen years. Why did we think we could do this with so little information?

There was the sound of a sliding screen door, and then another girl appeared in the doorway from the next room. She was taller than Beatrice, slender, with a pleasantly long face and straight, dark hair streaming past her shoulders. She was wearing an oversize tee over a bathing suit, the hem of the shirt falling to mid-thigh. She was the girl we'd seen on the chaise longue, which was now empty.

"What are you doing, loser?" she said to Beatrice, who was obviously her sister. "Who are these people?"

"This is Gracie," Beatrice said to us. She turned to the girl. "This is April and Eddie. They're the couple who picked up Rhonda Jean Breckwith the night she was killed."

The disdainful expression left Gracie's face and her eyes went wide. "For real?"

"For real."

"You should have told me, dork. I want to hear everything." Gracie strode into the kitchen and opened the fridge. "So you know about the murders?" she asked us as she pulled out a jug of iced tea.

"We just got here," I said.

"I'm *telling* them," Beatrice said. "They're from out of town."

"It's a cover-up." Gracie banged her empty glass on the counter a little too loud. "People get killed on Atticus Line, and the police don't want to do anything. It doesn't get written about in the papers. I called up three different people who write for the *Free Press*. None of them wanted to talk to me or write a story. Why do you think that is?" She looked around at us for dramatic effect. "It's because all of the murders were done by one serial killer, and the cops know *exactly* who it is."

"You don't think Rhonda Jean was killed by Max Shandler?" I asked.

Gracie turned to me. "You think Max Shandler, who has lived here all his life, just woke up one day and decided to kill a hitchhiker? I don't buy it. He hasn't confessed, right? Who says he really did it? What's the evidence? Whatever blood evidence they have, it's too soon for results. DNA takes months, unless you're O. J."

I glanced at Eddie and read his expression. *May as well tell her something*, it said. I turned back to Gracie. "Rhonda Jean was found wearing Max Shandler's coat. When we found her on the side of the road, after she'd been stabbed—that's what she was wearing."

I hadn't read the newspaper article Beatrice had shown us in the diner, but my guess was that the coat wasn't public knowledge. My guess was right. Gracie stared at me, and Beatrice squeaked in excitement in her chair.

I didn't know if I'd just broken a rule, telling the Snell girls that. But I needed information from them, and I had to give them something.

"What if it *was* Max Shandler!" Beatrice said. "So much for your serial killer cover-up, Gracie! He's too young to have done all of them."

But Gracie already had a comeback. "It doesn't mean anything, necessarily. Max could be a patsy. A setup. Steal his jacket and he looks guilty. It's pretty simple. I mean, Lee Harvey Oswald, right?" She looked around at us again.

"Hold on." Eddie raised a hand, palm out. He'd barely spoken during this whole exchange, and with those two words, the Snell sisters shut up instantly. "Before you bring the CIA and Oliver Stone into this, let's back up. April and I came here for information about the murders." He held up the photocopy of the Lost Girl article. "Is this all you have? Newspaper articles? Because we can find these ourselves."

It was the Snell sisters' turn to exchange a look of silent conversation. "We have more than newspaper articles," Beatrice said. She pulled out another set of photocopies. "We have these."

Eddie slid the papers over and looked at the top one. "Is this what I think it is?" He lifted the page, scanning another, and another, handing them off to me. "This is a police file."

His voice was just stern enough that Beatrice trained her gaze out the window and Gracie studied the fridge door. "We're resourceful," Beatrice said, her tone defensive.

I looked at the pages. Sure enough, they were photocopies of a police report—or what I assumed was a real police report, since I'd never seen one. It was old, too, with a lot of the information typewritten or handwritten in a squared, masculine hand. The date in the top right of the first page read April 30, 1976.

Eddie was a few pages further than me, deep in reading, his brow furrowed. "This is a description of the body," he said. He broke his gaze away and rubbed his forehead. I wondered if he was picturing the girl we'd seen, furious and desperate. It was her body he was reading about. He made himself glance down at the page and say, "Advanced decomposition."

"She'd been there at least a month." Beatrice's tone, normally so brassy, was much quieter as she spoke the words. "They couldn't determine if she was, um, raped. But the body had all its clothes on."

I scanned the pages as Eddie handed them to me. There weren't very many; there wasn't much to say about unidentified bones and scraps of flesh ravaged by animals. No fingerprints, no wallet or ID. No belongings found with her at all besides her clothes. No confirmed cause of death, though there were blows to her head that had cracked the skull. They'd taken X-rays of her teeth, in case they could match them with someone reported missing. The investigation had gone cold from there.

How did two teenage girls have a copy of an unreleased police file?

Gracie's voice came from behind the kitchen counter, where she was still standing. She recognized each page even from that distance; she must have known them by heart. "Go to the next section," she told Eddie. "The one dated in June."

Eddie turned the page, then frowned down at what he was reading. "They found a jacket?"

"Six weeks later," Beatrice supplied. "It was shoved into some underbrush. A hundred feet away."

Eddie scanned a page, then picked up a photo—or, more precisely, a photocopy of a photo. He held it up for me to look at.

"It's a letterman jacket," I said, looking closely at the fuzzy photocopy. The jacket had dark blotches of what was most likely dirt on it. It was hard to tell without color.

"A high school letterman jacket," Beatrice supplied. "From Midland High School in Midland."

Midland was farther south, almost at the Indiana border. "The Lost Girl was in her twenties, not a high schooler," Eddie said.

"They don't even know if the jacket was hers," Gracie said. "It could have been there randomly. It could have been the killer's. Or she could have owned it a long time. They couldn't find any evidence connecting it to the Lost Girl. No hairs or blood or anything. It had been there too long."

"The file says that Midland PD was contacted, and they didn't have any reports of missing women," Beatrice added. "And that was it. A dead end."

Eddie lifted the next set of papers. "Another police file," he said. "Katharine O'Connor's." He looked up, his eyes narrowed. "Tell me how you got your hands on all of this. Now."

The girls were silent, but I knew Eddie would get it out of them. I pulled the Lost Girl file toward me and flipped through it, reading for myself.

There was a standoff between Eddie and the two weirdest teenagers I'd ever met, but finally, Gracie caved. She rounded the counter and sat in a chair at the table, flipping her long hair behind her shoulders in a move I had done many times myself when my hair was long enough. I kept it cut just above my shoulders now, so hair tossing was much less dramatic. "Okay, so I got into some car trouble," Gracie said.

"You were totally speeding," Beatrice interrupted.

"Fine, okay. I was speeding."

"Like, six times." Beatrice looked at us. "They were going to impound her car."

"Shut up," Gracie snapped at her little sister. "Anyway, Dad knows a lot of people, and he arranged that I could volunteer at the police station to pay off the tickets. Like community service. Everyone thought it was this huge punishment, like I'd be bored. It's the *best*." She smiled. "Coldlake Falls isn't the most exciting town, but I get to see *everything*. I fetch coffee and order supplies, but what they really needed was help in the file room. It was a complete mess, stuff piled everywhere, nothing alphabetized or labeled the right way. Enter me." She grinned again. "I spent six weeks in there, and by the time my punishment was up, it was so perfect that they asked me to stay. Oh, and the photocopier is in the room next door."

"Oops," Beatrice said, her grin mirroring her sister's.

"Jesus." Eddie's tone was halfway between admiring and creeped out. "You two are a little scary."

"Just resourceful," Beatrice said. "If we don't do it, who will?"

Gracie's smug smile faded. "Some of those kids were my age. They got killed and dumped a few miles from my house. Over and over. Like garbage. Someone did that, and the police and the newspapers think that I don't have a right to know about it." She pointed to the file I was reading. "They didn't put anything about the letterman jacket in the papers. They didn't want it public because it was something only the killer would know. But they could write about it now. They could put out a story twenty years later: *Hey, do you remember a girl who went missing in 1976? A girl with this jacket? Do you know?* I bet someone knows, someone remembers her, but they won't do it."

"Why not?" I asked.

"Because we need tourists," Beatrice replied. "If there are stories about a serial killer in Coldlake Falls, the tourists go away. Which is why the cops could have planted evidence on Max Shandler, just like they did on O. J. Make it look like one guy went nuts and killed a girl, and they caught him the next day. Everyone's safe. No reason to cancel your vacation."

"They didn't plant evidence on O. J.," Gracie said.

"Yes, they did," Beatrice shot back.

Gracie shook her head, her tone imperious. "O. J. did it. Everything else, I question."

It was possible, maybe, but I had a hard time picturing Kyle Petersen and Chad Chipwell planting DNA evidence as if they were the LAPD. If the LAPD even *had* planted evidence. I didn't follow the case closely enough to know. Normally, I paid no attention to murder.

"It isn't just because of tourists," Gracie said, returning to the topic at hand. "It's because the Coldlake Falls PD know who the killer is, and they're covering for him. Framing Max Shandler is part of that."

"So who is it?" I asked her.

"If we knew, do you think we'd have all of this?" Beatrice waved to the pages strewn across the table. "We would have done something, told someone before Rhonda Jean got killed. We'd stop being obsessed. We'd go back to being normal."

There was something in Gracie's expression that said she had a theory she wasn't telling us, but I wasn't sure I wanted to know. A police cover-up in Coldlake Falls seemed far-fetched to me, the product of a teenager watching too much TV. Detective Quentin was odd and unsettling, but he had shown up in the middle of the night, determined to catch a murderer. He wouldn't be breathing down our necks so hard if he already knew who it was.

"I'm not sure you'd become normal all that easily, case or no case," Eddie said.

"I agree," Gracie said. She smiled. "What's normal, anyway? You two came into town and picked up a murder victim. Now you're still here, trying to solve it. I don't think normal is on your menu."

Eddie shifted in his seat but said nothing. Even from that small movement, I knew he was amused.

Holding Beatrice's gaze, I lifted up the page I had been reading. "This says that the Lost Girl was wearing a T-shirt with the tag ripped out," I said.

"Yeah," Gracie said. "The tag at the back of her neck."

"Did any of the others have that?"

She shrugged. "Not that I know of."

"How far apart were the murders?" Eddie was digging through the pile of files.

"Here." Beatrice flipped through her spiral notebook, then showed him her handwritten list. "The Lost Girl was 1976, and she was the only unidentified one. Tom Monahan was killed in 1982. Stephanie Wolfe was killed in 1989—she's the only Black victim. Carter Friesen was killed in 1991, then Katharine O'Connor in 1993, and Rhonda Jean Breckwith two days ago."

"Nineteen years," Eddie said.

If Max Shandler was twenty-eight, he would have been nine when the Lost Girl was killed.

Eddie flipped through the notebook, scanning the modes of death. "Beaten with something curved, possibly a tire iron. Stabbed with something resembling an ice pick. Beaten on the back of the head with something large and blunt, possibly a branch or rock." He flipped the page. "If a man is out hunting, why doesn't he just bring rope and a gun? And for that matter, a garbage bag?"

We all pondered that. "A gun is loud," I offered.

Eddie didn't blink. "So are screams. These methods of death are messy, slow if it isn't done right. The victim can scream and try to run, maybe get away. The reports don't say anything about restraint marks, so he didn't tie them up, which means they could fight him. It could take minutes for the victim to die, even longer.

Every minute is a chance he'll be seen and caught." He scratched his jaw. "A gun, yeah, it's loud, but it's fast. Atticus Line is a remote area. You take one shot, two if you want to be sure, and you drive off. People think someone is hunting or scaring a stray dog off their property. Before anyone can check out the sound, you're long gone."

His voice was so flat. This was the Eddie who had been overseas, who wasn't the same as the man who crooked his knees behind mine in bed every night.

Gracie spoke up. "Maybe he likes it. Making them suffer, making it hard. Maybe that's part of the fun."

"He had lots of time," Eddie said. "He killed them, and no one came. No one even found the bodies for a while. But they all had their clothes on. He could have abducted them, could have done a lot of bad things to them, but he didn't." He ran his finger down the writing in the notebook. "The death was the point. Just the death."

Something was niggling at me, trying to rise to the surface at the back of my brain. I turned to the Snell sisters. "Have you two heard rumors of the Lost Girl haunting Atticus Line?"

Beatrice rolled her eyes. "Everyone has heard those stories. They're so old."

"Don't let her see you, or you're next!" Gracie's eyes went wide and she waggled her fingers.

"So you don't believe it?" I asked.

"In ghosts? Of course not. Those are just legends."

So they could believe in the LAPD framing O. J., but not in old-fashioned ghosts. "Have either of you ever been out on that road at night?" I asked.

The girls laughed, as if I'd said something funny. "For real?" Beatrice said.

Gracie shook her head. "Of course I've never gone out there at night. I'd like to live to see nineteen. Or at least until I'm old enough to get out of here. It isn't ghosts I'm afraid of, though. Why not just stick a thumb out? What a great way to get murdered."

CHAPTER TWENTY-FOUR

After the night with the spaghetti and meatballs, Eddie and I weren't exactly dating. It was something simpler and yet more complicated than that. I had roomed with plenty of people who had been in half-assed relationships, who agonized over unreturned phone calls, confusing gifts of concert tickets (What does it *mean* if he invites me to see the Smashing Pumpkins with him?), and who made a mixtape for who. I'd seen a dozen dramatic breakups and a few engagements, which were also destined for eventual dramatic breakups. None of that described Eddie and me.

We spent a lot of time together. He helped me get my car fixed. I went with him to run his errands, because even his errands were interesting to me. We watched TV and he rubbed my feet—he was insanely good at it—and we talked about everything and nothing. I never, even once, wondered why he didn't call me back.

Was that dating? It didn't seem like it to me. Instead, under the quiet exterior of our time together, it felt like I was being pulled open, the threads of me unraveling as every part of my life came apart at the seams. I didn't recognize this life. I had run for so long since California, been so many women. I had never let a man help me fix my car or rub my feet. These things were momentous to me.

They were momentous to Eddie, too. At times I'd catch him looking at me as if he was happy to see me but wasn't quite sure how I'd come to be there. He was closed off and inside himself like I was, though his reasons and methods were different from mine, and he was equally baffled as to how all of this was happening. I didn't think he'd call what we were doing *dating*, either.

He didn't even try to sleep with me, not at first. Even though my skin hummed every time he touched me, even though we sat so close at the movies that our knees touched. Even though we were often alone in his bachelor apartment or in my shared living room, my legs curled underneath me as we watched TV.

We had dinner with his parents. His mother was polite and pleasant, though I could tell she wanted to open the top of my skull and dig around inside with a microscope, analyzing this girlfriend that Eddie had brought home. His father took refuge in hearty jokes and comments about politics that were targeted so widely, he obviously hoped to draw me in. *Taxes going up! You hear about that Russian space station? What's next?* Maybe he wanted me to reply with a joke about Bill Clinton playing the saxophone, but I didn't. I rarely watched the news—the roommates in my shared house changed the channel when the news came on, and no one subscribed to a newspaper.

After that dinner with his parents, Eddie said he was going to the bathroom. I followed him down the hall past the kitchen, where he passed the bathroom door and walked out the back door of the house.

"What are you doing here?" he asked in surprise when I joined him on the back patio, damp with melting March snow, the air frigid.

I didn't answer, and for a long moment I listened to him take deep breaths, one after the other. I had known that he wasn't going to the bathroom; I had known that he was going to escape for a few minutes to breathe. I had known it, and his parents hadn't. Eddie was lonely, even here, with these good people who loved him. His experience overseas, where he'd changed from a sweet young man into something else, was locked inside him; he couldn't let it out, and he couldn't get rid of it. No one in his life understood him anymore.

After a few minutes, I brushed my fingertips against his wrist. "Ready to go back?"

He was staring into the darkness, oblivious to the damp cold that must be seeping through his zip-up sweatshirt. "April, this is how it's going to be," he said.

"I know."

"It doesn't change; it doesn't get fixed. It just is. You understand?"

"I understand."

"If you want out, you have to say so."

I sighed. "Nothing about this scares me. It probably should. But it doesn't."

He nodded and we went back inside.

I watched him now as we sat at a picnic table outside a restaurant called the Ice Cream Queen. The handful of tables around us, unsteady on the uneven grass, were filled with families and kids. A hot breeze blew pine scent mixed with sugar and lifted the damp hair from my neck. Wasps buzzed over the garbage can. My head was spinning.

Eddie had ordered a banana split. This was his way of treating me, telling me that we were supposed to be on our honeymoon and I should eat something other than nonfat Yoplait, my usual staple. He picked up the long spoon and dug in.

"That was the weirdest afternoon I've ever spent," he said.

I picked up my own spoon. "I agree."

"Did you see that house? It was like something out of a magazine. Their parents have no idea." Eddie took a bite of syrup-covered vanilla ice cream and shook his head. "They could be in trouble over those photocopies. Those were confidential files."

"The idea didn't seem to bother them," I said. "Anything for the pursuit of justice, I suppose."

Eddie poked at a piece of banana. "I'm not sure we learned much."

I wasn't, either. We'd read Gracie's illegally photocopied files, one for each of the six Atticus Line murders. It hadn't been a huge undertaking, because the files were slim, filled with a bare minimum of information. We knew more now than we had when we met Beatrice, but not a lot more.

Six murders over nineteen years, all of them on Atticus Line. Not on a regular timeline, not at a regular time of year, not in a specific place along the road. None of the victims knew one another or anyone local that police could find. None had apparently been sexually violated, and all of them were found with clothes on. Some of them were missing their belongings and some weren't.

None of the cases were solved, and there weren't even any good suspects. None of the victims had been in the middle of a lovers' quarrel or other fight. None of them dealt drugs, owed money, or had anything to do with organized crime. None of them had told anyone they were being followed or stalked. Each one—except the Lost Girl, who wasn't identified—had been coming or going from their everyday life, taking a break from the world to hitchhike to Hunter Beach and pretend that nothing mattered for a little while. None of them carried enough cash worth robbing them for.

It was a lot of information, but there was no pattern. If it weren't for the fact that all of the murders were on one road, they would seem completely random.

But six people were dead, and there were no good answers to the puzzle. It was impossible to tell whether there was one killer, or two, or three, or six—could there really be six killers in one relatively small town? Or six murderers who happened to drive down one road, looking to kill?

"Hunter Beach is the one connection," I said, trying the theory by saying it aloud. "The victims were all coming or going from there. Is it worth going back?"

Eddie shook his head. "The police have probably been there by now. Everyone we talked to is most likely gone. Besides, no one stays there for long, especially for nineteen years."

He was right. The backpackers on the beach might not be breaking the law, but they would rather roll up their sleeping bags and leave than get into any trouble. It's what I would do if I were in their shoes. "Maybe we should track down the owner of the property," I said. "Kal said he lets the kids stay on the beach, even though the town doesn't approve."

Eddie thought it over. "It's an idea. Property records are easy enough to look up. If the property has had the same owner all this time, it could be the connection." He put his spoon down. "But I keep coming back to the Lost Girl."

"What do you mean?"

He spoke slowly, as if working the words out. "We assume she was a hitchhiker, headed either to or from Hunter Beach. But we don't know that. Not without knowing who she was. The police file doesn't have any mention of the police going to Hunter Beach at the time to interview the kids there. It looks like they didn't even check whether any of them knew about a missing girl. So how do we know that's what she was doing?"

I put my own spoon down, following his train of thought. "She's the only victim that wasn't identified."

"Right. And that was deliberate. Someone made it impossible to identify her on purpose."

"The tag torn from her T-shirt," I said.

Eddie nodded. "Whoever killed her ripped the tag out of her shirt because it could identify her somehow. The jacket they found might have been hers, or it might have been misdirection. What if the Lost Girl wasn't a hitchhiker at all? What if she was local?"

"There would be a missing person's report," I said. "Kal must have checked. *Someone* must have in all this time. The first thing to do would be to look at missing person's reports from the time of the murder."

"What if there wasn't a report?" Eddie asked. "She was in her twenties. Maybe she told her family she was leaving home. Maybe she'd done it before. Maybe someone in her family killed her, then told everyone she'd left town." His gaze focused on the distance, the banana split forgotten. "She was the first murder. She meant something to him. He didn't *want* anyone to know who she was, and he took steps to cover it up. I think it's because she knew her killer."

A trickle of worry started deep in my stomach. Not because Eddie was right, or because we might be looking for a killer here in town. I worried because this was the deep thinking mechanism I'd seen so many times by now: Eddie vanished inside his own head.

I didn't like it when he went so deep. When he went too deep, I couldn't follow.

And if I couldn't follow, who knew where he would go?

"Eddie," I said softly.

His gaze focused a little at the sound of my voice, but he didn't look at me. "She's still on that road, April," he said. "Just her. Not the others. She's been there since 1976, all alone. She's still on that road."

I reached across the table, put my hand on his. "I know."

CHAPTER TWENTY-FIVE

Eddie was still in Iraq when he started seeing things that weren't there. Someone standing just outside the shower door. A figure in the sunbaked distance, waving at him. One night he woke up with the cold metal of a gun pressed to his temple, the safety being clicked off. But there was no one there.

He talked to an army doctor about it. I didn't know anything about the inner machinations of the military, but somehow Eddie was discharged with a vague medical condition on his record and a prescription that eventually ran out. He didn't have enough money for expensive psychiatrists or treatments, and he was too ashamed to ask for more help from the army, so he went home to live with his parents and got a job fixing cars. He was physically fine, so the army was done with him. Case closed.

He didn't feel the gun pressed to his head anymore, but he heard dogs barking where there were none, and he had dreams in which he woke up to find his limbs gone. The shame of feeling like he was crazy stopped him from talking to any more doctors, because it was supposed to be over.

He told me about his "head problem," as he called it, early on. It wasn't something that happened all the time—just now and then. "I'm fine until I'm not," was how he explained it. "And then I'm fine again."

"Why do you think it happens?" I asked him.

"According to the army doctor, my brain thinks someone is trying to kill me," Eddie replied. "Because for a long time, someone *was* trying to kill me."

I didn't know what it was like to be in the army, to be deployed. I didn't know anything about what happened in Iraq aside from what Eddie told me. I didn't know what it was like to wake up with the feel of a phantom gun pressed to my head.

But I *did* know what it was like to have someone try to kill you. My father had done it plenty of times.

So I told Eddie the things I'd never told anyone else. I told him about my father knocking my mother's teeth loose, about him pulling his belt from its loops and hitting her with it as she crouched in the corner. I told him about how if I made a sound— or even if I didn't—my father would come for me when he was finished with my mother.

I told him about the night we'd left, about my mother pulling me from bed and putting me in the car, about how we drove and drove through the smoky night and I begged her to go faster. I knew, just as she did, that we had exactly one chance to get out of there. That our lives depended on how fast she could drive.

I told him about how we changed our names, our identities, so that we couldn't be found. How we had gotten by for a while, just the two of us. Then my mother was gone, and there was just me.

Eddie had listened, and then he had said, "So your name isn't really April Delray?"

"It is," I told him. "But that wasn't the name I was born with. That girl is dead."

Eddie hadn't questioned that, and when he spoke, his voice was flat. "I understand."

He knew what it felt like to leave your past self dead and buried, to leave the body of the person you had once been by the side of the road and drive away.

Eddie had left behind his childhood self. His birth mother had had him young, and had rarely been home, usually leaving him with neighbors. ("There was something wrong with her," Eddie said. "No one would ever tell me what.") When he was six, she abandoned him completely. He went into the system, and his parents adopted him.

He vaguely remembered his birth mother through the haze of fear and rejection, the stress-induced fog of waiting for her to come home, then going to live with strangers. He didn't even have a photo of her. The little boy he had been had disappeared.

And then he'd left his old self behind once again when he was deployed overseas.

I hadn't planned to keep running forever. For a long time, I didn't plan anything at all. People with normal lives didn't understand how you could live from day to day, from meal to meal, without ever thinking about what was ahead. People like me didn't think about career trajectories, property values, or retirement plans. I didn't even think about children, except to feel choking panic at the idea of getting pregnant by mistake. It was part of the reason I only dated forgettable men who didn't want anything from me and were easy to repel.

I would have killed April Delray, too, if I had to. If it was the only way forward, I would have left April by the side of the road, alongside the identities I'd used in the past. But after I met Eddie, I didn't want to do that. I wanted to be her, this girl who was with a man she had just met and yet somehow knew so well.

When I met Eddie Carter, I saw someone who was so different from me, yet whose darkness mirrored my own.

Reader, I married him. Because it should be me or no one.

By the time we got on the road to Midland early the next morning, Eddie was feeling better. He cracked a joke as we took one of the roads out of town that wasn't Atticus Line, heading for the interstate by the main roads instead of Atticus Line's deserted emptiness. "If we actually get there, should we just make a run for it?"

I rolled down my window and shouted into the wind. "We're just going to check out Midland, Lost Girl! See if there's anything there! We'll be back before dark, I promise!"

Eddie shook his head as I rolled my window back up. "We've got a three-hour drive," he said. "Find some good music, would you?"

I turned on the radio. When I didn't hear static like I had that first night, I relaxed a little. We found a country station, then switched to classic rock, changing stations as we moved out of range of one and into that of another. We talked about music as we watched the countryside go by, green and monotonous. We listened to radio ads for businesses we didn't know, located on strange streets we would never go to. We snacked on bologna sandwiches and Yoplait kept in a small disposable cooler Rose had dug out from under her kitchen sink, explaining that Robbie used to carry it to keep his lunch cool at work.

Despite everything—our ripped-up back seat and our hijacked honeymoon—I felt strangely buoyant for the first time, like I was bobbing on the surface of a lake. Eddie and I compared how many states we'd been to. He told me about going to the local water park when he was a kid, scraping his knees on the concrete on the side of the pool because there were no ladders to get out and how he still remembered the feeling of the chlorine stinging his skin. I told him about my first kiss at fourteen, when I realized too late that the boy hadn't spit out the gum in his mouth. My reenactment of my reaction made him laugh hard, his eyes squinting closed and his hands going tight on the wheel.

We didn't see any ghosts on the road. Maybe we should have kept going, all the way home to Ann Arbor. But neither of us suggested it.

Midland was mostly suburb. We passed a Denny's, a movie theater, and a cream-brick mall with a gold-and-glass centerpiece and an arched entryway announcing MIDLAND MALL. The neighborhood surrounding the mall was only half-built, new houses and spindly trees rising out of weedy heaps of construction dirt. Past that was an older neighborhood of bungalows with increasingly unkept lawns, and past that were streets lined with trailers.

Eventually, we found a few streets that were what passed for a downtown. There was a run-down pub, a used-record store, a tiny bookstore. The mall had sucked the life out of this area, draining it steadily, and there were few people here at this time of day. Eddie parked in a streetside spot and we got out to feed the parking meter.

We'd agreed that the police station was the best place to start. It was a long shot, but if we were charming enough, we might find a local cop who was willing to talk about missing person's reports from the seventies. We'd also passed the high school on the way to downtown—if the police wouldn't help us, we'd try the high school principal. The Lost Girl had possibly been wearing a Midland High jacket. Maybe, at the high school, someone knew of a student who had disappeared.

But as we stood on the downtown street, looking up and down, both of us were distracted by different things.

"There's a library," Eddie said. His gaze was on a surprisingly pretty brick building with a green lawn and garden and a sign that said MIDLAND LIBRARY above the doors.

I was staring in the other direction, at the bank on the corner. It was a branch of the same bank we used in Ann Arbor. I turned and followed Eddie's gaze. "You want to go to the library?"

Eddie was squinting behind his sunglasses, frowning. The heat wasn't so bad today, and a warm breeze moved over us. "Librarians know everything," he mused. "Let's try there first."

"Libraries are boring."

He shrugged. He had a lot more patience than I did. "What do you suggest?"

I pointed to the bank. "We need money, right? I'll go do a withdrawal."

My voice was steady. Casual. And Eddie was already distracted. "Good idea," he said. "We need to get through the next few days. You go, and I'll try the library."

I nodded, my throat suddenly so thick I didn't trust myself to speak. We split up, and I gave myself only a few seconds to watch him walk toward the library with his long, easy stride. Then I turned and walked to the bank.

Pushing my sunglasses to the top of my head, I filled out a withdrawal form and waited in line for the teller. I kept the withdrawal amount small—two hundred dollars, even though the account I was withdrawing from had a lot more in it than that. Eddie thought I was withdrawing from the account my paycheck went into, and I didn't want him to get suspicious.

The teller took my slip and walked into a back room, then came out again as the printer buzzed. "I'm sorry, I can't fill this," she said, handing the form back to me. "The account doesn't have any funds in it."

I stared at her in shock. "Pardon?"

She shrugged. "There are no funds." The printer finished and she tore off a sheet, handing it to me. "Looks like there was a withdrawal a week ago."

I stared blindly at the printout of account activity. A week ago, there had been seven thousand dollars in the account. Then, a withdrawal of all of it. And now there was nothing.

My heart raced and I felt my pulse in my neck. The money was gone. My secret money. The money I had been relying on to keep me afloat, just in case.

"Did you not do this withdrawal?" the teller asked, mildly curious at my obvious panic.

I shook my head. My voice was a croak. "No."

"Oh. Well. It says here it's a joint account, so maybe it was—"

"I know who it was." I shoved the paper back at her. "It's fine. I'll do a withdrawal from a different account." I'd have to use the account my paycheck went into after all.

"You'll need to do a new slip."

Twenty minutes later I exited the bank and stood on the street, my mind racing. *Think, April, think. You've dealt with surprises before.* For a moment the old panic rushed over me, mixed with hurt and a searing, cleansing blast of anger. That money had been promised to me. It was supposed to be mine. *Mine.*

I gathered myself and walked slowly toward the library. I waited out front for a while, sitting on the stoop next to the garden. From here I could see the front door of the Midland police station, a squat concrete building with glass doors. Nothing was happening there; it was quieter than the library was. Maybe I should try the police station alone. Some men responded positively to requests from women who looked like me, especially if I could convince him I was helpless.

I was about to try it when the library doors opened and Eddie came out. He had a piece of paper in his hands. When he saw me, he grinned, raising the paper so it could flap in the breeze.

"I told you," he said. "Librarians know everything."

CHAPTER TWENTY-SIX

What he'd found was a classified ad in the back of the local Midland newspaper in November 1977. *SHANNON HALLER, PLEASE COME HOME*, it read. *I last saw her in Midland in March 1976. Twenty-six years old, long brown hair. If you are Shannon, please call, I am worried. If you know Shannon please call Carla.* Then a phone number.

I stared at the photocopy Eddie had taken. "How did you find this so fast?" I asked. I pictured him wading through a pile of old newspapers.

"Luck," Eddie replied. "I took a shot that someone might have looked for her. Also, the Midland paper was only published once per week back then. And the classified section was less than a page long."

Maybe this wasn't the Lost Girl. Maybe this was a completely different girl who had disappeared from Midland in 1976, a month before the Lost Girl's body was found. Maybe Shannon Haller had simply left town, gotten married, and started a new life without telling her friend Carla. But it was something.

We walked to the phone booth on the corner, and Eddie dialed the number from the classified ad. "It's ringing," he whispered to me, the phone to his ear. "We're lucky today."

"Grow a mustache and you could be Magnum, P.I.," I said.

He waggled his eyebrows at me, then schooled his features as someone on the other end picked up the phone.

The woman who answered wasn't Carla, but her daughter. The phone number was still Carla's—Midland was that kind of town— but Carla wasn't home. She was at her job as hostess at the Wharf, a seafood restaurant. The daughter was very helpful and had no problem giving her mother's information to the polite man who had called out of the blue. Carla's last name was Moyer, she had three teenagers, and she had worked at the Wharf for nearly ten years. Lunch hour was usually pretty busy, but since it was a weekday, it would be quieter and we might luck out if we wanted to talk to her.

"Did you get some money?" Eddie asked after he hung up.

My throat tried to close again, thinking of what had happened at the bank. "Yes," I said.

Eddie smiled at me. He was in his element, I realized. He was having fun.

"Let's go have lunch," he said. "I'm in the mood for seafood."

S hannon is dead," the woman across the table from us said. "She's been dead since 1976. I didn't let myself believe it at first, but now I do. In the back of my mind, I think I've always known she was dead."

The Wharf had high ceilings, dim lighting, and deep booths. Fishing nets and paintings of boats decorated the walls, but to see them you had to squint. Weekday lunch hour meant there were a few tables of retirees spaced through the large dining room. It was a relatively new restaurant, built just outside the orbit of the mall.

Carla Moyer was somewhere in her forties. Her dark hair was cut to her shoulders and worked over with a curling iron, her bangs carefully pieced out and sprayed. She wore black dress pants and a black satin blouse with shoulder pads. Rimless glasses were tucked in the breast pocket of her blouse. When we told her we had found her ad from 1977 and wanted to talk about Shannon, she had immediately taken a break and joined us in a booth as we ordered lunch.

"Why do you think she's dead?" I asked her.

Carla looked past us into the distance, recalling. "We met in rehab. Actually, it was called a 'dry-out camp,' if you can believe that. You signed up and went to summer camp for a week, cabins and all. No booze and no drugs. You went cold turkey while you played Frisbee and took canoe rides with your fellow campers. And when you got home, you were supposed to be cured. That was the kind of rehab you could get in Michigan in the early seventies."

The waitress put two plates of shrimp and rice in front of us. "I'm guessing it didn't work," I said to Carla.

"God, no," she replied. "It was doomed to failure, starting with the fact that half of us snuck alcohol to camp. Shannon was my cabin roommate. We'd do the stupid Frisbee games, then drink vodka after lights out." She gave us a smile that didn't have much humor in it. "Vodka has no smell, so no one knows you're drinking it. We were just young and stupid enough to think that nobody noticed. In fact, nobody cared."

I pictured two girls in a cabin in the early seventies, sunburned and half-drunk. "Except for the dry-out part, it sounds fun," I said.

"Oh, it was," Carla agreed. "The funny thing is, we'd both signed up with good intentions. I'd been arrested for a DUI, and Shannon had a baby she wanted to dry out for. But once we got to dry-out camp, we forgot about all of that." She sighed. "You said you think she might have ended up north somewhere? Why are you looking into this?"

I gave her one of my best smiles. "We're on our honeymoon," I said. "It turns out the town we're staying in has an unsolved mystery of a murdered girl from 1976. We thought we'd try our hand at solving it."

Carla's eyes, lined with black eyeliner, looked from me to Eddie and back again. "That's a strange honeymoon," she said, her voice flat. She'd been excited at first that someone was interested in hearing about her friend. Now she was thinking twice.

"It's kind of a hobby," Eddie said. "We heard the locals talk about the mystery. There's even a legend that the girl's ghost haunts the road where she was found. We got caught up in it and thought we'd try to solve it. I guess we got tired of playing Scrabble."

When you're lying, use as much of the truth as possible. When he had to, Eddie was as good at it as me.

"A ghost?" Carla straightened a napkin on the table. "Jesus. In all this time, I never thought about Shannon's ghost being somewhere, wandering around. That's gonna keep me up at night."

"The girl in Coldlake Falls was found with a letter jacket from Midland High," I said.

"Sure, Shannon had one of those." Carla adjusted the napkin again, unaware that she had just made Eddie and me sit up straight in our seats. "She dropped out of high school in grade ten, but she got the jacket from some boyfriend or other. Wore it one day and never gave it back. I loved Shannon, but you had to watch your things around her, especially nice things. She had a habit of taking them." She finally stopped fidgeting with the napkin and put her hand to her cheek as a wave of emotion came over her carefully made-up face. "My God, it's been so long since I talked about Shannon. Since I thought about these memories. Sometimes I feel like she wasn't real. She was gone one day, and it was like she was erased. No one even cared."

"Why not?" Eddie's voice was gentle. "Did she have family?"

"Her mother was dead," Carla said. "She stayed with her father sometimes, but they fought. He got mad when she got pregnant with no boyfriend in the picture. She'd met a guy at the movies one day, and a couple hours later, she was pregnant. She said she did it because he seemed nice." She sighed again. "She never saw the boy again, didn't even have his last name. Her father said she should have an abortion. Shannon said no." Carla shook her head. "She had a hard time when the baby came. She tried to stay sober, but nothing ever took. She was doing drugs, too. I mean, there was no question that she was kind of crazy. But I liked her because I was crazy, too."

"Crazy how?" I asked.

Carla raised her eyes to mine, ready to be defensive. Whatever she saw there made her change her mind. I didn't judge crazy. I never would. I knew it too well.

Carla shrugged, closing off the question. "She didn't talk much about it, but I knew she'd had episodes. She'd been given medication, but she hated it and stopped taking it. She'd tried to kill herself twice before we met." She pressed her lips together briefly. "I'm not going to go into my life, but let's just say we understood each other. And I've been much better since Prozac came along."

"What happened to her?" Eddie asked.

Carla shook her head. "I don't know."

"We want your version."

There was a pause. Carla pressed her hand briefly to her cheek again, then dropped it. "We kept in touch after dry-out camp. She was the person I called whenever I felt like the rest of the world didn't understand me, would never understand me. When I thought it was all too hard. I was that person for her, too. She was trying to take care of her baby, but she was having a rough time. He got taken and put into foster care, and she wanted to get him back. When she was in her right mind, she knew she needed help." She looked into the distance again, her face hard. "She got clean. She told me she'd been clean for nearly three months, and I believed her. She was going to take some courses, get a job, turn her life around. Things were going to change, she said. She was determined."

We waited. "And then?" Eddie asked.

"And then she stopped calling. When I called, her phone was disconnected. I thought maybe she hadn't paid the bill, so I went to see her. And I found out she was gone."

"Gone," I said.

Carla nodded. "She'd left, saying she was going on a trip to find herself. She was going to have one trip to see the country, to live life. Then she was going to come home and get her kid back. The phone bill and the rent on her apartment were due, so the landlord had moved in and the phone had already been shut down. And that was the end of Shannon, forever. I never heard from her again." She turned her head and looked at us, her jaw twitching. "I know what you're thinking. You're thinking that Shannon just took off and never came back. You're thinking she was irresponsible, an addict, and a bad mother." She leaned forward, eyes blazing. "I know she was sober, that she was planning to come home. No one has ever believed me, but I know. She was planning to start a real life, a happy life, one that included her son. You think she left her kid for *twenty years* and never came back to find him? She didn't. Because she's dead."

I thought of that unidentified body in a ditch at the side of the road, all those years ago. A body with a Midland High jacket. If you wanted to lose the real world and find yourself, Hunter Beach was a place to go.

Was it possible that the Lost Girl was Shannon Haller? The dates matched and the jacket matched. But hundreds of people had a Midland High jacket. And the police weren't even certain that the jacket had belonged to the unidentified girl.

Maybe we were chasing shadows.

"Can you think of anyone who would have wanted to kill Shannon?" I asked.

That got us a bitter smile from Carla. "What do you want me to say? Let me guess. 'No one would ever have wanted to hurt Shannon! She was so beautiful, so kind! She rescued baby animals!'"

She shook her head. "Here's the truth, honey. Before she got sober, Shannon was a liar, a thief, and an addict. She neglected her baby and she liked to get wasted. She didn't work often, and when she did, she blew the money. She was sick in the head, like I was. Anyone could have killed her—a drug dealer, an ex-boyfriend, someone she stole from. She was the kind of person the world just throws away."

"But you cared about her," I said.

She put her hands on the table, as if she was about to push out of the booth and leave. "Yes, I did. I still do. You know why? Because we were the same, Shannon and me. I'm the kind of person the world throws away, too. The only difference is that I managed to live longer. I managed to get sober and raise kids and get a prescription for Prozac. Shannon got to die, and I got to work in this restaurant until they tell me I'm too old to hostess anymore. Shannon lost her gamble, and I won mine. Look around you. This, for me, is what's considered winning." She slid to the edge of the seat, then paused. "I hope you find the bastard that killed her. She deserved a shot, like me."

CHAPTER TWENTY-SEVEN

The long drive back to Coldlake Falls left us exhausted. Eddie was keyed up; he was used to constant physical activity in the army, and exercise was how he got out of his head. Almost as soon as we parked the car in Rose's driveway, he said he was going for a run.

I nodded. Rose wasn't home, and the house was empty. "I'm going to call the bowling alley," I said. "They're expecting me back. I'll tell them it will be a few more days."

Our honeymoon—the one we'd originally planned—was almost over, but there was no discussion of going home yet. Eddie nodded and said, "I should call Paul, too. I'll do it later. He won't mind." Paul was his boss at the garage.

After Eddie left for his run, I took a seat in the phone nook in the corner of the kitchen. This was a chair with a padded seat next to a table with a telephone on it. Predictably for Rose, the phone was the ornate kind, the headset resting on two upstretched hooks. She probably imagined it was the kind of phone they had at Buckingham Palace. Still, even as I squeezed into the fussy space, I realized I was getting used to Rose and her aesthetic. It was almost calming. I let my gaze rise to a picture of Princess Diana on the wall as I picked up the phone and dialed. Since the number was long-distance, I made a mental note to pay Rose for the charges.

My boss at the bowling alley in Ann Arbor wasn't happy to hear what I had to say. "I had you scheduled for tomorrow night," he complained.

"Sorry," I said. "We've been delayed. I won't be back by then."

"This is inconvenient. I was counting on you, April."

"I know it's—"

"You're being irresponsible."

I stared at Princess Diana, and suddenly I was gripped with an exhaustion so deep it was almost transcendent, an exhaustion I had never known I was capable of. How many arguments had I had in my life, with how many useless bosses, at how many dead-end jobs? I wasn't being paid for my days off—it made no difference to his bottom line whether I showed up or not. I was disposable, and yet I was treated like a disappointment for acting that way. Just like every other job I'd ever worked.

The thought bubbled through my mind, unbidden: *I don't want to do this anymore. I want more.*

Surviving to tomorrow wasn't good enough. Not anymore.

"I'll be back when I'm back," I said, unable to keep the sharpness from my voice.

"I might have to let you go."

I should care. I had to pay rent, bills. The bank account had been emptied. I needed a job. I should care.

Rhonda Jean had bled out in the back seat of my car, scared. Her bloody hand had gripped mine as the life seeped out of her. And the Lost Girl was still on the road, murdered and unidentified, begging for help.

"I'll be back when I'm back," I said again, and hung up.

I let the silence seep into my brain as I steeled myself. If I was let go from my job, we would need money while I looked for another one. I picked up the phone again and dialed a number I knew by heart, one I had been dialing for years.

It took a few minutes to connect. I had to talk to an operator, then another, and then wait as beeps sounded in my ear. But finally, at long last, the phone on the other end was picked up and I heard the familiar voice.

"Hello?"

"Mom, it's me," I said.

There was a beat of silence, enough to tell me everything I needed to know about the money. "Hi, baby." My mother's voice was rough, a smoker's voice. She had been a smoker for as long as I'd known her. I supposed she still smoked in prison, too.

Even though I was angry at her, maybe as angry as I'd ever been, the first words out of my mouth were the usual ones. "Are you all right?"

"As good as I can be." This was her usual answer. "How sweet of my girl to ask about me. I tell the others here that my daughter calls me regular. I don't know if they believe me, but it's true."

My throat was dry, and I licked my lips. I had to get this call finished before Eddie came back from his run. "Mom, I'm calling for a reason."

Her voice went cold. "Don't start."

"I'm starting." My voice was as icy as hers; she was the one I'd learned it from. "I went to the bank. You cleaned the money out of the account."

The money was ours, Mom's and mine. Seven thousand dollars, sitting in a bank account that had both of our names on it. It had been nearly twenty thousand dollars once, but I'd withdrawn half of it over time to pay for Mom's first set of appeals. It was a mistake I wasn't going to make again.

Where did the money come from? If you asked Mom, you would get a different answer each time. She'd say it was left to her by a distant relative, or it came from the sale of her dead mother's jewelry. She'd never even told me the truth, most likely to protect me—and herself—in case I was ever questioned about it. One of Mom's rules was that whatever I didn't know, I couldn't tell the police under questioning.

But since Mom had left my life when I was eighteen, taken back to California to stand trial for what she'd done the night we left, I'd done a little digging. I couldn't trace most of the money, but some of it, incredibly, was my father's life insurance. I didn't know how she'd gotten her hands on it, or how she'd managed to siphon it into a bank account the police couldn't find. The rest—well, I didn't know exactly where it had come from, but as my mother's daughter, I could make an educated guess.

She'd had plans for that money, I was certain. Then the police had found her when we lived in Fort Lauderdale—they'd tracked her somehow through the life insurance check. She'd been arrested while I was working a shift at Olive Garden. When I got home to find her gone, I'd had to pack up and get out of town. Alone.

After spending half of the money trying to free Mom, I'd been careful with the remaining half, reluctant to use money that dirty unless I had to. I'd withdraw a hundred or two at a time, only when I needed it. The fact that it was my father's blood money didn't bother me—I had a cracked molar and a badly healed broken pinkie finger because of him. It was the rest of the money that made my conscience stir.

And yet that money, that number in the bank, was my buffer against starvation, against homelessness. Just knowing it existed helped me sleep at night. It was the barrier against me taking a man home and taking his fifty bucks so that I could eat. I earned my own way, but if things ever got bad, I could still withdraw a hundred bucks' worth of dignity. And now that dignity was gone.

"My lawyer says we can appeal. But appeals take money," my mother said.

Cold sweat made my hand slick on the receiver. "We spent so much on the first appeal, and we wasted it. It isn't going to work."

"It could work," she argued. "My lawyer says it could be self-defense. People pay more attention to that than they used to. Ever since that woman cut her husband's dick off. And O. J. is on TV nonstop. It's all over the news."

Here's one thing: I loved my mother. It sounded crazy after all she'd done, but I did. I really, truly loved her. For most of my life, she was the only person in the world who understood me.

Here's another thing: My mother was a murderer.

My earliest memories were of my father hitting my mother, my father hitting me. I had lived in a constant state of fear, the only state I knew. All I had ever wanted, as a child, was to get out of that house.

So maybe it was self-defense. If Mom had shot Dad while he was coming at her, it could have been.

But that night when I was twelve, Mom had bludgeoned Dad to death with a baseball bat while he slept. She'd set the bed on fire to try and cover it up. Then she'd pulled me from the house and we'd escaped, my mother driving, me egging her on.

I'd told Eddie we had escaped my father and changed our identities that night, that my mother was dead. Because when you tell a lie, you should stick to the truth as closely as possible. We *had* escaped that night; we had just left behind a dead body instead of an angry abuser. Years later, after they'd finally caught her, when she called me collect from California, her instructions to me were clear: *Cut your losses, baby. I'm dead to you now. Do you understand?*

I'd disobeyed her, just a little. I called her regularly in prison, made sure she was all right. I couldn't help it; she was all I had.

But if I had followed her instructions—if I had withdrawn our shared funds from the bank account and never contacted my mother again—I would still have the money. How hilarious was that?

"How did you do it?" I asked her now. "How did you get the money out from inside? You've never been able to access the money before without me."

"People help me," Mom said, and in her voice I could hear my own flat inflection, the tone I used when I was a shiny, hard surface that no one could penetrate. I hated myself so much in that moment that I felt bile in my stomach. "It doesn't matter how I did it, honey. We always said that money was for emergencies. This is an emergency."

"I needed that money," I croaked.

"For what?" She waited, and when I didn't answer, she kept talking. "You don't tell me anything about your life, do you know that? Not ever. You think I don't notice?"

"I have told you," I argued. "I live in Ann Arbor. I work in a bowling alley."

"Uh-huh. So what's the money for? Rent? A house? Clothes?"

"It doesn't matter."

"Is there a man?" Mom paused, as if I'd spoken. "My God, there is, isn't there? Who is he? Tell me everything."

My temples were pounding and my eyes stung. Leave it to Mom to be able to smell a man from prison a thousand miles away.

"There's no man," I said.

"There's a man." She was sure of it now. "Who is he?"

"There isn't a man," I said again. "I date every once in a while. That's it."

"Liar." Her voice was flat with anger. "That's what you wanted the money for? To spend it on some man? I taught you better than that. I taught you the hard way."

She had. The way she taught me the lesson of her life—never let anyone in—was very, very hard. She had been beaten bloody for that lesson. She had killed for it. She had fled her life, changed her name. She had left her old self dead by the side of the road, along with the husk of the little girl I had been. She was sitting in prison now for that lesson. She had sacrificed everything for it.

She had taken all of our money in her final lesson to me. I should never let anyone in—even her.

And for what? The day I married Eddie, I had gone against everything she taught me. I'd thrown away every word of her hard-won advice. I'd done it the day I'd first seen him in the hall outside my bedroom, to tell the truth.

If she knew about Eddie, I had no idea what my mother would do. But I knew her first instinct would be to destroy him in any way that she could. Now that she'd stolen my money and was asking about my husband, I was relieved that I'd never told my mother the name April Delray. She still didn't know it, and she didn't ask. When she used my name—which was almost never— she called me by the name of the dead girl she'd given birth to, who I'd left behind in California.

"There's no man," I repeated, because she had to believe it. She simply had to. I had finally learned my lesson. "I wanted that money. I earned it as much as you did. I never told on you. I never went to the police. I kept your secrets. You know that."

"Then make more," Mom said. "I taught you to be resourceful. This appeal is life or death. I hate to be a Prime Bitch, but if I lose this time, I lose. I looked out for you long enough. I have to look out for me."

I closed my eyes. She had robbed me—my mother had robbed me. I didn't know why even a small part of me was surprised. I didn't know why it stung. I didn't know who I was anymore. I didn't know why it mattered.

"I'm in a situation," I said. "I don't know if I'll get out of it."

My mother's words were sure, her confidence the only mothering she could give me. "You'll get out of it. Do you know how I know? Because I made you, in more ways than one. And if it was me in your situation, no matter what it is, I'd get out of it. I'd do whatever it takes."

CHAPTER TWENTY-EIGHT

Eddie and I slid the dresser against the bedroom door again. Rose wasn't home, but she could be here any minute.

He was sweaty after his run, but I didn't care. After the phone call with my mother, I needed him. I met him halfway across the living room when he came through the door, put my hands on his damp shoulders, kissed him, and said, "Eddie Carter," in his ear. He was happy to oblige.

Afterward, we lay catching our breath in the twisted sheets. Eddie had a dazed expression on his face that made me smile.

"Okay," he said at last. "That was like a real honeymoon."

I stared at the ceiling and said nothing.

"We should probably shower." His voice was lazy. "I'm so goddamned tired."

My heart was thumping in my chest, and it wasn't only because of what we'd just done. I felt raw, exposed. Panicked. The money being gone, then the conversation with my mother, had shaken something loose in me. I hated it, and I couldn't stop it.

I was so good at not thinking about the things I didn't want to think about. Except right now, I wasn't.

Tell him, I thought. *Tell him.*

If I told him, I'd lose everything. I didn't have much, but I wasn't willing to risk it. Not yet. Not now. I had worked too hard for it. It *mattered*. Eddie mattered. This marriage mattered, and I wasn't used to having something in my grip that I didn't want to let go of. Something I wasn't willing to leave behind.

"Do you ever wonder about your parents?" I asked into the quiet. "Your real ones?"

Eddie's voice was slurring. He was drifting off into sleep. "I used to. Not so much anymore."

"Do you ever wonder if you're like them? If being like them is inevitable, even if you don't know who they are?"

"That's an intense question," Eddie said, but of course, he answered. "Yeah, I've wondered that. I don't even know if I look like either of my parents. I don't have a picture of my mother, and I don't remember my father at all." He rubbed his forehead slowly. "Maybe one of them was a genius. Or a psychopath, you know? Maybe that's why there's something wrong with me. Maybe I would be like this, even if I hadn't gone overseas."

I was quiet, staring at the ceiling. My eyes were dry as sand.

"It was getting better for a while," Eddie went on, his voice quiet. "But lately . . ." He trailed off.

"Lately what?"

"It isn't getting worse, exactly. It's changing. I don't see the stuff I used to see. I see different things—or at least, I think I do.

The nightmares have stopped, but sometimes I feel like I'm dreaming."

"Dreaming?" I asked.

"Dreaming everything," Eddie said. "That I'm here, living this life, with you. Like I woke up and I was just here one day, and I don't know how I got here. Logically, I know that I came home, I met you, we got married. But I get confused. The police kept asking me why I made the turn and ended up in Coldlake Falls, and I don't have an answer for them. I don't know, because I don't really remember. I honestly don't know how I got here."

My heart was still beating in my throat. Because I didn't remember, either. I had dozed off when we made the turn onto Atticus Line. Or had I? Did I remember that, or was it the story I told myself? What did I really remember for sure?

I was here, with this man, and I didn't know how I got here, either. How well did we even know each other? We had met less than six months ago. I had changed so much since we met. How much had he changed, too?

"The memories I have of my mother," Eddie said, "maybe I dreamed those, too. I remember her holding my hand at a playground, urging me to climb the ladder to the slide. I remember the feel of her hand in mine, the way I never wanted to let it go. I had no way to tell her that I just wanted to hold her hand, more than I wanted to play with the other kids, more than I wanted just about anything. I wanted to be wherever she was and hold her hand. And she thought I wanted to slide down the slide, like any other kid. So eventually, I did." He paused. "Maybe that memory isn't real. Maybe it's a dream. Maybe it doesn't matter."

"I know you think it makes you crazy, but to me it sounds nice," I said. "I don't dream."

He shifted next to me. "What do you mean? Sure you do. Everyone does."

"Not me. I wish I did. I remember everything." I blinked at the ceiling, thinking about my mother, the years of our life together. If that were a dream, I would gladly wake up, but it wasn't. I remembered every gritty detail, every exhausted late night on the road, every cheap apartment, every time I ate a candy bar for breakfast. I remembered the face of every man my mother dated, no matter how briefly. The facts of my life were relentless, unending, and none of them would leave my head, even for a minute, to leave room for a nicer dream.

I remembered the churning fear in my gut that one day I'd come home and my mother would be gone. Then it had actually happened, and I remembered that, too.

So, yes, I remembered everything. Until I met Eddie, and for the first time my life slipped by me like water. Until we'd made the turn onto Atticus Line, which I didn't remember at all.

"What brought this on?" Eddie asked me. "The question about my parents? It was the conversation with Carla, right? About Shannon leaving her son."

I was supposed to be the calm one, the one that soothed Eddie through his panic attacks. I wasn't supposed to quietly fall apart while he lay next to me. "It's a coincidence," I said. "The fact that she left her son, like your mother left you. Carla said he went into the foster system. It has to be a coincidence, right?"

"I know," Eddie said. "As soon as she started talking, I

wondered . . . I guess that's how my mind works, how it'll always work. Always looking for clues. I remember living out in the country—I don't remember Midland. Even being there today, it wasn't familiar to me." He stared at the ceiling, thinking. "The math doesn't add up. Shannon had a baby, not an eight-year-old in 1976. That was some other kid. Not me."

His hand moved across the bed and took mine. Maybe it was supposed to be a gesture to comfort me, but it felt like a gesture to comfort himself. To reassure himself that I was still there.

"There's nothing wrong with wondering," I said.

He squeezed my hand. "I guess you think about the same things since your mother died. Wondering how things could have been different if she'd lived."

I closed my eyes. They stung with guilt. "I don't want to think about my mother," I whispered.

"But you do think about her." He sounded so certain. "You always will. You went through a lot with her."

"Eddie."

"I'm going to have a nap." His thumb moved over the back of my hand, stroking it. "Then we'll talk about it some more."

When he had drifted off, I got up, showered, and dressed. When I came out of the bedroom I found Rose sitting on a stool at the kitchen counter, a magazine open and unread in her hands. She stared at me hard.

"Don't give me that look," I said. "We're married."

"I have to wash your sheets, missy," she said.

"Fine." I grabbed a glass from the cupboard to pour myself some water. "I'll wash them myself. Weren't you married to your precious Robbie for years?"

"You leave Robbie out of this. Where were you both this morning?"

This morning? It felt like a long time ago. "Midland," I said, taking the cheap plastic ice cube tray out of the freezer and twisting it so the cubes would pop up. "We had a lead that the Lost Girl might be from there. We found out there's a missing girl from Midland named Shannon Haller."

"That hitchhiker from the seventies?" Rose said. "That's what you're up to? You're not going to get anywhere. Robbie never did."

I put my glass down on the counter. "Robbie investigated the hitchhiker murders?"

Rose made a sniffing sound that eloquently told me I was an idiot. "Of course not. I told you, they wouldn't make him detective because he was Black. He was a beat cop. They give detective jobs to men like Quentin. Didn't mean that Robbie didn't know what was going on, though. It's hard to miss a bunch of murders happening in your town. He had his own questions."

"And what did he think the answers were?"

"If you think you're going to solve it, you're not," Rose said without answering my question. "We don't have a crazed killer running around Coldlake Falls. We have irresponsible kids who hitchhike to Hunter Beach and back, and sometimes they get in trouble."

I sifted her words in my head. "So you think it's random, but Robbie thought there was a killer."

"He had to knock on doors and ask questions," Rose said. "That's what beat cops do. No one knew those kids, and none of them had family here. I always told him—they're just kids who had bad luck."

I pulled up the chair next to her and sat down. "And he never agreed with you."

Rose put the magazine down and adjusted her glasses. "He said that those kids were perfect victims," she told me, reluctantly. "Old enough to have left home by their own choice. They were on the outs with their families, or they'd told everyone they were going on a trip, so no one expected them to come home. Hitch-hiking on a remote road, sometimes at night. Robbie said it was the perfect setup for someone who's hunting."

Hunting. It made sense, except that you'd have to drive Atticus Line every night for years, looking for a hitchhiker. Who did that? Wouldn't they be noticed?

And as Eddie had said, if a man is hunting, why wouldn't he bring a knife or a gun? He'd strangled them or bludgeoned them with rocks. Max Shandler had supposedly used the knife he kept in his car in case of an accident. I was no cop, but that sounded impulsive to me. Like Max—if it had been Max—had seen Rhonda Jean hitching, and had suddenly decided she was going to die.

And then each victim had been left, forgotten. Like Eddie said, the death was the point.

I looked at Rose. She was pretending to read her magazine, like she didn't care about this conversation. "I heard a rumor," I said. "I heard that the Coldlake Falls PD know exactly who the killer is, but they've covered it up all these years. Did Robbie ever say anything about that?"

Rose snapped the magazine shut. "Beatrice Snell," she said, angrily. "And her crazy sister."

That surprised me. "Um, maybe."

"I worked with her at the grocery store." Rose sniffed. "It's hard to shut that girl up and get a word in edgewise. UFOs, Roswell, the CIA giving people drugs—I never got a minute's peace. Beatrice is morbid, but Gracie is the really crazy one. I'm not surprised they got their hands on you somehow. They're going to get in real trouble one of these days, talking like they do."

"Who does Gracie think the killer is? She had a theory she wasn't telling us."

"Probably because she doesn't trust you enough, and she knows she'll get in trouble if she repeats it too often. She thinks the killer is Detective Quentin."

My jaw dropped open. "Holy shit."

Rose looked like she smelled something bad. "I don't like swearing. I had to remind Robbie all the time. I don't care what you say outside my house, but leave your swears at the front door, under the mat."

"It fits," I said, ignoring her lecture. "He might be old enough. He's in good shape. No one would suspect him." Gracie, in her way, was kind of a genius. "It would explain why the murders haven't been solved. It would also explain why he showed up at the hospital so fast at three o'clock in the morning, already dressed."

"Wasn't Beam there, too?" Rose asked.

I didn't reply. I wasn't in the mood for holes in the theory. "So the police have covered up the fact that one of their own is a killer. Maybe they needed someone to blame this time, so they framed Max Shandler. They could have put Rhonda Jean's backpack in his truck, planted the knife they say they found."

"Quentin isn't a murderer," Rose said. "Robbie was Coldlake PD. He would never have taken part in a cover-up like that—never. He would have died first."

The bedroom door opened and Eddie came out, dressed in jeans and a tee. "Mrs. Jones," he said, greeting Rose. Rose pressed her lips together and nodded at my husband without speaking. Eddie ducked his gaze away, embarrassed, and opened the fridge. Honestly.

"Mrs. Jones, would you like us to make dinner?" Eddie asked, still staring into the fridge. "I see hot dogs in here. I could barbecue them."

"That grill out back hasn't been used since Robbie died," Rose said. "Two years."

"Then I'll clean it up and get it going for you."

An hour later, we were finishing our meal and stacking the dishes. I was rinsing plates in the sink when I felt the light touch of a hand on my shoulder. "What is it?" I asked Eddie, not lifting my head.

"What is what?" Eddie asked. He was standing at the kitchen table five feet away, crumpling the used napkins.

My hands went still. I stood there, wondering what had just happened. Wondering who had touched me. Wondering why.

Eddie frowned at me. "April? Are you okay?"

Why?

My hands dropped to the counter. My stomach twisted. Cold sweat started on my back, but it wasn't the same cold I'd felt on Atticus Line, the icy breath in the hot, sweltering air. This was a different cold, the cold of pure dread. The cold of fear blooming inside me.

Something bad is about to happen.

Was it a thought, or a voice?

"April?" Eddie said again.

Something bad is about to happen. I opened my mouth to say it aloud, to warn Eddie or Rose, or maybe to warn myself. I had the urge to turn and run out the back door of Rose's house, to make for the trees and keep running as fast as I could until I was so deep in the darkness that no one would see me. But I gripped the counter and stayed still.

There was a knock on the front door.

"I'll get it," Rose grumbled, crossing the room.

I looked at Eddie, but he wasn't looking at me. He was throwing out the napkins, then turning toward the door.

Rose opened the front door, and her tone was disdainful. "Oh. It's you."

"Good evening, Rose," Detective Quentin said. "Can we come in?"

CHAPTER TWENTY-NINE

Detective Quentin sat in one of the fussy chairs in Rose's living room, one with curled arms and upholstery of pinkish-brown flowers on a cream background. He was wearing dark blue dress pants that were cut close to his slim figure, in contrast to the boxy, pleated suit Detective Beam wore. Once again, Quentin had skipped the jacket and tie for only a crisp, white shirt, the top button at the throat undone. The entire effect should have been dandyish, but it only made Quentin look otherworldly, as if he had been ported to Coldlake Falls, Michigan, from some other place and time. He regarded me steadily with his eerie blue eyes and ignored the Diana portrait behind his shoulder. The fear roiled in my stomach as I looked at him.

Detective Beam took a seat on one end of the sofa, and I took the other. Rose sat in one of the chairs turned away from the abandoned kitchen table. Eddie had declined to sit and instead stood by the entrance to the kitchen, his arms crossed over his chest.

"My apologies for the disturbance," Quentin said. "My partner and I have come across some information in our investigations, and we have questions."

"We're done with your investigation," Eddie said. "We already established that."

Quentin raised a hand, the movement oddly graceful. "The questions aren't for you, Mr. Carter. At least, the first questions aren't. The first questions on our list are for your wife."

I went still as he turned his dark blue eyes to me. On the other end of the sofa, Beam fidgeted. I had never seen him fidget before.

"We've learned," Quentin said, "that a long-distance call was placed from this house this afternoon. We traced the number to the Central California Women's Facility."

There was silence in the room.

"Luckily for us," Quentin went on, "phone calls placed to prisoners are logged in the CCWF system. We cross-referenced the time the call was placed with the calls that came in, and we found a match. The call was placed to a prisoner named Diane Cross, who is currently incarcerated for the murder of her husband, Ron, in 1981."

"What the hell are you talking about?" Eddie said.

For the first time I could remember, I couldn't look at him. *Diane Cross.* It had been years since I'd heard that name; it wasn't the one Mom was using when she was arrested. Diane Cross had been left for dead a long time by then. I dropped my gaze to my knees.

Think, April. Think.

"That's an excellent question, Mr. Carter," Quentin said. "What connection could the Diane Cross case have to the people in this house? The answer was easy to find when we looked at the case itself. After Diane bludgeoned her sleeping husband to death in his bed with a baseball bat, she set the bed on fire and fled with their twelve-year-old daughter."

Stupid. It had been so stupid of me to call Mom—I should have known that Quentin would have some way to find out. But I had needed that money, and my feelings had been hurt. My mother could still do that to me after all this time.

I raised my gaze and locked it with Quentin's. "I called my mother," I said clearly. "She's in prison for murdering my father. Is that all you have to ask?"

Quentin's hard, blue eyes flicked to Eddie. He'd gambled that Eddie didn't know, that I'd lied to my husband. He'd gambled correctly. He looked back to me. "You were interviewed by us at length, Mrs. Carter. You never mentioned this."

"Because it has nothing to do with what happened to Rhonda Jean."

"Leave the question of what's relevant to us," Quentin said.

"Our job is to gather information." This was Beam, speaking for the first time. He sounded angry. I didn't look at him. "We can't do our jobs if the people we interview withhold information."

"Do you think I'm a serial killer?" I asked Quentin, my voice snapping with anger. "Do you think I've been lurking on your stupid road since the seventies, killing hitchhikers, because of my mother? I was a toddler when the first murder happened. Do you think I did it?" The anger had me now, and I was in its grip, unable to stop. "You don't even know whether there's one killer or ten.

You don't know why the murders are happening, or what will make them stop. You can't find a pattern. You don't know who will be next, or when. You're chasing me and my mother, and you don't know *anything.*"

"How did you get my phone records?" Rose added angrily. "That's violating my privacy."

Quentin gave her barely a look, as if her question was beneath his notice, before he turned back to me. "The FBI had some interesting information about Diane Cross," he said. "They got involved once it was clear that she had left California. Murderers who cross state lines become their concern. It took some time, but they tracked down several of Diane's aliases. There were likely more."

I was silent.

"The aliases they did find," Quentin went on, "were in some trouble. It seems that, under several different names, Diane Cross was good at defrauding people of money. She started with a house-sitting scam, giving customers false references, then robbing them when she got access to their house while they were away. Then she moved up to stealing people's bank and credit card information instead of simple theft. She'd collect the information while house-sitting, then clean out their accounts several weeks or months later, leaving them to backtrack to figure out who it could have been. There were other scams. Do you want to hear about them?"

The blood was roaring in my ears. I had known about the scams—there was no way I couldn't have known. But Mom had kept the details from me, not out of consideration for my tender feelings, but because that way I couldn't tell on her if the police ever picked me up. She was sentimental like that.

Still, I knew that the money in our joint bank account came from something illegal. I never asked. And I never told on her. I didn't have the luxury of being moral. I had needed my mother to survive.

Quentin didn't seem to need any answers from me. He was reciting all of this from memory, without even a notepad to read from. "Diane's daughter was even more elusive than she was. Even the FBI could find almost no information about her. We do know that when she left California with her mother, her name was—"

"Stop."

"I beg your pardon?" Quentin asked.

I ground the words out. "I don't want to hear that name. Not now, not ever. Don't say that name."

There was a second of surprised silence, but then, with perfect inexorability, Quentin spoke the words. "Crystal Cross."

My stomach rolled, and I wondered what it would be like to get sick right here in the sitting room, in front of everyone. It might happen. That name—that stupid name that my mother had thought was a great idea when I was born—was a burden I'd thought I'd dropped forever. "Crystal Cross is dead," I managed.

"She was very much alive in 1981, when she presumably left California with her mother," Quentin said. "After that, she disappears nearly into thin air. The FBI assumed she took a new identity. However, Diane was clever enough not to give her daughter's new identity the same last name as any of her own new identities. She likely changed her date of birth, too. And since a teenage girl wasn't implicated in any of Diane's money scams, the FBI wasn't interested—unless Diane had murdered her daughter, too, and she wasn't alive at all."

"My mother would never murder me," I said. "She killed my father because he abused her. Because he abused both of us."

"There were no police reports to that effect," Quentin said. "However, I've been a policeman long enough to give you the benefit of the doubt on that. I'm not completely heartless."

Anger seethed through me. The gall of him, to think he knew anything about what it was like to be me. To be my mother. To live in that house day after day.

"I talked to one of the original detectives on the Cross murder case." This came from Detective Beam, on the other end of the couch. I'd almost forgotten he was there. "He told me that there were reports from the neighbors. The abuse was most likely true." He cleared his throat. "He was probably doing it for years."

"Thank you, Detective Beam." Quentin's tone was icy. "I'm certain all of the evidence was presented at trial." He turned back to me. "Mrs. Carter—though that isn't actually your name—I admit I'm curious about you. About why you're here in Coldlake Falls. About why you haven't left yet. About—"

"Enough."

Eddie spoke from his position in the doorway. I gathered my courage and looked at him. He was tense, his arms crossed over his chest, his jaw hard, his eyes blazing with anger. Eddie was rarely angry.

"Stop harassing my wife," he said, his voice rough.

I wasn't stupid enough to see this as a loyal defense. Some of that anger, I knew, was directed at me. Eddie's trust was hard-won, and I'd broken it. What the damage might be, I had no idea.

"Mr. Carter," Detective Quentin said.

"Leave her alone," Eddie told him. "We've cooperated with

your investigation. We've been interrogated twice. You've gone through our car, our luggage, our lives. None of this has anything to do with Rhonda Jean or your other murders on Atticus Line."

Detective Quentin was looking at Eddie with his sharp, crystal gaze, his attention leaving me behind. "Are you sure about that?" he asked.

"Of course I am." Eddie's temper was rising. It was obvious, at least to me.

There was a moment of silence, and I panicked. I knew what was coming—not exactly what, but I had an idea. Enough to be sure that I didn't want to know whatever the detective was going to say next. I opened my mouth to shut him up, to tell him to get out of here, to tell him to get out of our lives. This was over. I never wanted to see Detective Quentin again. But the detective spoke first.

"We've been given some interesting information about your discharge from the army," Quentin said to Eddie.

Eddie went still.

"There were some incidents on your record," Quentin said, again from memory. "Psychiatric incidents. A disagreement with another soldier. Behavioral problems. When you were discharged at the beginning of this year, an unauthorized handgun was found in your personal effects. I believe it was a .22."

"I got rid of that gun," Eddie said, his voice dangerously quiet. "It was legal."

"But it wasn't legal to have on base, was it?" Quentin's tone was chillingly polite. "However, the gun is not what interests me about your record. What interests me is that you were stationed at Fort Custer in 1993, before you went overseas. Fort Custer is a few hours from here. You were on authorized leave from March 1 to March 4, 1993. Katharine O'Connor was killed on March 2, 1993, and her body was left on Atticus Line."

There was not a single sound in the room except for the ticking clock. Rose was perfectly still, her knuckles white as her hands fisted in her lap. Eddie and Detective Quentin had locked gazes, Eddie's expression hard and defiant. I glanced at Detective Beam to see him looking at Quentin. His expression was dark and almost impossible to read, but it looked a lot like hatred.

"So," Quentin said, as if we were all having a conversation, "you can see where my interest is piqued when a man with your . . . *issues* appears at my murder scene. A man who claims he was going to a resort miles away in the wrong direction. When the same man was stationed nearby, on leave, at the time of my last unsolved murder. When he appears in town with a woman who has quite possibly made a living as a con woman since childhood." Quentin looked at me. "I don't know where you were in March of 1993, Mrs. Carter. I don't even know what your name was that year. Maybe you'd care to enlighten me."

"You need to leave."

This was Rose. She pushed her kitchen chair back, the scrape of it making a loud sound.

"You need to leave," she repeated, speaking to Quentin. "This is my house. Go away."

Quentin's voice was soft, yet somehow carried command. "Rose."

"Go away," she said again, louder this time. "This is my house, Robbie's house. He was a good cop, and you never gave him the time of day. Go."

Quentin looked like he was going to argue again, but Beam stood from the sofa. "Good day, Rose," he said, nodding politely at her. Without another word or a look at his partner, he walked out of the house, the door clicking shut behind him.

There was a pause, and then Detective Quentin stood. "I'll be in touch," he said to us, then followed his partner outside.

CHAPTER THIRTY

here was silence in the room after the detectives left. I had a splitting pain in my chest, as if someone had run a blade down my sternum. It was shame and heartbreak and crippling fear, and it was so strong that for a moment I couldn't move or speak.

I turned to Rose. "I'm sorry," I said to her, my voice cracking. I was saying it to Eddie, too, but I couldn't look at him. Not yet. "I'm sorry that you ended up tangled in this. I'm sorry that there was so much that you didn't know. If you want us to leave your house, we will."

I expected her to kick us out, using the tone that said everyone she spoke to was clearly an idiot, but instead she frowned. Emotions crossed her face—anger and bitterness, mixed with exhaustion that seemed similar to the kind I felt, exhaustion with everything in life. When she spoke, her voice was uncharacteristically rough.

"I hate that man," she said. "He ruins people."

Quentin. She meant Quentin. For the first time, I saw Rose as a woman who had been married and widowed, who had been through gut-wrenching pain. "What did he do?" I asked, my voice low. "To Robbie? What did he do?"

"Not just him. All of them." Rose blinked, her expression becoming hard. "The way they treated him, the grunt work they gave him, the low pay. The entire department just loved to gang up on Robbie. The names they'd call him—to his face, if they could get away with it. If they got in trouble for that, then they'd say the names behind his back, as if he didn't know." Her hands twisted the cotton of her thin cardigan, her small wedding ring gleaming in the dim light. "But it wasn't just that. Robbie was good—really good. He could have done so much, solved so many cases, helped so many people. He had a perfect record. He applied for every promotion, every raise, and it was like he was throwing his energy away. Nothing Robbie did mattered—not to them. It didn't make a difference how hard he worked, how smart he was, how kind, how he followed the rules, that he was a model cop, the kind that any force would beg for. It never mattered at all."

I screwed up my courage and glanced at Eddie. He was still leaning against the doorframe, his arms crossed. His gaze was on Rose, listening. He wasn't looking at me. His expression was so perfectly blank, I couldn't read it.

"I believed in him," Rose said. "I believed in Robbie. I knew how good he was. I was a spinster before he came along, and we were mismatched. People made fun of us behind our backs, but we didn't care. I married a good man." She swallowed, her eyes cold. "And then one day, we decided we'd plant cucumbers in the garden. We'd put up a trellis. Why not? Cucumbers would be nice. So we went to the backyard, and I started to dig—you know, a hole so that Robbie could put the trellis in. And he said, 'Rose, I have a headache.' And that was all. That was the end of everything. Those were the last words he ever said to me." She blinked. "It turned out that one of the neighbors saw it from his upstairs window, me digging while Robbie was on the ground. So the rumor got out that I'd killed Robbie and just dumped him there while I dug his grave in the garden. Like what happened wasn't cruel enough. Like I hadn't had to call an ambulance and sit with him until they came. Like I didn't wish every day that I'd lain down next to him and gone where he went."

My God. I felt cold, my fingers numb. "Rose," I said.

"They made it a joke," she continued, ignoring me. "The department. After Robbie was gone, after they'd treated him like that all those years, they made a joke of how he died. And Detective Quentin, the great genius? He doesn't care. He does nothing to stop it. He knows I didn't kill Robbie. Everyone knows. It's been years, and he's never said a word. Quentin is cold. He sucks people dry, like a vampire. Robbie was a piece of dirt under his shoe—he still is. So as far as I'm concerned, he can get out of my house. Nothing he has to say is of any worth to me. If your mother killed your father, she probably had her reasons." She looked at Eddie. "And you? You're no serial killer. I don't care where you went for a weekend in 1993. So, no, you don't have to leave. I'll leave this house in a pine box before I let Detective Quentin, or any of them, manipulate me."

"You don't deserve this," I told her. "You didn't ask for it."

"I'm not afraid," Rose replied. "The only thing I was ever scared of was Robbie dying, and that already happened. Nothing you bring could be worse than that."

My stomach twisted. Rose had lost her husband in the space of a few minutes. If that happened to Eddie and me, it would end me.

The door to our bedroom closed. Eddie had gone inside without a word.

He had lied to me. Or had he? He had told me about the visions, about the nightmares, about the medication he'd been given. He hadn't told me about the incidents that led to his discharge, and he certainly hadn't told me about owning a gun. But had he lied? Had I?

Yes, oh, yes, I had lied. Every time I mentioned my dead, dearly departed mother, I had lied to him. That night when he cooked me spaghetti and meatballs, I'd told him that my mother and I had fled my abusive father, my mother driving as fast as she could into the night. I'd never said that before we got in the car, my mother had smashed my father's head in while he was sleeping, then set his dead body on fire.

As recently as our wedding, when Eddie's mother had told me how unfortunate it was that my mother couldn't be there to see me married, I'd agreed with her. She was a nice woman with a nice family. None of them needed to know about Mom, locked up in prison in California, buried under the weight of her many crimes.

My mother had done what she had to in order to survive, sure. But then she'd done other things. She'd scammed and stolen because she liked it. And I'd kept every one of her secrets, until today.

Rose stood from her chair. The sour look was back on her face, every trace of grief or sympathy gone. "You need to make that right," she said to me, gesturing toward the closed bedroom door. "That's on you. I'm going to watch TV in my bedroom." She turned and left, and I was alone.

She was right. I had to make it right with Eddie, and I would. I would make all of it right. I wouldn't run or hide. If I wanted this life, life as April Carter, no one was going to give it to me. I had to make it myself, and I had to hold on to it so it couldn't be taken away.

I looked at the closed bedroom door, my mind spinning. Back, back to that first night, when we'd taken a wrong turn off the interstate. Back through everything that had happened since.

The Lost Girl was keeping us here. First, she'd physically kept us from leaving town, and then she'd kept us here in other ways, by drawing us into her secrets. We were tangled up with her now in ways I couldn't understand, and even if we left Coldlake Falls right now—if we got in our car and started driving—we wouldn't fully escape. The Lost Girl was too powerful, and sooner or later, we'd come back.

I'd made a promise to the Lost Girl, whoever she was. I'd also told her she owed me. It was time to settle up.

I couldn't fix everything with Eddie and build the life I wanted so badly. Not until I fixed what was happening on Atticus Line.

CHAPTER THIRTY-ONE

Dusk was falling when I parked Robbie's Accord on the side of the road, under an overhang of trees. The sky was purplish gray, and mosquitoes flitted past my face as I got out. The sound of the driver's door closing was loud in the silent air.

I had left a near-empty house. Eddie, still silent, had gone for a nighttime run an hour ago and hadn't come back. Rose was in her bedroom, watching TV. Quentin's visit had left a crater, as if he'd dropped a bomb among the three of us.

I didn't know what Eddie was thinking. Was he angry with me? With himself? Was he rethinking everything that had happened since we left the interstate? Was he rethinking everything that had happened since the moment we met?

I zipped up my navy blue windbreaker and put my hands in the pockets. I was wearing jeans and sneakers, the clothes I'd brought in case it rained on my honeymoon. I had tied my hair back in a ponytail, and though I sweated into the tee I was wearing under my jacket, I kept the windbreaker zipped up. It made me feel less exposed and it kept the mosquitoes away.

Atticus Line was dim and silent, stretching away in both directions. There was no sign of a car. My feet crunched on the gravel as I walked away from Robbie's Accord. I had parked just off the interstate, near where I had seen the strange light in the trees that first night. The first time I'd had an idea that something was wrong with this place.

I was in no hurry, so I walked slowly. The light faded moment by moment, and I touched the small flashlight I kept in the pocket of the windbreaker. I'd found it in the toolbox in Rose's garage—I assumed it had been Robbie's. So, too, was the folded pocketknife I carried in my back pocket. A girl couldn't be too careful, alone on a deserted road at night.

When my mother had roused me from sleep that night all those years ago, she'd taught me one of her important lessons— that helplessness gets you nowhere. She may have taken it to a demented extreme, but that night, my mother had taken charge of her life instead of waiting for someone else to run it for her.

Now, though the situation was different, I was facing the same kind of decision. With Eddie withdrawn from me and my future as April Carter in the balance, I could either wait around for something to happen, or I could go and get answers. You can't run from your demons forever—sometimes you have to walk into them head-on.

Despite everything—the insanity of my situation and the crashing hopelessness of my life—I settled into a rhythm, my sneakers making a beat on the gravel. A breeze blew, drying the sweat on my neck. I heard a single bird in a tree high overhead, and then nothing.

There was something very, very wrong with this road.

The landscape didn't change as I walked, moving slowly past the trees. I wondered how many hitchhikers had come before me over the years on this same road. I wondered how many sets of sneakers had made this noise in the silence. Had the others felt the same disquiet that I did? Had Katharine O'Connor or Carter Friesen felt fear as they walked, not hearing any sound in the trees? Had they hoped a car would come along to take them off this road?

Maybe this was a fool's errand. But as a waft of icy cold air hit my spine, crawling under the hem of my windbreaker, I knew it wasn't. The Lost Girl hadn't shown herself yet, but she knew I was here. She knew every time someone walked this road, and she certainly knew me.

If you see her, you'll be the next one found at the side of the road.

Well, I'd seen her already, more than once, and so far I was still alive. I started to whistle, the sound carrying through the dead air.

The sky grew darker, and then I saw it—the light in the trees. It started dim, then flared up, like a lantern. I was cold now, my neck prickled with gooseflesh. I stopped whistling but I kept my pace, one foot in front of the other.

Far overhead, lightning flickered in the sky between the clouds, a midsummer storm. The air was expectant, and I wondered if I would see her from the corner of my eye. I wondered if I would turn my head to see her walking next to me. I thought I heard the sound of leaves swirling to my left, but before I could turn to look, I heard the far-off sound of a car, coming down the road.

I turned and started to walk backward. When I could see headlights, I put out my thumb. Was this part of the game? The Lost Girl liked to kill hitchhikers, right? Fine, then. She could try and kill me.

Or I would try and end her, any way I could.

The car slowed as the driver obviously caught sight of me in the headlights. Because of the light shining in my eyes, I couldn't see the driver. I kept my thumb out. I kept my chin up.

The car slowed more, pulling up beside me. "Come and get me," I whispered into the darkness. Crystal Cross. April Delray. April Carter. She could come and get all of us.

I stopped walking, lowering my thumb. The passenger window rolled down. "Are you out here all alone?" It was a woman's voice.

I wasn't sure what I had been expecting. Another unnatural storm? A girl screaming and running in the road? A different ghostly trick? I paused for a beat too long, wondering how the Lost Girl was trying to trap me, before I spoke.

"Yeah," I said. "I'm headed to Hunter Beach."

"That's another hour's drive up the road."

"Do you think you could take me at least part of the way? However far you're going? It would help me out a lot, and I'd appreciate it."

There was a pause as the woman in the car thought it over. I still couldn't see her clearly in the dark, just a shadowy shape. She was alone.

"I suppose I could do that," she said. "But I can't take you all the way."

"I understand."

"All right, then. Get in."

I opened the passenger door and got in the car. The woman driving was wearing jeans and a navy blue sweatshirt. She was around forty, Asian, her black hair worn down. She gave me a smile that was polite and a little worried.

"I've never done this before," she said, "but I couldn't just leave a woman alone on the road. My name is Trish."

I turned to glance in the back seat, which had no one in it. Then I looked at the road ahead, which was also empty.

"I'm April," I said.

"You're going to Hunter Beach? You don't have a backpack." Trish's voice was curious, even kind. Her eyebrows were drawn down in a bemused frown. She wore a wedding ring on her left hand.

"I'm staying there. I took a day trip today, and now I'm going back."

Trish hesitated, and just like I had done to her, she glanced down at my left hand, where my wedding ring was. I didn't seem much like a Hunter Beach kid with a ring on my finger. Too late, I realized I should have taken it off.

"My husband is there, at Hunter Beach," I explained. "We got married only a few days ago, and then we decided to travel for a little while. We wanted to get away from real life, I guess."

"Congratulations," Trish said, though she still looked wary. She hadn't put the car in gear.

"Thanks." A heavy feeling dragged at the pit of my stomach,

telling me something bad was about to happen. And despite the fact that I'd come here specifically to find the Lost Girl, and this seemed to be part of it, I said, "It's fine if you don't want to give me a ride. I understand. I can just get out of the car and walk. No hard feelings."

"No." The word was sharp and immediate. Trish shook her head, as if pushing a thought away. "It's fine. I'm not leaving you in the dark." She put the car in gear and stepped on the gas, jerking us onto the road in an uncoordinated movement. I braced myself by putting a hand on the passenger door.

"Thanks," I said again. I turned and looked in the back seat once more, noticing this time that there were kids' toys back there but no car seat. One of the toys was in the shape of a tooth, plush and white, with a cartoonish smiling face on it. It bore the logo of a mouthwash brand and the words *Dentists keep you smiling!* Trish accelerated in silence.

"Have you seen anything strange on this road?" I asked her.

Trish frowned as she drove. "Strange?"

"Yeah, strange. Like lights or anything like that?"

"No, I don't think so. Why do you ask?"

"I've heard stories," I said, trying to keep up the fiction. "You know, about this road. About hitchhikers here."

"You're a hitchhiker," Trish pointed out.

Oh, great—now I was giving her the creeps. "I guess it's just spooky, since a girl was murdered here a few days ago."

"What are you talking about?" Trish sounded bewildered.

I looked more closely at her. Except for her confused expression, she looked like a normal woman, and yet something was wrong. "I assumed you were a Coldlake Falls local," I said.

Trish said nothing. Her hands had gone tight on the wheel, and there was sweat on her forehead.

"Are you all right?" I asked.

"I'm fine."

"Where are you going?"

"I'm going home."

Something was definitely wrong. I shivered as cold crept down my neck, under my jacket. I looked at the knobs on the dashboard that controlled the temperature and saw that the air-conditioning wasn't on.

"Are you cold?" I asked Trish.

"I'm going home," Trish said a second time, her tone distracted. She put her foot on the gas and the car sped up.

I was freezing now, the chill numbing my cheeks and my fingers. Outside, lightning flickered high in the clouds again, flashing light into the car. I turned the air-conditioning knob one way and then the other, but nothing changed. I tried to roll down my window, but the roller wouldn't move.

"You can let me out here," I said.

Trish didn't answer.

I tried the window roller again, jerking it, but it wouldn't turn.

I looked in the rearview mirror and there was the Lost Girl, sitting in the back seat.

I had expected this, possibly even wanted it, but still, when I saw her pale face and long, brown hair, my chest seized with fear. My breath stopped and we locked eyes in the mirror.

She was a girl, but she wasn't. She was a person, but she was also an empty hole where a person should be, sucking all the air through it and spreading darkness. I could see how thin her arms were, and I thought I could hear her breathe. But she wasn't breathing, was she? She'd been dead a long time, and this close I caught the faint scent of rot, earthy and sweet. There was blood trickling from her ear.

Then the Lost Girl smiled.

A sound left my throat that was part gasp, part helpless moan. I knew that smile. It wasn't the amused kind, or the friendly kind. The Lost Girl's lips formed a pressed line, a smile that said, *You're going to suffer, and I'm going to enjoy it.*

"No," I breathed. And it crashed through me, what I had done, how the Lost Girl had tricked me. I'd thought I would be facing her alone. But the Lost Girl didn't play by my rules, and she'd never intended that at all.

The car slowed down. "I need to pull over," Trish said.

"Trish, something's wrong." I had to try. I had to get through to her.

The car slowed to the shoulder of the road, and when Trish looked at me, her eyes were black, her pupils blown all the way open. Her features were slack.

"I have to get something from the trunk," she said. "I'll just be a minute."

"Don't," I said. "I'll get out, and you keep driving. Please. Just put your foot on the gas and keep going. Drive to Coldlake Falls and don't stop for anything you see. She'll give up and leave, and this will all be over. You probably won't even remember it. Get out of here. *Please.*"

Trish didn't seem to hear me. She had turned back to the road as she stopped the car and put it in park, turning the key in the ignition. "I'll just be a minute," she said again.

She got out of the car and walked to the back. I heard the thump of the trunk opening. "You bitch," I said to the Lost Girl, and when I spoke, my breath curled in the air.

She was gone from the back seat. It was empty except for Trish's children's toys. I slid into the driver's seat and turned the key, which was still in the ignition, my hand slick on the metal—maybe if I could get away, the Lost Girl would follow me and leave Trish behind. Nothing happened. The motor didn't turn, and there was no sound.

I tried again, cursing. There was another thump as Trish moved something in the trunk. In my mind's eye I saw the Lost Girl's smile, knowing and cruel. She had made Trish leave the key in the ignition on purpose. She wanted me to hope, to think I could end this nightmare. She wanted me to waste my time.

How many people had this happened to before me? A lonely hitchhiker gets a ride. The driver says they need to pull over for a minute. How many knew by this point that something was wrong? All of them? How many tried to get away from whatever was going to happen? How far did they get?

Beaten with something curved, possibly a tire iron. Stabbed with something resembling an ice pick. Beaten on the back of the head with something large and blunt, possibly a branch or rock. That was how the others had died—killed with whatever was at hand. The killers hadn't brought a gun, because when they got into their car that day, they hadn't known they were going to kill someone. How many of them knew what they were doing, even though they couldn't control it? How many of them remembered?

I opened the driver's door and slid out, trying to keep low so that Trish wouldn't see me.

I had waited too long. From the corner of my eye, I saw a movement. I jumped to my right just as something whistled past my head and hit the pavement.

A tire iron. Trish, her eyes black and her face dead of expression, had swung a tire iron at me. And she was lifting it to swing it again.

I ran.

CHAPTER THIRTY-TWO

My sneakers hit the gravel on the shoulder of Atticus Line as I pumped my legs, sprinting back the way we'd come. I didn't scream, didn't utter a sound. I saved all of my breath for running. Overhead, lightning flashed in the sky. The wind, hot and damp, picked up.

I heard Trish's footsteps behind me, and then they stopped. She didn't speak, either, didn't call my name or curse. The Lost Girl had nothing to say about killing me. She just wanted it over with. My death was the point. It always had been.

A few seconds later I heard the car start, then turn around on the road. I changed course, leaving the shoulder of the road and running through the trees. It was dark in here, and I ducked to avoid the low branches that were only shadows, hoping I wouldn't trip and fall. I tried to keep my footsteps quiet as Trish's car pulled to the side of the road again.

When I heard the car door open and Trish get out, I slowed my pace. I was far into the trees now, hopefully hidden in the dark, and I didn't want her to hear me. My breath was sawing in my chest, and I silently gasped for air, feeling a cramp low in my stomach. I could see the opening through the trees, far to my right, where the road was. I could see the glare of headlights.

Would she come after me? I couldn't think of her as Trish now; I had to think of her as the Lost Girl, because that was who she was. And if the Lost Girl wanted me dead, I had to think she wouldn't give up. She would find me.

I wasn't safe hiding in the trees, waiting for her to go away. Even if I could find a good hiding spot in the dark, I still wouldn't be safe. Now that Trish had a weapon, I had to assume she was carrying it. I took the jackknife from my back pocket and unfolded it, pausing to listen for footsteps.

"Hello?" Trish's voice came from the road. "What happened? Where did you go? Are you okay?"

A lie, or was that really Trish? Had the Lost Girl let her come back for a moment, long enough to trick me into showing myself?

I hesitated, not sure which way to go. And then I turned and saw that a man was standing next to me.

He was young—twenty, maybe. He was wearing worn jeans with a hole in one knee and a jean jacket. On the lapel of the jean jacket were pinned buttons, the round, plastic kind that had graphics or sayings on them. One was dark blue, with the words *May the Force Be With You* in yellow letters. The other was a Union Jack with the words *Punk's Not Dead* over it. The man's hair was blond and tousled, and he was so close that if he had been alive, I would have been able to hear him breathe.

"Carter Friesen," I whispered.

He didn't seem to hear me. He didn't speak. He turned away, walking into the shadows, and then he was gone.

I wanted to follow him, to find him again, but it wasn't possible. Carter Friesen was gone; he'd been dead since 1991, when he'd been stabbed on the side of Atticus Line, maybe where I was right now. Maybe he'd tried to run. Maybe he'd almost gotten away. But he'd died anyway.

Who had his killer been? Someone with a slack expression and black eyes. Someone who, I realized now, hadn't known what they were doing. Someone who had no urge to be a killer, who maybe didn't even remember doing it. Which was why they had never been caught.

Damn it. Why had I come all this way? Why had I sought out the Lost Girl, just to lose my nerve? I wasn't going to run.

Instead, I circled through the trees, making my way slowly toward the road again. Trish's car was still there, the lights on, but I didn't hear her voice again. Had she left the road, looking for me? Or was she still there, waiting for me to show myself?

I was still holding the knife, though my hand was slick with cold sweat. I was behind the car, and I couldn't see anything moving, though the car was running and the headlights were on. My sneakers crunched the gravel at the side of the road.

"I'm here," I said, my voice a croak.

Nothing moved, and I heard no sound. Lightning flashed overhead, illuminating the road. Trish was nowhere to be seen.

I walked slowly to the middle of Atticus Line, giving the car a wide berth. "She's got you," I said, louder now. "This is what she does, Trish. She takes innocent people and makes them killers.

She's making you do something you don't want to do. Don't let her."

Still nothing. I turned in a circle, looking all around me, but the shadows didn't move. I didn't hear a footstep.

"Shannon?" I called out into the darkness. "Is that who you are? You lived in Midland. You wore a jacket from Midland High. You had a son." The wind kicked up, making the sweat on my neck prickle. "Carla was your friend," I shouted. "She still thinks about you. She looked for you, put a notice in the paper. She wonders where you are."

I walked toward the front of the car, keeping a distance from it. As always, there were no other cars on Atticus Line. This place was wrong and dead. It was the worst road in America. It deserved to be destroyed and plowed under, replaced with an ugly freeway. I was sure that there were more bodies here, left in the woods and never found. Atticus Line was that kind of place.

I had no idea how Eddie and I had come here. Eddie was driving, and I'd dozed off, and when I opened my eyes, we were—

I froze, and this time I didn't know whether the chill at my back was the ghost or whether it was me.

I thought I was going the right way, Eddie had told the police. But as Quentin had pointed out, there was no sign, and he wasn't using the map. Why had he ended up on Atticus Line, thinking he was going the right way?

"Shannon?" I shouted.

You were going the wrong direction, Mr. Carter. Quentin's voice in my head.

And then, Eddie: *I know this place.*

He didn't, though. He didn't know this place at all.

Shannon did.

"Shannon, what did you do?" I cried. "How did you get us here? Why?"

There was the scrape of a shoe on gravel, a low moan.

I walked slowly toward the car, holding the knife in front of me. The wind brushed the trees, making them sound like rain. I moved one foot, and then the other.

Sitting against the side of the car, her back to the closed passenger door, was Trish. Her knees were up, her hands in her lap. She tilted her head back to look up at me. When lightning lit the sky, I saw that her eyes were normal, her expression drawn in pain. Both of her hands were gripping the tire iron in her lap. Her knuckles were white.

Our gazes locked, and her look was pleading. She couldn't speak, and she didn't have to. I knew what was happening. She was fighting it.

She was fighting the Lost Girl as hard as she could.

I thought of Rhonda Jean. I thought of Max Shandler in his big, black truck, going out to pick up beer. Was this how it had been? Had Max felt a chill on the back of his neck as he picked up Rhonda Jean? Had he felt the compulsion Trish was feeling now? Had he fought it?

How scared had Rhonda Jean been when she realized the man who had picked her up was pulling a knife?

The jacket she had been wearing—Max Shandler's jacket. Had he awoken from a horrible fever dream and realized what he'd done, just like this? Had Max, the real Max, put his jacket on her and told her to run?

Had she stumbled away, bleeding, until Eddie and I pulled

over? While Eddie and I were talking to Rhonda Jean, deciding what to do, Max Shandler had been losing his struggle with the Lost Girl. He had been getting back into his truck to chase us down. To finish the job.

I closed my knife and pocketed it. In one quick motion, I took the tire iron from Trish's hands and threw it as hard as I could into the trees. It landed somewhere in the darkness in a hush of leaves.

I grabbed Trish's hands and pulled her up. She was freezing, her skin like ice, her body stiff but unresisting. "Move," I told her.

I pushed her around the front of the car, making her legs move. She moaned softly, but I didn't let her go. I shoved her into the driver's seat and put her hands on the wheel of the running car.

"Drive," I told her. "As fast as you can."

I slammed the door.

Trish found strength somewhere, and with a roar, the engine opened and the car took off. The back fishtailed briefly on the gravel, and then the taillights faded as she drove away.

I didn't wait to see if the Lost Girl was still there, if she would come for me. I turned and ran, heading back down the road the way I had come, running down the middle of Atticus Line. When there were footsteps behind me, I didn't look. When there were footsteps beside me, matching mine, I didn't look.

When lights appeared in the trees by the side of the road, I didn't look.

When I saw my car at the side of the road, I felt like weeping in relief. And still, I didn't stop. I kept my feet moving, my legs pumping, and I didn't slow down. Not until I had opened the door, the key in my hand.

CHAPTER THIRTY-THREE

When I got out of the car at Rose's, the front door banged open and Eddie came out. He strode down the front walk toward me. "Where the fuck have you been, April?" he shouted. "It's late. I came home and you were gone."

His voice was ragged, his expression frantic. He was still wearing his running clothes. His hair was tousled, as if he'd been running his hands through it. He was army big, furious, and coming rapidly toward me, but I never had a whisper of fear. All I felt, looking at him, was that I loved him so much I could barely stand it.

I had never loved any man in my life, but Eddie had changed all of that.

I was bone-tired, and my legs felt like they were on fire. It was full dark now; I had no idea what time it was. I unzipped my windbreaker and slid it off, letting the warm night air cool my sweating skin.

Eddie stopped in front of me. "Well?" he said. "I was going to call the cops."

"It's her," I said.

He frowned, confused. "What?"

"The Lost Girl. All of the murders—they're her."

His gaze searched my face. "Where have you been?" he asked, his voice lower now.

"Where do you think? I drove to Atticus Line." I dropped my jacket and stepped forward. "Tell me how we got here, Eddie." I raised my hands to his jaw, cupping his face, feeling the scratch of his stubble on my palms. "You were driving. Tell me the truth. Tell me how we got here."

His gaze locked on mine, and I looked into his eyes. Eddie Carter's eyes. I watched the emotions at war in them, fear and confusion and the lingering anger over my leaving. The worry about me. Part of him had thought I'd left him. He didn't have to tell me that—I already knew.

"I thought I was going the right way," he said.

"Why did you think that?" My voice was almost a murmur. "We were going the wrong way. Didn't you know? Did someone tell you which way to go?"

The words made him flinch; I felt it under my hands. "April."

"Tell me the truth."

"No one told me." He ground the words out. "But I was so sure."

I dropped my hands to his shoulders. The muscles were bunched, his body tense, but his skin was warm and familiar beneath the cotton of his T-shirt. "She brought us here," I told him. "It wasn't a mistake, and it wasn't random. It wasn't a wrong turn. She brought us here, and she just tried to kill me."

Our gazes locked. "Tell me," he said, calmer now.

"I will. I'll tell you everything."

He was still under my touch, our gazes still locked. "Who's crazier, April?" he asked. "Me or you?"

"I don't know, but you don't have to worry. I'm going to fix everything."

"You can't fix it." He closed his eyes. "You can't."

"Eddie," I said, "you haven't seen me try."

CHAPTER THIRTY-FOUR

Neither of us were sleeping. I was halfway into a doze as gray dawn crept into the sky outside our bedroom window, and Eddie was on his back on the bed next to me, his breathing even and his body still. I knew he was awake.

We had talked, speaking in low voices in bed for a long time. I told him what had happened to me, about Trish and the tire iron. Eddie had been rigid as he listened, and he barely spoke.

"Jesus," he said when I finished. "So that's why they can't solve it. It was someone different every time. Someone random. Someone who doesn't remember."

"All of them except for the first one," I said. "The Lost Girl. We don't know who killed her. That's the key."

We'd pretended to sleep then. But now, as dawn light began to edge into the sky, Eddie said, "April, I want to explain."

I was too tired to follow. "Explain what?"

"What happened before I was discharged. The things Quentin said."

I had to reach back into my memory. "You mean the fight he said you got into? The gun?" I let out a humorless laugh. "Are you sure you don't want to talk about my mother being a convicted murderer first?"

"You didn't trust me with that," he said softly, and those were the only words he needed to make my rib cage feel like it was closing in on itself. "You're protective, April. You think I don't know that? I've always known there are pieces of you I can't see. You told me what you could. I feel like I should have seen the rest."

"My mother was a criminal," I said into the graying darkness. "I was never part of it. You can believe me or not if you want, but that's the truth." I could barely breathe, the words were so hard. "But I didn't turn her in, either. I spent the money she made. There was a lot of money, sitting in a bank account that I never told you about until my mother cleaned the account out. But until then, I kept that money. And I lied for her over and over again."

Eddie laced his hands on his chest, his gaze still fixed on the ceiling. "When I bought the gun, I didn't know whether it was to use on me or on someone else. I couldn't decide."

I rolled onto my side, facing him, listening.

"I couldn't sleep," he went on. "I was dreaming about terrible things. No one I talked to could help me. It just seemed like if there was a way forward, I couldn't see it. I couldn't see anything."

I wanted to touch him, but I knew he didn't want me to. So I stayed still.

"I didn't like guns as a kid," Eddie said. "Didn't even like them as toys. And there I was, years later, and I knew how to kill people.

It was one of the skills I'd learned. I didn't want to be the man I was. But I was. They were going to send me on another tour, so I bought a gun. I figured if they came for me, I'd kill either them or myself. Because I knew how. And then I got in that fight—which I never do, but I did that day. I don't know why. That led to my discharge, and they weren't going to send me back anymore. I was ashamed of it, so I didn't tell you. I thought I could leave it behind."

"You can." This time I did touch him, putting my hand on his shoulder. "Leave it behind, Eddie. It isn't easy, but I think you can do it. I think we both can."

"Those days of leave Quentin talked about—"

"Don't," I said. "Don't think for a second that I'd believe you're a murderer."

"Why did she draw us here?" he asked. "We just wanted to get married and move on, both of us. Why are we here?"

"I don't know."

There was another moment of quiet, and then Eddie sat up in a swift motion, his legs swinging over the side of the bed. "Did you hear that?" he whispered.

I blinked. "Hear what?"

"I heard something."

I hadn't heard anything, but I rolled off the bed and stood as Eddie strode to the bedroom door in his old tee and boxer shorts. I recalled the things I'd heard—or thought I'd heard—in this house. Had Eddie heard them, too?

In my short nightie—it was cotton, but it was lacy, because when I packed, I thought I'd be on my honeymoon—I followed him into the main room. Darkness had started to fall away, and the furniture in the living room was just visible, the hump of the sofa and the dark squares of pictures on the walls. Nothing moved, and except for the ever-present ticking of the clock on the wall, there was no sound.

I followed Eddie's back as he walked slowly toward the front door, listening between steps. "Out here," he whispered.

Maybe it was Kal again, or maybe it was one of the other cops who was supposed to keep an eye on us at night. Were they still out there, sitting in their cruiser, or had Quentin and Beam reassigned them? Were Eddie and I still a threat?

Eddie stood at the front door. He put his hand on it, as if he could sense vibrations, and suddenly I had a bad feeling. *Don't open the door*, I thought. I wanted to grab him, to tell him that opening the door was a bad idea.

"They're gone," Eddie whispered, letting out a breath. Then he unlocked the door and swung it open.

Outside was an empty porch and gray sky. The warm, damp air of a summer dawn. A breeze rustled the trees. There was no other sound in the silence.

Eddie stepped onto the porch and looked around. "Someone was here," he said, and this time he sounded confident, completely sure. He walked barefoot down the steps to the front walk, looking left and right. "Maybe they went around back," he said, holding up a palm briefly in my direction. "April, stay there."

I crossed my arms over my breasts, hugging myself as he strode off through the grass around the side of the house. I could barely breathe. Far off in the sky, a starling called. I edged my feet forward, letting my toes touch the threshold of the front doorway, feeling the warm air on my bare legs. It was a beautiful morning for someone who hadn't almost been murdered a few hours ago.

Then I saw it.

"Eddie, here," I said, keeping my voice calm so I didn't alarm him. "Come back and look at this."

He reappeared instantly from the other side of the house, because he'd done a swift circle through the backyard. "What?" he asked.

I pointed.

Rose had a black mailbox affixed to the brick wall next to the front door. The corner of the mailbox was propped up by something that had been shoved inside. It could have been a flyer, or it could have been the mail, but I had the feeling it wasn't either of those. I could see an edge of bright pink lettering, a familiar typeface I'd seen many times before.

Eddie walked back up the steps, lifted the lid of the mailbox, and pulled it out.

He unrolled it, and Alicia Silverstone's face looked up at us. Someone had left us a copy of *Seventeen* magazine.

In Rose's kitchen, Eddie and I turned on the overhead light and opened the magazine. It wasn't much of a mystery how the magazine had arrived—it had to have come from the Snell sisters. Rose sure as hell didn't have a subscription to *Seventeen*, and neither had Robbie.

"Why the subterfuge, do you think?" Eddie asked, opening the pages. "If there are cops watching Rose's place, they'd see her putting the magazine in the mailbox."

I flipped past a Benetton ad, a thick card with a perfume sample on it. "I don't think there are cops watching the house. The Snell girls work in mysterious ways."

"What are you doing?" Rose came into the kitchen, wearing her neck-to-feet housecoat and an irritated look. "It's early." She caught sight of the magazine. "Why are you reading that?"

"It was left in the mailbox," I said.

Rose huffed. "Beatrice Snell." Her voice dripped with disdain. "She's probably in trouble with her parents and her phone privileges are cut off. Or she thinks someone is listening to her phone calls. What did she put in it?"

The magazine flipped open to the middle, where the subscription card was. Taped to the subscription card was a small envelope. Eddie detached it and opened it. I was starting to realize that no one had a sense of drama like a teenage girl—especially a Snell sister.

Eddie unfolded the paper inside the envelope and read it over. He didn't say a word. Then he handed the paper to me.

"What is it?" Rose asked, impatient.

I scanned the page, which was a photocopy. "It's a missing person's report," I said. It had been filed by a man named John Haller, stating that his daughter, Shannon Haller, had not been seen or heard from since March of 1976. Shannon was aged twenty-six at the time. The report was filed in December of 1977.

Shannon Haller's father had filed a missing person's report.

"I don't get it," I said, handing the page to Rose to read. "When we were at the Snells', the police file said that they checked with Midland and they had no record of a woman missing."

"Look at the dates," Eddie said, his voice calm. "The Lost Girl's body was found in April of 1976. The missing person's report was filed in December of 1977. There wasn't a report filed when the police file was written. Not until over eighteen months later."

"You think this is the girl whose body they found?" Rose asked, her eyes reading the page from behind her large glasses. She read the description that John Haller had filed in the report. "'Brown hair, past shoulder length. Five-five, slender build. Brown eyes.'"

Eddie and I exchanged a glance, both of us remembering the Lost Girl's face. "We can't assume it's her," I reminded him. "There are millions of girls with brown hair."

"How many of them are from Midland, and how many of them died in 1976, aged between twenty and thirty?" he asked.

I shook my head. "How did the Snell sisters get this?"

"I have no idea." Eddie picked up the magazine and leafed through it. "There's more."

Rose and I moved closer and read over his shoulder. In the margin around an article about the five best eye shadows to buy this season was handwriting scrawled in ballpoint pen. An address in Midland.

At the bottom of the page was written: *You're welcome*, punctuated with a heart.

It must be John Haller's address. Shannon's father still lived in Midland. I was exhausted, so bone-deep tired, yet my pulse started to pound in my throat. We had to go talk to Shannon Haller's father. We had to do it right now.

The ghost on Atticus Line had tried to kill me. I had to know who she was, once and for all. I had to know if she was Shannon.

I grabbed a pen from the phone nook. I flipped the pages of the magazine to an ad for Calvin Klein perfume and wrote along the edge, since this was the Snell sisters' preferred form of communication. *Trish*, I wrote. *Age around 40, Asian, drives a dark green Toyota.*

Married, has at least one child that is old enough not to need a car seat anymore. Possibly a dentist or works at a dental office. If you can locate her, please check on her and make sure she's okay. Then I ripped out the page with the Midland address on it. I put it with the photocopy of the missing person's report. I walked to the front door, opened it, and put the *Seventeen* magazine back in the mailbox.

I walked back into the kitchen. Rose was frowning. Eddie's gaze met mine, and his expression was stark and determined.

"Let's get dressed," he said.

CHAPTER THIRTY-FIVE

We took Robbie's car, because the metallic smell in Eddie's Pontiac was so bad we couldn't bear it. I took the first hour driving while Eddie slept in the passenger seat. Then we switched. When I woke up, we were more than halfway to Midland. Eddie was silent in the driver's seat, his jaw set.

"What's the matter?" I asked him.

He tapped one finger to the rearview mirror. "See for yourself."

I leaned to look in my side mirror. Driving behind us, not bothering to hide, was a police cruiser. There was a single driver inside, a cop in uniform. Officer Kal Syed.

"Are you *kidding* me?" I said.

"I spotted him right after you fell asleep. He must have been farther back before, but he's been following us all the way from Coldlake Falls."

"Does he have nothing better to do?" I rolled down my window, letting the summer wind blow into the car, and adjusted my mirror. Kal didn't move, but he would clearly be able to see my hand. I gave him the finger.

Beside me, Eddie cracked a reluctant smile, the first one I'd seen in a long time.

I let my rude gesture linger for a moment, just so that Kal would get the message. Then I brought my hand back into the car and rolled my window up. "Do we just let him follow us?"

"I don't see why not. We're not doing anything wrong. If he wants to waste his time, we may as well let him."

"What is he thinking?" I looked in the rearview mirror again. "Maybe he thinks we'll kill a hitchhiker right here on this road while he watches. Shouldn't he be questioning Max Shandler about Rhonda Jean? Looking for evidence? Arresting drunk kids? Doing some kind of police work?"

"I don't know," Eddie said. "Where is Max Shandler? Did he confess? Are they processing the evidence they found? If they're doing all of that, why is he following us? I'm tired of having questions. Maybe we'll finally get some answers of our own."

"Maybe Detective Quentin sent him," I said.

The silence in the car grew heavy, and then Eddie said, "April, I need to know. How much of what you told me was a lie?"

He meant about my mother, about the story I'd given him. I owed him the truth.

"I was asleep," I said. "My mother woke me up and told me we had to run, just like I told you. I packed my things, just like I told you. But the house was too quiet, and Mom had just had a shower.

I wondered why, if it was such an emergency, she had taken the time to have a shower before getting out of the house."

Eddie was quiet, driving and listening. I glanced at Kal in the rearview mirror.

"We left in the dark, and their bedroom door was closed." I made myself say the rest, made the words keep coming. I owed Eddie this. "Mom only told me it was over, but that we had to run or we'd be in trouble. She was jumpy and her hands were shaking. She smoked one cigarette after another. As we drove away, I saw the flames through the windows. She'd set the fire right before waking me. It was only later that I wondered how much blood there had been if she felt the need to take a shower. It must have been a lot."

"Jesus," Eddie said softly.

"I didn't let myself think about it for a long time," I admitted. "I didn't ask questions. I probably should have, but I was twelve. She was all I had. We moved around like we were scared Dad would find us—changed identities, changed states, changed jobs. That was the story—that we didn't want Dad to find us. That was the story I told myself, at least for the first few years. After a while, I admitted to myself that I wasn't scared of Dad tracking us down, and I never had been. It was the police we were running from. Because Dad had been dead since that first night."

"Did you ever talk about it with her?" Eddie asked.

"No, and she never confessed to me. She never confessed any of it, because the more she told me, the more I could tell the police if I got picked up. Maybe I would have forced it at some point, but when I was eighteen I came home and she was gone. I knew the police had caught up with her, that she'd been arrested, and I knew what she'd been arrested for. Part of me always knew. From the moment I saw her damp hair and her fresh clothes, I knew. So I packed my things and ran again."

There was a long moment of silence. Behind us, Kal Syed followed steadily, never out of patience.

"You could have told me," Eddie said.

I blinked back the tears that lurked deep behind my eyes. "I thought you would be disgusted. I thought you would leave. I was planning to tell you—honestly I was. I had it all planned out. Then you proposed before I could get my nerve up, and I said yes. And it felt like it was too late. I couldn't make the sacrifice. I couldn't lose you anymore."

"You could have told me," he said again, his voice rough. He was torn. "It wasn't your fault, what happened. I would have understood."

Maybe. Maybe not. Maybe he didn't understand, even now. I rubbed a hand over my face, thinking of all the mistakes stretching back through my life, a long chain of them. "You're the opposite of my mother," I said. "She was all I had for a long time, and it was killing me. *She* was killing me. I was becoming something I didn't want to be. You're everything she's not. I think that's why I fell for you so fast. What would I do if I told you and you hated me?"

Eddie frowned, his eyes still on the road ahead. "That visit from Quentin was deliberate. Showing up at Rose's, dropping information on us. He was trying to rattle us. Maybe there's a reason Max Shandler couldn't have killed Katharine O'Connor. He's solved Rhonda Jean's murder, or at least it looks like it, but when it comes to the others, he has nothing except us."

There was no discussion of telling Quentin the truth, of what I'd seen on Atticus Line last night. We had nothing concrete to tell. If the Snell sisters found Trish, would she even remember what had happened? If she remembered, would she confess to trying to kill me? It would be my word against hers, and if it came to that, which one of us was untrustworthy, a liar, and possibly crazy?

Me. Only me.

Even if Quentin bought my story, I didn't want Trish to get in trouble. I hadn't meant to involve her, or anyone. She'd had no choice in what she'd done. She was innocent. It was strange to say that about someone who had tried to smash in your skull with a tire iron, but it was true.

"So he was trying to rattle us," I said. "Trying to turn us against each other."

"Trying," Eddie said grimly.

I turned and looked at him, focusing on every line of his body. Trying to read his thoughts. If I could put my hands on him right now, I would know everything, as if he telegraphed his feelings to me through his skin, through my palms. As if he always had.

"Is it working?" I asked him. Because I was done going along with things, not asking questions. I needed to know.

"April." Eddie reached to my lap and took my hand. He raised it to his lips and kissed the back of it, like he had that first night. Then he let me go. "I don't hate you," he said roughly.

I couldn't speak. I didn't know why I felt like crying.

A sign for a gas station appeared ahead, and Eddie switched on his signal. "We're almost out of gas," he said. "Let's see what Kal has to say."

H e was waiting for us when we came out of the gas station kiosk after we paid for our gas. The police cruiser was parked at the edge of the lot, away from the pumps, and Officer Syed was leaning on Robbie's car in full uniform, his arms crossed. The other people at the pumps gave him wary looks and a wide berth.

Eddie and I had both put our sunglasses on, and I felt the heat wafting off the sunbaked pavement as we walked toward the car. "Are you taking a day trip?" Eddie asked Kal.

Kal watched us approach, his expression stoic. He wasn't wearing sunglasses, and I could see his handsome brown eyes perfectly clearly. "Just doing my job," he replied.

"Your job is to follow us around?" I asked.

He didn't answer that. "According to my information, you two live in Ann Arbor. Yet you're not going in the direction of Ann Arbor. Can you tell me where you're going?"

"Midland," Eddie said. There was no point not telling Kal; he would know soon enough if he followed us.

"Okay. And what is so important in Midland?"

Eddie's tone was matter-of-fact. "We're looking for the Lost Girl. We have a lead."

Kal's expression went slack with shock. "What are you talking about? That case from '76? The unidentified girl?"

Unidentified girl. I thought of all the times I'd seen her—in the back of Max Shandler's truck; screaming for help at our passenger window, pulling my husband across the front seat; in the back seat of Trish's car. I might not be sure of her name yet, but she didn't feel unidentified to me.

"We have some information," Eddie said. "We're checking it out."

"You have information, and you didn't pass it to the police?" Kal looked from Eddie to me and back. "You didn't pass it to me?" When we didn't answer, he said, "Where did you come across this so-called information?"

The Snell sisters had gone to lengths to stay secret, so I said, "We're not going to tell you that."

Kal's expression turned grim. "And what is this tip?"

"We're not going to tell you that, either." Eddie was firm. "You can follow us and waste your time if you want. Can we get back into our car now?"

Kal looked between us again and shook his head. "I don't get it. I thought for sure that when I picked you two up this morning, I'd see you go home. That's what I was doing—making sure you went back to Ann Arbor, so I could tell my superiors that you were gone for good. You could walk away from this mess if you wanted, and we wouldn't be able to stop you. Both of you know that. So why? Why are you doing this instead of going back to your lives? What are you looking for?"

"We got a visit from Quentin and Beam last night," Eddie said. "Quentin has spent a lot of time and energy looking into both me and my wife. He's even had the phone line from Rose's place monitored somehow. He's gone to a lot of trouble. Why do you think that is?"

Kal didn't answer. He looked frustrated.

"I was on leave from Fort Custer the day Katharine O'Connor was killed," Eddie went on. "From what I remember, I checked into a cheap hotel, ordered room service, watched TV, and slept for three days because I didn't want to go home to my parents. It's pathetic, but it's true. Quentin thinks that makes me a murder suspect. I know I didn't murder any of those people, and neither did my wife."

"Because you know who did?" Kal asked. "Or you think you do. You think you've solved these cases that have been happening for nineteen years." He sighed. "Please don't tell me you think Quentin is a serial killer. We've had that tip called in more than once, always anonymous. It sounds like a great theory if you're an armchair detective, but I can assure you, it's bullshit."

"If we thought Quentin was the killer, why would we go to Midland?" I asked.

Kal looked frustrated again. "Goddamn it. You're not going to tell me anything, are you?"

"No," Eddie replied.

"And you're not going to turn around, or change course for Ann Arbor."

"No," I said.

Kal pressed his lips together. Then he moved away from our car. "Fine. I guess I'll see you in Midland."

CHAPTER THIRTY-SIX

Kal was as good as his word. As Eddie and I drove through Midland, looking for the address Beatrice Snell had left us, he followed politely in his cruiser. Eddie shook his head as I studied the map in my lap.

"Turn left up here," I said.

"What should we do with him?" Eddie asked.

"I don't know," I admitted. "Maybe it isn't the worst thing in the world to have a little help."

"He'll never believe us."

"Then we don't tell him everything." I followed our progress on the map. "We tell him the less crazy parts."

"Which parts are those?" Eddie's tone was dry. "I can't decide."

"The house is on this street. Number forty-seven. Just up there."

We were pulling up to a town house complex, a string of small homes attached by the garages. The complex wasn't new, and the small yards were weedy, with bikes and kids' toys abandoned next to the porches. An old man smoking a cigarette on his porch watched us as we drove by.

Eddie drove past John Haller's house and parked farther down the street, next to the curb. Kal Syed's cruiser parked behind us. I glanced in the rearview mirror and saw the old man promptly stub out his half-smoked cigarette and disappear into his house.

"Haller isn't going to talk to us," I said. "Not with a cruiser here. He probably won't even answer the door."

Eddie sighed.

Kal got out of his car and walked up to my window, which I rolled down. "Hello, Officer," I said with one of my fake smiles. "Fancy meeting you here."

"I'm not leaving," Kal said. "Are you going to tell me what you're up to? I can sit here all day."

I pushed my sunglasses up on my head and took the folded photocopy of the missing person's report from my purse. I handed it through the window to Kal.

He unfolded it, reading in silence for a minute. "Goddamn it. How the hell did you get this?"

"Check the date," Eddie said.

"I know, Mr. Carter. I know. A year and a half after we found the body in Coldlake Falls. So there wasn't a missing person's report at the time."

"There's more," Eddie said. He took a folded paper from his pocket and handed it over. It was the copy of the classified ad Carla Moyer had placed in 1977.

Kal read that, too. "Do you have any leads on this Carla Moyer?"

"Already talked to her," Eddie said. "She's in the phone book."

"I hate you both." Kal sighed. "You make me look bad. Were you planning on knocking on John Haller's door and asking questions? Because I assure you, I'm not going to let you do it. From this point on, I'll ask the questions."

"Be our guest," I said. "We'll wait right here."

Kal ducked and looked in my window at us. "You think this is going to get me closer to finding a serial killer? Or do we even have a serial killer? Do you want to give me a clue?"

"From this point on, the clues are your problem," Eddie said.

"I hate you both. Please turn around and go back to Coldlake Falls now. Or better yet, go home to Ann Arbor."

"No," I said.

Without another word, Kal stood and crossed the street to John Haller's door. We watched him knock, then knock again. The door opened and a man with gray hair in a ponytail opened it. He wore old sweatpants and a T-shirt, flip-flops on his feet. He gave Kal a hostile stare as the policeman spoke, and then his expression changed. He said something back to Kal, an argument of some kind, and when Kal persisted, he stood back and let Kal in.

Twenty minutes later, Kal emerged from the house, putting his hat back on his head. He strode across the street to our car. "John Haller answered all of my questions," he said. "His daughter, Shannon, left home in 1976, wanting to travel and find herself. She was an addict and an alcoholic with mental problems. He never saw her again. He waited over a year for her to come home, and then he filed a missing person's report. Nothing ever came of it."

"Can Shannon be connected to the unidentified body you found?" Eddie asked.

Kal sighed. "The dental records would do it, if we still have them. We'd have to track down Shannon Haller's dentist and find out if he still has nineteen-year-old records. If that's a dead end, I'll check if any blood or tissue samples were taken from the body and kept all this time. If not, the unidentified girl was buried in one of the graveyards in Coldlake Falls. We'd have to exhume her, which takes a ruling by a judge and a lot of money. And even if we do have samples saved from the postmortem, we'd have to run DNA tests, which take a lot of time and cost a lot of money. We'd also have to run DNA from John Haller to match the results, if he even agrees to give a sample. All of this is above my pay grade. But I'll try." He looked at us. "This is in the right hands now, and there's nothing else the two of you can do. You can turn around and go back to Coldlake Falls now."

I glanced at Eddie. He had turned to look at John Haller's house, which was quiet. He seemed to be deep in thought, so I turned back to Kal.

Our eyes met. We were thinking the same thing: Even if the body could be proven to be Shannon's, her murder still wasn't solved. Max Shandler was a child when Shannon was killed. I knew now—or had an idea—how the others had been murdered, if not who the killers were. But who killed Shannon?

"You could help, you know." Kal's voice was low. "If you tell me what you know, or what you think you know. We're no further ahead than we were before—you know that. You could change that situation."

Right. Go into the Coldlake Falls police station again? Sit in that little room with Quentin and Beam and tell them what happened to me last night? Tell them that their serial killer was a literal ghost? That wouldn't help anyone, least of all me.

"I can't help you," I told Kal, because I owed him something that wasn't a lie.

His brows drew down in concern. "Is someone threatening you?"

What a loaded question that was. "In a way," I said. Shannon's ghost was definitely threatening me.

He tried not to look defeated. "I have to go back," he said. "I'll write a report and start the process of identifying her the best I can. That poor man lost his daughter. I ask that you please don't bother him."

"Of course we won't," I said.

Kal gave a reluctant nod, and then he got back into his cruiser, started it, and drove away.

Eddie was still staring at the house, unmoving.

"Eddie?" I asked. We'd been sitting in this hot, still car for too long. Sweat was soaking my back.

"Just wait." Eddie's voice was calm, detached. He didn't move.

I opened my mouth to say something else but stopped. For once, I agreed with Kal—we should go back to Coldlake Falls. I wanted to see if the Snell girls had found Trish. I wanted to know if she was okay, if she remembered last night. I wanted to know if there was a way to find out how the case against Max Shandler was progressing.

But Eddie was so still, it was scaring me. He was watching for something, for someone. For a second I pictured him just like this in the desert somewhere, waiting for the enemy, and despite the heat in the car, I shivered.

A minute ticked by, then another. The front door of John Haller's house opened and he came out. Without looking left or right, he got in his car and pulled out of the driveway, heading in the opposite direction from Kal.

"Perfect," Eddie said, his voice still as detached as a robot's. "Now."

"Now what?" I asked.

"Now we go in."

He couldn't be serious. "To the house? What are you talking about?"

Eddie turned and looked at me. "She lived in that house, April. Grew up there, maybe. Had a bedroom there. He probably still has her belongings, old photos. There's still a lot more to find."

"That's breaking and entering!" I hissed. "Eddie, we're done here. We need to leave."

But he didn't hear the end of my sentence. He was already out of the car, moving swiftly across the street toward the house. I had no choice but to get out and run after him.

He was fast—army fast. He moved down the attached row of houses with silent speed, his feet making barely a sound on the pavement. Around the corner was a gate opening to the narrow lane behind the houses' backyards. As if he'd been here a dozen times, Eddie unlatched the gate and slipped through.

I followed, trying to keep pace. I had never seen Eddie move like this, as if he was on a mission. He knew exactly what he was doing.

We passed the back gates of several houses, and Eddie stopped at one, pressing his hand to it. It was locked from the inside. He gripped the top of the wooden fence, hoisted himself over, and dropped down. A second later, the gate opened for me as he unlocked it.

"Eddie, stop," I tried to whisper, but he was already gone.

The screen door creaked as Eddie opened it, trying the handle of the back door. Locked. He moved to the nearest window, which looked into the kitchen. He ran his hands over the edges of the screen, feeling with his fingertips. He popped the screen off and dropped it to the ground, leaning it against the house. He fiddled with a latch in a way I couldn't see, lifted the window, and disappeared inside.

The whole operation had taken seconds.

My heart was pounding, and cold sweat had replaced the heat from the car. This was wrong, all wrong. We weren't supposed to be here. Eddie wasn't a thief; I had never seen him act like this. I hadn't thought he knew how to break into houses. Why was he so determined to break into this one? What did he think he was going to find?

I hesitated, glancing around. What if a neighbor saw us from a window? The police could be here in minutes. I walked to the window and pulled myself over the sill, swinging my feet down to the kitchen floor inside.

The house was dim and quiet. It was small, untidy, run-down—the house of a man who lives alone as he grows older, year after year. Empty beer bottles lined the kitchen counter, and my sneakers touched something sticky on the yellowed linoleum floor.

I couldn't see anything unusual. There were auto magazines

on the kitchen table, an ashtray with cigarettes stubbed out. An empty can of baked beans in the sink. John Haller had no wife, no photos on the fridge. His daughter had left long ago, and Carla had said that Shannon's mother was dead.

Eddie had moved to the front room, where he was looking at a shelf of dusty old books. He bypassed the sparsely filled liquor cabinet and opened a cabinet door, peering in.

"Eddie, we need to leave," I said.

"This will be fast." He was still peering into the darkness of the cabinet. "We'll just find Shannon's things and go."

"She left years ago. How do you know he still has her things?"

"Where else would they be?" He closed the cupboard and looked around the living room. "Nothing here, I think. Probably upstairs."

"Eddie!" I tried to keep my voice low in case the neighbors could hear through the walls. But what could I do? He was already moving up the narrow stairs, taking them two at a time.

I looked around the living room, debating whether to follow him. There were no photos in here, either, no framed family pictures on the end tables or above the TV.

My eye caught on something—a cabinet below the TV, the door partly open. Inside I could see the thick pages of a photo album.

I crouched down, sliding the door open. The album had been pulled to the front of the cabinet, as if it had been taken out and carelessly put away. Despite the urge to run, I opened it.

There were loose photos inside the album, along with some stuck to the pages and covered with cling film. I picked up the top loose photo and looked at it.

The photo was of two young women of maybe twenty, their arms around each other's shoulders. I immediately recognized Carla Moyer, though her hair was cropped just below her ears in the photo and her face was round, babyish, carefree.

The other girl had brown hair, worn past her shoulders. She was smiling widely at the camera, grinning in the sunshine, but I immediately went cold.

It was the Lost Girl. It was Shannon Haller.

I didn't need Kal Syed's evidence—dental records, DNA, blood tests. I already knew that the body on Atticus Line was Shannon's because I'd seen her last night in Trish's rearview mirror.

The album had been moved recently because Kal had just been here, talking to John Haller. He had probably asked him for a photo of Shannon, and John had picked one from this pile. Then he'd hastily put the album back.

I picked up the second photo. Shannon carried a small boy on her hip. She was pointing to the camera, trying to get him to smile at the lens. She wore a ringer tee, and she was too thin, her cheekbones sharper than in the other picture, faint shadows under her eyes. The boy had been caught as he turned his face away from the camera, and his features were blurred. He looked about four or five years old.

I stared at the picture for too long. I'd thought Shannon had a baby when she disappeared, not a little boy. *Shannon had a baby she wanted to dry out for,* Carla had said. But she hadn't specified when that was, what year. I'd just assumed she was talking about the year Shannon had disappeared, and so had Eddie. *The math doesn't add up*, Eddie had said. *Shannon had a baby, not an eight-year-old in 1976. That was some other kid. Not me.*

He was wrong. Shannon hadn't just given birth when she disappeared. She had a little boy, who had been taken away from her and put in foster care. I squinted at the photo, but it was too blurry, and the little boy was turning away. I couldn't see his face.

A muffled thump came from upstairs. I shoved the photo in my back pocket, pushed the album back, and closed the door. We'd been here too long. We had to get out of this house.

CHAPTER THIRTY-SEVEN

Upstairs, Eddie was in the main bedroom, looking in the closet. His footprints were clear on the old carpet, and the items in the closet had fallen on the floor.

"Eddie!" I grabbed his elbow, trying to pull him. "Get out of there now!"

"I found her things." He had pulled the lid from an old banker's box and was going through it. I looked over his shoulder and saw a small stuffed baby toy, a few child's drawings. The things that John Haller still had left to remind him of his daughter.

The photo I'd found burned in my back pocket. What would Eddie think if he saw it? Would he have false hope? I didn't understand why he was acting like this. At the same time, if it was possible that Shannon Haller was Eddie's mother, we needed to know. And we wouldn't be able to do anything if we were arrested for breaking and entering.

Eddie's big hands were moving quickly, going through the items. There was a high school diploma, a small silver ring. "It's here somewhere," he said.

"What? What is?" I grabbed his shoulders from behind, trying to shake him. "Please, Eddie. Let's go. *Please.*"

He paused. He held a small Nikon camera in his hands. He ran his fingers over it, turned it over.

"Eddie!" I cried, not bothering to be quiet anymore.

He touched a button, and the camera made a whirring sound as the film wound. Then he touched a button on the top of the camera, opening the back. He took out the roll of film.

He dropped the camera and everything else back in the box, put the lid on, and shoved it in the back of the closet. Then we ran.

W e were silent as we drove back to Coldlake Falls, the air in the car thick with tension. I stared out the window at the passing landscape, feeling sick. We'd come so close, taken too big of a risk. Eddie had behaved more like the man who had picked fights before being discharged from the army than the husband I knew. I didn't recognize him.

We had broken into a man's house, left evidence that we'd been there. If John Haller called the police to report the break-in, it could be traced back to us. Our car had been parked in front of Haller's house. Kal Syed—a cop—had followed us there, talked to us. We had left footprints, fingerprints. It would take only a few phone calls before our names came up.

The panic oozed through my stomach, crawled up my back. The familiar feeling I'd had so many times in my life, every time

Mom said we had to pack and run yet again. The fear that had pulsed through my skull in every motel room and long stretch of highway as Mom and I stayed a step ahead of the police. It was so close I could practically hear her voice. *Relax, baby. Everything will be fine. We'll just keep going. When we stop for gas, don't let anyone see you and don't use the bathroom. Try to sleep. The state line is just a few hours away.*

The threat was as real as it had ever been. If we were arrested, we couldn't afford lawyers. We had no defense. If we were convicted of robbing John Haller, we'd both have criminal records. We could do prison time, and then who would hire us? I might be finished at the bowling alley already, and there was no way Eddie's boss would give him his job back if he was a convicted criminal.

One of the ways I'd survived this long was by never crossing the line into breaking the law. Staying invisible, especially to the police, was my best line of defense. Eddie had just smashed a hole through it.

I glanced at him. His jaw was set, his gaze fixed straight ahead on the road. There was no scrolling through the radio dial this time, no laughing at my stupid jokes. Sweat was beaded on Eddie's temple, and his knuckles were white as he gripped the wheel. The silence was so suffocating it felt stuffed down my throat.

It wasn't until we saw the first sign for the Coldlake Falls city limits that Eddie spoke. "If you want to leave, April—if you want to cut and run—I won't hold it against you."

I closed my eyes. It would be easy. I knew where the keys to the Pontiac were. When we got back to Rose's, all I'd have to do was get in and drive. I knew how to get a new identity, start over.

I knew how to leave April Carter dead at the side of the road if I had to. I had done it so many times.

Think, April. Think.

"You believe I'd do that?" I asked him, unable to keep the hurt from my voice. "You believe I would just abandon you? Maybe Quentin got to you more than you think he did."

"What are you thinking about me right now?" my husband shot back. "You think I'm crazy. The way I just acted was nuts. So Quentin got to you, too."

I flinched at his words. "Tell me why we just risked getting arrested. Can you do that much?"

His voice was a roar that filled the car and made me flinch again despite myself. "*I don't fucking know.* Okay? I can't explain it. I am nuts. You know that. I always have been."

"Don't say that!" I shouted back at him, my feelings raw, my eyes stinging. "If you're nuts, then so am I. We've been through too much, Eddie. Too much. So just man up and tell me what's going on."

It was his turn to flinch, but when he spoke, his words were shockingly calm. "She's in my head."

I stared at him. "Shannon?"

His hands gripped the wheel even tighter, and he looked tormented. "I don't know how she got into my mind, but she's there. I'm starting to think she's been there since that first night, and it's getting worse. Or maybe I've just completely lost my sanity after all this time. That wouldn't surprise me. Either way, it's probably better for you if you leave."

Technically, he was right. I was good at cutting my losses.

But these murders were my fight. Shannon was my fight. My

life as April Carter was my fight. And most of all, Eddie was my fight.

"Why did she pick you?" I asked Eddie. "Why you, of all people?"

He shook his head. "I don't know."

The stolen photo sat in my back pocket, practically screaming into the silence. I couldn't show it to Eddie now, not when he was hanging by a thread. But he'd need to see it. We had to know.

I looked around and realized we were driving through downtown Coldlake Falls. "Where are we going?" I asked.

"I'm trying to find a one-hour photo place. There has to be one around here."

We passed a pizza place, a strip mall with a tiny video store and a nail salon. It was late afternoon now, and everything would close soon. "What if there's nothing on the film you took?" I asked.

"There's something."

"You don't know that."

"I know it."

The stress was throbbing in my temples, mixing with the heat. When was the last time I ate? I didn't even know what day it was anymore. I had long ago lost track of this honeymoon.

I turned in my seat and looked out the back window. Was that a police car a few cars back? It was hard to tell. Was it a coincidence, or was the Coldlake Falls PD keeping tabs on Eddie and me? Had Kal made a report about seeing us in Midland? It was likely that John Haller had come home by now from wherever he'd been. He would see the removed back screen and he'd know that his home had been broken into. If he called the police in Midland, that wouldn't necessarily connect to us in Coldlake Falls.

"Stop thinking, April," Eddie said. "Everything is going to be fine."

I gave a bitter laugh at that. "There was a police car behind us," was my reply. "It just made a left."

"Then it wasn't following us. We aren't doing anything wrong. We just have to find a way to get this done quick."

I turned back around, but I kept looking in my rearview mirror. Cold sweat was sticky on the back of my neck. I was starting to panic. I never panicked—never.

And then I saw it in a parking lot up ahead—a familiar car. Blue and brand-new, gleaming in the late-afternoon sun.

"Turn right," I told Eddie, pointing.

He saw the car, too, and for a second he hesitated. Then he signaled and pulled into the lot, parking a few cars away from Beatrice Snell's shiny new car.

A minute later, Beatrice came out of the drugstore, carrying a small bag. She was wearing jean shorts, a camisole, and a black vest. Her hair was twisted on top of her head and she wore her silver sunglasses. Without seeming to notice us, she unlocked her car and got in.

I glanced back at the street, looking for another police car. I was probably being paranoid. Still, my hand was icy as I pulled the handle to get out of the car. I walked briskly to Beatrice's car, which she hadn't started yet. I could see through the window that she had taken a tube of lipstick from her shopping bag and was putting it on, looking at herself in her rearview mirror.

The sound of the driver's door slamming behind me was my only indication that Eddie was following me. I opened Beatrice's car door and slid into her back seat. Eddie opened the other door and slid in, too.

In the front seat, Beatrice went still, her lipstick in midair. She pushed her sunglasses up, watched us get into her car, and her eyes went wide.

"Hi," I said.

Beatrice twisted in her seat to look at us. Her expression was surprised, and then it warmed into a big smile. Her lips were cherry red.

Something about that smile made the tension ease from my temples for the first time in hours. I couldn't have said why.

"Mr. and Mrs. Carter," Beatrice said. "It's so nice to see you. What are we up to? Whatever we're doing, I'm in."

CHAPTER THIRTY-EIGHT

'm not saying you're being followed by the police," Beatrice Snell said. "But then again, I'm also not *not* saying it."

"They could have put a tracking device on your car," Gracie said. "It isn't that hard to do. It gives off a radio signal. You were smart to come to us."

We had picked up Gracie at the movie theater as she came out of an afternoon showing of *Dolores Claiborne*. ("Not bad," was Gracie's succinct review.) As we drove, I talked.

I told them everything—about the encounter with Shannon Haller's ghost on Atticus Line, about going to John Haller's house, about Kal seeing us there, about breaking in. As I spoke, Eddie stayed silent.

The Snell sisters listened intently to everything I said as Beatrice drove through Coldlake Falls, making random left and right turns. Then we started talking about what to do.

"Okay," Gracie said. "So you have this roll of film, right?"

I looked at Eddie. He spoke for the first time. "I have it."

"And we don't know what's on it."

"It could be nothing," Beatrice said. She had put her sunglasses back on and was frowning as she drove. I hadn't told them that Eddie believed that Shannon Haller might be in his head, but both sisters had accepted without question that we'd broken the law to steal a roll of film, as if it seemed logical to them. "What would Shannon have left behind on film that we need to see? If she was leaving home, she would have taken everything important with her."

"Well, we won't know until we develop it," Gracie said. "Maybe it's like the Zapruder film."

"Where should we get it developed?" Beatrice asked.

"I was looking for a one-hour photo place," Eddie said.

Gracie clucked her tongue. "The only one I know of is Bickle's Photo." She checked her watch, a thin band on her narrow wrist. "It closes in ten minutes."

"Can we get in after hours?" Beatrice asked. "Who works there?"

"Mark Sankowicz." Gracie made a face.

"Yuck," Beatrice said. "I turned him down for homecoming last year. He probably won't let us in after hours. Besides, I don't trust him."

"Me, neither," Gracie agreed.

I was melted into my seat, oddly relaxed. It felt good to let someone else take over, to stop making decisions for a little while. The Snell girls were only too happy to steer the ship. The tension had left Eddie, too, and while the sisters talked in the front seats, the distance between Eddie and me could be forgotten. We had a task to do, and for better or for worse, we were committed to it now. We would see it through.

"Did you get my magazine?" I asked.

"Got it," Gracie said. "We're on it. That's why you wanted to find this Trish woman? Because she's the one you met on the road last night."

"I just want to make sure she's okay," I said.

Gracie nodded. "We'll find her. If she was driving away from the interstate on Atticus Line, she's probably local, because Atticus Line ends at Hunter Beach and there are no other towns along the way. There are less than a dozen dental offices here. I hope she's all right." She shuddered. "I can't imagine what it would be like to have the Lost Girl inside you, making you do things."

I grasped Eddie's hand and curled my fingers around it, but he looked away.

Beatrice sat up in the driver's seat. "I have an idea. We can develop the film ourselves at the high school. There's a darkroom there for photography class."

Gracie put a palm on her forehead. "Why didn't I think of that? It's perfect."

"But it's summer," I said, "and it's late. Isn't the school closed?" I wasn't sure I had the stomach for any more break-ins.

The sisters exchanged a look. "Okay, I *might* have an illegal key," Gracie said. "I *may* have used the school newspaper's ditto machine after hours to make an anonymous pamphlet about UFO abduction cover-ups, but it was important. People need to know."

"We found seventeen people in Coldlake Falls who say they were abducted," Beatrice added. "Some of them weren't even high."

"Do either of you know how to develop film?" I asked.

"I got a B-plus in that class," Gracie said.

"A-minus," Beatrice added.

I looked at Eddie. He seemed to pull himself out of his thoughts. Reluctantly, he shrugged.

"It's as good an idea as any," he said. "I'm in."

Coldlake Falls High School was a small, redbrick building, a perfect cube with a square of green lawn in front and a running track behind it. The parking lot was empty, and the building looked abandoned in the lengthening summer sun. Darkness wouldn't fall for a while yet, but the long shadows made the school look lonely and sad, like every school does in summer.

Gracie had picked up her key at the Snell house while the rest of us waited in the car, parked out of sight. Now she unlocked the school's side door and it swung open with a soft click. The experience was anticlimactic, to be honest. Still, my stomach turned as Eddie and I took part in our second break-in of the day.

The lights were off in the halls, and the only light was from the lowering sun through the windows. The air-conditioning was off, but the air wasn't unbearably hot. I looked at the announcement board with curiosity as we walked past it, taking in the old notices of play auditions and student council meetings from last school year. High school had been a very distant experience for me, as if I'd spent time on another planet. Mom and I had moved so much that it had been a struggle to graduate, and I'd never gotten involved in football or yearbooks or math clubs like other students. It went without saying that I had had no friends.

Beatrice led us down one hall, then another. In the dim light and the silence, my exhaustion nearly caught up with me, and I had the urge to lie down and take a nap. High schools in summer, it turned out, were strangely peaceful places.

"In here." Beatrice whispered, even though there was no one else in the building to hear. Her hand was on the knob of a door labeled PHOTOGRAPHY LAB. She turned it experimentally, and it gave. The lab wasn't locked.

We slipped inside, all of us moving like fugitives. Gracie flicked on the light, showing a classroom with several tables instead of desks, a chalkboard on the front wall. Gracie clicked the door shut behind us.

"Okay," she said in her normal voice. "The darkroom is over here."

As the girls opened the door labeled DARKROOM, I imagined years of students passing through this room, the happy ones and the miserable ones, the smart ones and the stupid ones, with their small rivalries and petty resentments, on their way toward a destiny they couldn't see. Though we'd never talked about it in depth, I knew exactly what Eddie had been like in high school—big, shy, quiet, overlooked by most of the girls, doing his best to get good grades because he didn't know any other way to be. I knew Eddie so well that I could see it, see *him*, his hair overgrown and his shoulders slouched at sixteen.

Our gazes caught, and a flicker of a smile touched his mouth. He guessed what I was thinking. For a second, everything fell away and it was just us—no secrets, lies, worries, or unsolvable problems. Just Eddie and me.

"Come on," Gracie hissed, and Eddie gestured for me to precede him into the darkroom.

Eddie took the canister of film from his pocket. "Let's do this fast," he said.

The girls got to work, preparing the equipment and the chemicals. They whispered directions to each other. Eddie and I waited.

Somewhere outside, I heard the snap of a door closing. We all froze.

I put my hand on the doorknob. There was no mechanism to lock the door from inside—probably a measure to prevent teenagers from locking themselves in to fool around. Anyone could open the door and find us.

The four of us looked at one another. "You heard that, right?" Beatrice asked, her voice a whisper again.

Our faces said that we all had. We waited in silence for the sound to come again.

Ice-cold air crept up the back of my neck, like fingers. Somewhere down the hall was a thump, as if something heavy had been dropped.

"Do it," I hissed at the girls, my voice coming out harsh. "Do it fast. Right now. Go."

The girls blinked, and then they nodded. Gracie looked at Eddie, who was standing by the light switch. "We're ready. You can turn out the light."

My hand tightened on the doorknob. I didn't know who—or

what—was outside this darkroom, but it wasn't going to open this door. If the door opened, this would all be for nothing.

What did you take pictures of, Shannon?

I looked at Eddie, nodding to him that I was ready.

Eddie turned off the light.

CHAPTER THIRTY-NINE

For a second, the darkness was total, sucking us all down. Then a red light came on. Beatrice had pressed a button next to one of the tanks.

She and Gracie worked quickly. I didn't watch; I focused on the door I was holding, even though there was nothing to see. The back of my neck was still cold. I strained my ears, listening.

Minutes ticked by. The sisters bickered under their breaths, trying to remember the correct sequence, hissing about canisters and fixing agents. I felt time narrow down to a fine point as I waited, knowing it was coming. And then I heard it.

There was a sound outside the classroom door, as if someone was standing there, waiting, shuffling as they lingered. I heard Gracie's harsh intake of breath.

"If they come in here, they'll know we're in the darkroom," she whispered. "When the red light goes on, a sign lights up above the door that says DARKROOM IN USE."

In the red light, we all looked bathed in blood. Whoever was outside already knew we were in here. She seemed to always know where we were, wherever we went. But the Snell sisters didn't know her like we did.

"There's nothing we can do," Eddie said, his voice flat. "Just keep working as fast as you can."

They did, and seconds later I heard a soft creak as the classroom door drifted open, as if by a gentle hand. My palm was slick on the doorknob, and I closed my eyes, listening to her steps outside the door—the touch, maybe, of a rubber sneaker sole against the polished floor. There was the scrape of a chair, or maybe a desk, moving. I pictured her long hair, her eyes. The way she'd screamed at us in the dark that night, grabbed Eddie and tried to drag him from the car.

"What do we do?" Beatrice sounded panicked. I had never heard her sound afraid before.

Eddie's voice was calm, and in the darkness behind my eyes, I wondered what he looked like. "Keep going," he said. "As fast as you can."

She was outside now, only a foot away through the door. I was cold, so cold. I thought she might try the doorknob, but she didn't. Instead, I felt the gentle brush of something against the door, a scraping sound. One of the girls made a soft whimper in the back of her throat.

"She won't hurt us," Eddie said softly. And even though my pulse pounded in my throat, I didn't think she would, either. If she wanted to, she would have done it already. Could she enter one of us and make them kill the others, like she had done so many times on Atticus Line? Perhaps she could. She could certainly force this door open, whether I held the doorknob or not. And yet she didn't try.

The scraping continued, and then there was silence. A strange, sinister smell. Something popped, too loud. I wondered what she was doing out there.

The Snell girls were breathing hard as they worked, close to panic. "We have to dry the negatives," Gracie whispered, her voice shaking. "There's a—a dryer thing. There's only four negatives. But the dryer makes noise."

"Do it," Eddie said.

I didn't open my eyes. I didn't have to. I kept my hand on the knob and listened to her outside, doing something I couldn't figure out. There was a tinkle of glass. Then the cold started to recede. "She's leaving," I whispered.

There was a repressed sob, which sounded like it came from Beatrice. I admired her restraint. It was hard not to scream when Shannon Haller was only a few feet away, dead and not dead at the same time.

The dryer whirred, painfully loud. When one of the girls clicked it off, we heard another footstep in the hall and the classroom door opened. "Is anyone in here?" a voice said.

It was a man's voice. A real, live, actual man. Even though we were about to be caught, the sound of it was comfortingly sane. Still, we all froze, and I kept my grip on the doorknob.

There was a minute's pause, and then the man's voice came again. "If you're in here, say so. You won't be in trouble. I just want you to leave."

I opened my eyes and turned to look at the others. Beatrice was frozen in place, and Gracie had a strip of negatives in her hand. The negatives wavered in the air as her hand shook.

Eddie was standing still, his brows furrowed in confusion. The man outside must be able to see the sign lit up above the darkroom door, but he didn't come to the darkroom. Instead, we heard him come into the classroom and straighten the chairs, grumbling under his breath. He was the janitor, doing a daily sweep of the building. He had to be.

There were more footsteps, accompanied by more grumbling. Then the classroom door closed and the janitor was gone.

"Oh my God," Gracie breathed. "I think I'm going to pass out."

"What do we do next with those?" Eddie motioned to the negatives. His voice was tight and calm. Iraq calm.

"There were only four exposures on the roll," Beatrice said. "We can print them if we're fast."

"Do it," Eddie said.

So the girls took paper from a stack on the shelf. Eddie moved to stand next to me at the door, so close I could feel his breath against my neck as liquids sloshed. It seemed like a long time before Beatrice said, "Okay, we're done."

She clicked the red light off, and I opened the darkroom door so we could all exit. I didn't want to look at the photographs in there; I didn't want to be in there for even one more second. I felt like I was suffocating.

"We need to get out of here," Eddie said in his perfectly calm voice. "The janitor is still in the building somewhere, and he'll probably be back."

He moved to the door, but Gracie said, "The light."

I turned to see her staring at the light above the darkroom door, the one that said DARKROOM IN USE. It looked slightly crooked.

"Bea, turn on the light," Gracie said. Her sister walked back into the darkroom, and we heard the click of the switch. Nothing happened. The light didn't come on.

I walked to the darkroom door, reached up, and touched the light. It tilted against my fingertip, and then it fell to the floor. The glass from the broken bulb scattered at our feet. Behind the disconnected light, the wall was burned and black, the outlet incinerated. There was a plastic-smoke smell in the air.

"Shannon," I said. That's what she had been doing outside the door. Of course she hadn't tried the doorknob—she didn't want to interrupt us. She didn't want the janitor to interrupt us, either. Whatever was in those photos, she wanted them developed. She wanted us to see.

Beatrice made a strangled noise and grabbed her big sister's hand. She had always been so bold and confident, but right now she looked young. She looked like a scared sixteen-year-old who had just seen something she didn't understand. She stared up at the scorch marks on the wall, her eyes wet with unshed tears.

I took her other hand. It was cold, not with the presence of Shannon Haller, but with fear. I squeezed it, telling her I understood.

The four of us left the room in silence.

CHAPTER FORTY

Twenty minutes later, Beatrice drove her car into an empty parking lot outside a closed Kmart. She pulled the prints from under her shirt, where she had hastily stuffed them as we made our escape from Coldlake Falls High School.

"So? Are we going to talk about that?" she asked, turning in her seat to look at the rest of us.

She had regained some of her composure, but she was still shaken. In the passenger seat, Gracie was pale and silent.

Oddly, I felt calmer than I had since I watched Eddie climb through John Haller's window. The pulse in my throat had slowed, the sweat drying against my shirt. "I told you what happened," I said. "You said you believed me."

"Are you kidding me?" Beatrice's voice was high-pitched with leftover adrenaline. "We did, but that was before—oh my God."

"I think I might throw up," Gracie said.

"I want to look at the photographs." Eddie's voice was calm. "We need to do that before we talk about anything else. Turn on the light."

Dusk had fallen, and it was shadowy inside the car. Beatrice reached up and turned on the interior light, throwing us all into a glare.

There were four photos, so she passed them around, one to each of us. We all looked at our photographs, the ones that Eddie and I had broken the law for, the ones that we'd risked everything for.

"Mine's unreadable," Gracie said. She flipped her photo so we could see that it was a blur. "She must have moved when she pressed the shutter."

"Mine's Shannon with a girl I don't recognize." Beatrice flipped her photo, too. In it, Shannon Haller had her arm around another girl's shoulders, big smiles on both of their faces. It was a lot like the photo I'd seen at her father's house, though the woman was different. An everyday photo of a young woman hanging out with a girlfriend, taking a picture because they were having a good time.

I looked at my own photo, my hands cold. I couldn't speak.

Eddie was silent, too, staring at the print in his hands.

"Well?" Beatrice's voice was sharp with excitement. "Don't keep us in suspense."

I was frozen, but Eddie slowly turned his photo around. It was of Shannon, by herself, standing on a set of concrete steps. She looked serious, solemn, her slim body held tensely. She was wearing jeans and a Mickey Mouse T-shirt, a backpack on her back.

"That's my mother," Eddie said, his voice low and raw. "I remember her face. That's her."

"Eddie," I said softly, and he looked at me.

Had he always known? Had I? Shannon was a little too thin in the photo, her cheeks hollow, her eyes too large. But I saw the shape of Eddie's nose, the angle of his eyebrows in that picture. I saw the tentative expression on her face, the quiet way she held herself. In death, Shannon was terrifying. But in life, she resembled her son. She was a woman who'd had hard luck and struggles, one who had made decisions both good and bad and paid for them. A young woman who just wanted a better life and wasn't sure of how to get there. Lost, just like the rest of us.

"She brought you here," I said to Eddie. "That's why we can't remember exiting the interstate."

His voice was close to a whisper. "I'm so sorry, April."

"She was looking at you," I went on. "That first time, when she was in the back of the truck. And outside Max Shandler's barn. I thought she was staring at us, but she wasn't. She was staring at you. Only you."

"What are you talking about?" Beatrice nearly shrieked.

"Bea, be quiet," her sister said.

"She grabbed you from the car," I said. It was falling into place now. "She reached across me and grabbed you, because it was you she wanted. It was so weird that no one had ever seen her like that, remember? The storm, and the light, and the way she banged on the car. It seemed so strange that no one else had ever seen that, but now we know why. Because she wanted you. When I was alone, she tried to kill me—but not when I was with you. She never wanted to kill you."

"I'm so sorry," Eddie said again. "You didn't ask for this, but you got dragged in anyway. It's my fault."

I took the photo from my back pocket and handed it to him—the picture of Shannon and the little boy who was Eddie. He took it and looked at it for a long moment.

"I always thought I didn't remember her," he said, the words coming slowly. "I thought I didn't know her face. But now I think it was because I was trying not to remember. I was trying not to recall her face—I've been doing it for years. I remember staying with neighbors, wondering when she would come home. Wondering if she would ever come home." He put a hand to his forehead and rubbed slowly, closing his eyes. "There's so much I don't remember. The day they took me away—I don't remember that. I worried about her so much, wondered if she was all right. I wondered if she had been hurt or was in the hospital. If she would ever come back for me. Then she didn't, and I think I tried to forget everything."

"I think she would have come back for you," I said. "If she had lived. She wasn't perfect, but she was trying. Carla said she was sober before she disappeared. She just didn't get the chance."

We were all quiet for a moment. Beatrice seemed to have calmed down, and she was biting her lip, her expression solemn. She and Gracie may not know all the details of Eddie's story, but they could guess enough.

"She's really pretty," Gracie said.

Eddie looked at the photo of his mother holding him as a boy again, and then he raised his gaze to me. "April? Your photo."

The picture in my hand felt like ice. I had the urge to tear it up, throw it out the window, as if that could keep everything the way it was in just this moment.

But we'd come all this way—so, so far from the road we'd thought we'd travel—and there was no other way to go but forward.

"There's more," I said.

Eddie nodded, as if he expected it.

"Take another look at that photo." I pointed to the picture of Shannon standing on the steps. "She's wearing a backpack." I held up my photo. "And then there's this."

Shannon was smiling in this picture, too. She was standing with a man and a woman I didn't recognize, her brown hair lifted by a breeze. Despite the smile, her eyes were shadowed and unhappy. But that wasn't what mattered.

In the background of the photo was a familiar house, one that Eddie and I had visited a few days ago.

"Hey," Beatrice said as she recognized it. "That's Hunter Beach."

Eddie's expression went carefully blank as he recognized the cabin on Hunter Beach, the one the backpackers had been using since the seventies and were still using today. His mother was standing in front of it, posing with her friends.

She had been there in 1976, right in the spot we'd stood to talk to the kids around the fire.

I saw his face change when he saw it. Behind Shannon and her friends, a backpack was lying in the sand. A pair of sandals was tucked beneath it, a sweatshirt folded on top of it. Lying on top of the sweatshirt was a letter jacket from Midland High.

The photo had been taken after Shannon left home to find herself. She would have been carrying the camera, with the film in it, when she died.

"Her father had this photo in his house?" Beatrice asked, breathless. "Her *father*?"

"Oh my God," Gracie said. "She's the Lost Girl. The Lost Girl really is real."

"Her father had her camera," I said. "He was there when she died."

CHAPTER FORTY-ONE

Detective Quentin leaned back in his chair. "That was impressive, Mr. and Mrs. Carter. You've spun quite a tale."

It was the next morning, and we were back at the Coldlake Falls PD, sitting in an interview room. Quentin was talking to us alone; Beam was nowhere to be seen. Quentin was wearing black dress pants and a dress shirt with the sleeves rolled up. When we'd called the police station to request a meeting with Quentin— we would talk to no one else—we weren't even sure he would get the message, and if he did whether he would come. Maybe he was done with us. But within forty-five minutes, we got a call back at Rose's to say we should come to the station because Quentin was on his way.

Eddie and I had decided to tell him everything—about Shannon Haller, about seeing the Lost Girl, about breaking into

John Haller's house and finding the roll of film with the photograph on it. We'd told him about ghosts and Eddie's adoption and the strange way we'd ended up here without really remembering it. It didn't matter that we sounded delusional and possibly unhinged. Eddie and I were done carrying the mysteries of Atticus Line around, letting them weigh us down.

We had only left out one part of the story—the attack on me. Whoever Trish was, wherever she was, she didn't deserve questioning by police and possible attempted murder charges. Quentin might not believe us, but if he could find Trish, he would sit her down in this very room and try to figure out the truth. I didn't want her to go through that. She'd been through enough.

Quentin crossed his arms, looking at us with his uncanny blue eyes. He had listened to us in silence. As usual, he had taken no notes, as if every word we said was immediately locked into his brain. On the table between us was our only piece of evidence— the photos we'd taken from John Haller, including the one shot on Hunter Beach.

"Mr. Carter," the detective said crisply, as if he was told ghost stories all the time. "You're saying that this woman"—he gestured to Shannon in the photographs—"is your birth mother."

"Yes," Eddie said. As strange as this interview was, he looked more relaxed than he had when we started, as if he was unburdened.

"You also claim that this woman's father possessed a camera with this photograph on the film, which means the camera was obtained after she left home. This, to you, proves that the father saw the daughter at least once after she left, contrary to his missing person's report. And from this, you conjecture that he must have killed his daughter on Atticus Line. In effect, your grandfather murdered your mother. Am I following this?"

"Yes," Eddie said.

"Mrs. Carter," Quentin continued, turning to me. "You have stated that your husband broke into the house of a man named John Haller in Midland, and that you followed him. Both of you illegally entered the man's house through a window while he wasn't home. In searching John Haller's home, you found the camera with the alleged film inside, after which you produced these photographs."

"That's right," I said.

"And by the two of you committing this crime, you both claim to have solved one of my oldest open murder cases, a case that—please excuse my word usage—haunts my career even now, nineteen years later, as a blight on my record, even though it happened before my time."

I looked into his chilly blue eyes as I answered him. "Yes."

Quentin leaned forward across the table. "I can make one phone call. One. I can call the Midland PD and ask if a man named John Haller has reported a break-in at his home, and the answer will be yes or no. If it's yes, I will tell the Midland PD that I have two suspects here who are confessing. If it's no, your entire story disappears. Neither of those options is very good from your point of view. So please explain, Mrs. Carter, why did you tell me any of this in the first place?"

He was hard to read, but I read enough. It was in the undercurrent of anger in his voice at the idea that we were wasting his precious time. "You don't believe us," I said.

"Believe you?" He tapped the photograph. "This photo could be of anyone. It could have been taken at any time, and it could have come from anywhere. You could have brought it with you from Ann Arbor, for all I know. It isn't evidence. To solve a murder case, I require evidence. You've given me nothing."

Eddie shifted in his seat beside me, because he didn't like the way Quentin was speaking to me. But I held still and kept my gaze on the detective's. "You don't scare me," I told him, my voice almost as icy as his. "Make your phone call. Do it."

"I am not susceptible to women like you," Quentin said as Eddie shifted in his seat again, getting angry at the phrase *women like you*. "Maybe everyone else you meet is, including your husband. They react to your blond hair, your looks, your smile. Pretty, but not too pretty, correct? The way you dress manages to show off your legs without being too showy. You don't talk too much or too little. You don't push. You pretend to be agreeable and obedient, and then you do whatever you want. Women like you can keep secrets for years—decades. Until death, if they have to. They never get drunk and slip up or get stupid over a man and tell him too much. And woe to anyone who crosses you. You think I don't see it? Because I saw it from the very first second I walked into the room the night that Rhonda Jean Breckwith died in your back seat."

His words fell hard, and I kept my face from flinching. I'd thought I'd been so careful. I should have known.

"You get off on this," I told him, firing back. "Unnerving people, scaring them. Keeping them off-balance so they talk too much. You think you're so powerful, but this room gives you most of that power. If you weren't a detective, we'd be even, which drives you crazy. Because you like to intimidate women. You find that especially fun."

"Unnerving people is how I solve cases, Mrs. Carter. On most people, it works."

He meant that it didn't work on me, but I didn't care for the compliment. I pointed to the photo on the table, to Shannon Haller's face. "That's your unidentified murder victim from 1976. Her name is Shannon Haller. Maybe you believe that her ghost haunts Atticus Line, killing other hitchhikers, or maybe you don't. But as we told you, we already gave this information to Officer Syed. He said he can check the dental records from the post-mortem. If you can match the dental records—or her blood—then you have evidence. And the identity of your unknown victim is solved."

His jaw tightened. He didn't have to tell me that none of it would happen quickly, not in a case this old. Whether the results came in a month or a year, it would still be proof one way or another.

And in the meantime, John Haller's missing person's report matched the description and time frame of the murder of the unknown girl. It was a lead he hadn't had before, and Quentin was a detective. He would follow it.

"Are you going to arrest us?" Eddie's voice broke into our standoff. "I've never confessed to a crime before. I don't know how this works."

Quentin's look was calculating as he turned to Eddie, and then he seemed to make a decision. He shook his head.

"I don't have time for this." He picked up the photos from the table and put them into his breast pocket. Eddie flinched, and I knew he wanted to protest, because aside from the picture of Shannon and Eddie—which we hadn't given up—those were the only photos he had of his mother. But we had the negatives, and we could print them again.

"What do you mean, you don't have time?" I said.

"Old legends. Ghost stories. Unprovable theories." Quentin pushed his chair back. "I don't deal in those things. I deal in facts and evidence, and that's all."

"You're not going to investigate?" I asked.

"Investigate what? There's nothing here. What I'm going to do, Mrs. Carter, is go back to my other cases—cases that need my attention—and pretend this meeting never happened."

Eddie and I exchanged a look. He didn't have to believe us about the Lost Girl, but we had confessed to a crime. Didn't he care?

"What do you want us to do?" Eddie asked.

"That's easy, Mr. Carter. I want both of you to pack your bags, go back to Ann Arbor, and never come here again."

"A few days ago, you told us not to leave town," I snapped.

"I changed my mind. This is over. We have someone in custody for the murder of Rhonda Jean Breckwith, and both of you are cleared as suspects. Go home."

What if John Haller reported the break-in? I was about to ask it, but I didn't. Maybe John Haller wouldn't report the break-in if it meant questions about what was stolen. He had secrets to cover up.

Quentin stood, and Eddie pushed his chair back and stood, too, tense with anger. "My mother was murdered. Her killer is still out there, free."

"That is your theory, Mr. Carter," Quentin said. "It's a theory with no proof, and I've heard plenty of those—including the theory that I committed all the murders myself. Maybe you'd like me to investigate that one next?"

"So that's it?" I stood, too, and the three of us faced one another over the table. "You just pretend that none of this ever happened?"

"Because none of it *did* happen. Nothing that you can prove." Quentin looked from me to Eddie. "The two of you were drawn into a difficult and stressful situation the night you picked up Rhonda Jean. It made your imaginations overreact. Mr. Carter, you've wondered about your birth parents all your life, have you not? You'd grasp at anything that seemed to answer your questions and let wild theories fill in the blanks, especially considering your precarious mental state. It's unfortunate, but it's what happened. I'm not going to investigate this supposed break-in, and in return, you're free to go."

He didn't wait for us to argue again. He turned and left the room.

Detective Beam was standing in front of the Coldlake Falls police station, smoking a cigarette and waiting for us. He took in our surprised faces and asked, "What did he say to you?"

Eddie and I exchanged a look. "We're leaving town," I said, skipping over the confession we'd given that Quentin had discounted. "He told us to go."

"Oh, did he give his permission?" Beam gave a bitter laugh and tapped his cigarette ash to the sidewalk. "How generous of him."

I took in his expression, his tired, bloodshot eyes. "Why do you work with him if you hate him so much?" I asked.

Beam exhaled smoke and dropped his cigarette to grind it out. "I don't have much choice, do I? He closes cases, and that's all that matters. No one cares that he's a soulless bastard. Besides, it's nothing to me anymore. I'm taking retirement next month. Some other detective can deal with the great, almighty Quentin." He trained his gaze on Eddie. "I heard how he talked to you at Rose's, tried to make you feel like you're crazy. He doesn't know what the hell he's talking about. He doesn't *know*." He nodded at my husband. "I did two tours in Vietnam, son. I know what crazy is, and you aren't it."

Eddie held Beam's gaze. "My discharge papers disagree," he said quietly.

"Because they're trash," Beam replied. "Put them in the trash where they belong. Whatever's going on, Carter, you're not the crazy one, and neither am I. Men like us know the truth. It's the world that's crazy. We're the only ones who are sane." He took a step toward the doors of the police station, then turned back. "Don't let anyone tell you different," he said to Eddie. "Not doctors, not Quentin, not anyone. The things we've seen mean the world is crazy. Not us."

CHAPTER FORTY-TWO

Back at Rose's, I pulled my small suitcase from the corner of the bedroom and opened it. I picked up clothes and started folding and packing them.

Outside in the kitchen, I could hear Eddie and Rose. Eddie was trying to pay Rose for our stay; Rose was arguing that we could mail her a check when we got home, after we "got our feet under us" as she put it. As I folded one of my bras and tucked it into the suitcase, I had no illusions—if it had been me negotiating our bill instead of Eddie, she would have given me one of her looks and demanded her money. I could at least give Rose credit for having good taste in men.

Their conversation continued, never quite blowing over into an argument. Eddie reluctantly gave in to the check-mailing solution, but he insisted on hauling the last of the debris from Rose's backyard before we left.

We had no choice but to leave. Detective Quentin had shut us out, and we couldn't afford to stay in Coldlake Falls forever, looking for answers. We had Shannon Haller's name and the photo of her with Eddie. We knew who his mother was now, who his grandfather was. We didn't have justice, but we were just two people with no connections and almost no money. I might not have my job at the bowling alley anymore, and we couldn't afford for Eddie to lose his job, too.

Stories don't always end the way they're supposed to. They don't always end at all.

I snapped my suitcase shut and walked out of the bedroom to see Rose folding her grocery store apron into her bag. "I'm going to work. I guess I'll see you," she said, not making eye contact and pushing her glasses up the bridge of her nose.

"Bye, Rose," I said. "Thank you."

She gave me a narrow-eyed look and made a disapproving sound in her throat. Then she left, and Eddie and I were alone.

I crossed my arms and leaned against the bedroom doorframe, looking at my husband. He was wearing the only pair of clean jeans he had left on this trip, and a gray tee with a brown plaid flannel shirt unbuttoned over it. He'd brought the shirt, I knew, in case the nights on our honeymoon got cool. His short hair was tousled and he had two days' scruff on his jaw. He looked exhausted, and the whole effect should have looked disreputable, but somehow Eddie never truly looked disreputable. Even in the depths of chaos, while his life was falling apart, he looked like a man who would hold the door for you and ask if you were okay. It was just how he was.

He was looking at me, too, and I wondered what he saw. I

wasn't that girl in the blue bra anymore, drifting aimlessly through life. I wasn't even the same April who had gotten married in a secondhand dress. I wasn't sure what I was anymore. What I was going to be.

"I'm sorry my mother stole all of my money," I said.

"I wouldn't have wanted it anyway," he replied.

Of course he wouldn't. "It was a lot of money."

"Too bad."

I cleared my throat. I'd never told him I was sorry—I had never said the words. There was only one person that I was capable of apologizing to, and he was standing in front of me. "I'm sorry I didn't tell you about my mother. It was the wrong thing to do. I should have told you."

"Well." He scratched his jaw, his gaze wandering up to the ceiling. "Considering I broke into my grandfather's house and my grandfather murdered my mother, I guess I've dragged you into a few problems of my own."

His tone was so casual I had to bite my lips to keep in a laugh.

"April, don't laugh."

"It's uncomfortable laughter. Like at a funeral."

"I know, but still."

I put a hand over my mouth, trying to keep the amusement in. The urge was uncontrolled, and I felt my stomach squeeze. I lifted my hand long enough to wheeze, "Eddie, don't ever take me to a funeral. I mean it."

"April, this is very serious."

Those words made me want to laugh even more, and my eyes watered. I kept my hand over my mouth. Eddie didn't crack a smile, but I caught the ghost of a twinkle in his eyes as he turned away.

"I'm going to the backyard," he said. "We'll leave in twenty minutes."

I nodded mutely, still trying not to giggle. I took a deep breath and turned back toward the bedroom. That was when I saw the man.

He was fiftyish, stocky. He wore a red plaid shirt tucked neatly into a pair of light-blue jeans. I could see him so clearly that I could make out the gray at his temples and the wrinkles in the dark skin at the corners of his eyes. He was standing by the bedroom window. A breeze blew outside, and I watched the leaves on the tree outside the window move behind him, as if the man was made from transparent film.

His mouth moved, mute. Then I heard it.

"Get down," the man said.

His hands rose. I didn't see him move, but I felt two hands shove my shoulders, so hard I lost my balance. The hands pushed me to the floor.

"*Get down*," said the voice in my ear.

I opened my mouth to scream.

There was a crack outside, and the bedroom window broke, shards of glass falling to the floor.

A second crack. A third. My ears hurt. Something hit the wall, and plaster exploded, sending decorative knickknacks falling to the floor. I stared at the hole in the wall and realized that someone was shooting through the window.

"Eddie!" I screamed.

There were footsteps outside the window. "I can hear you in there," a man's voice said, harsh and angry. "Stand up."

The back door banged; Eddie had been in the backyard. His shout was hoarse. "April!"

"Get down!" I screamed as the gun went off again. The footsteps outside receded, running for the back of the house, and I cried out, "Lock the back door!"

I crawled on my hands and knees across the bedroom floor toward the doorway. Eddie was crouched in the corner of the kitchen, his hands on his knees. The back door was closed. His gaze crawled over me. "Are you all right?"

I nodded. Eddie opened his mouth to say something else just as a blast hit the back door, making me jump.

"Come out, you two!" the man's voice shouted. "You think I couldn't track you down? You parked your car in front of my god-damned house while you broke in! I know exactly who you are!"

John Haller. My mind went blank with shock. Instead of calling the police on us, John Haller was here, right now, shooting at us. He'd come around the side of the house to fire through the window at me while Eddie was in the backyard. How close had he come? If he had walked a few more feet and looked into the yard, Eddie would have been an open target, defenseless. He would have died right where Robbie had.

Another shot hit the back door, but the door didn't break. I watched Eddie's gaze move to the front window, the front door. His eyes were blank, calculating. He had gone somewhere in his head that his training had taken him, somewhere he'd gone during his months in Iraq. He didn't even look afraid. My hands were shaking.

A hot breeze blew through the broken bedroom window like a breath, lifting the fussy curtains. I heard the footsteps coming back, and I forced one of my trembling hands up to signal to Eddie. He gestured for me to get out of the bedroom, outside the door.

"It was Shannon's film you took, wasn't it?" John Haller shouted. I crawled outside the bedroom door and put my back to the wall. I wondered if the neighbors would call the police, how long it would take the police to come. "Took me a minute to figure it out. I bet you think you're smart. I bet you thought I'd crawl in my hole and not say anything, didn't you? Get out here."

This was insane. We were under siege, right here in Rose's house in the middle of a summer morning. The police had to be coming—but how many? Two cops? Three? I had seen the size of the Coldlake Falls PD. I pointed to the phone in the phone nook on the other side of the living room, but Eddie shook his head. "No time," he said.

I heard an intake of breath outside as Haller heard Eddie's voice. "This isn't going to end how you think it is," Haller said, his tone calmer. "I knew from the second that cop knocked on my door that it was over, and I'm ready. Are you? Because I'm not waiting around."

The footsteps moved away again, this time toward the front door.

I heard a scraping sound. Eddie had taken a kitchen knife from the counter and slid it across the floor toward me. I stopped it with my foot and grabbed it by the handle. "He's coming in," he said calmly. "We can't stop him. You have one chance, and then I'll take him."

I looked to the front of the house. Eddie was right—there were both the front door and the front windows that looked out over the street. The door would be hard, but the windows would be easy. A couple of shots to the glass, and Haller could get inside, where Eddie and I were sitting here, waiting, unarmed.

"Should we go out the back?" I asked. My voice was weirdly normal, like it had been that first night, when I realized that Rhonda Jean was bleeding to death. I was still shaking, but it didn't matter. My thoughts had stopped scattering like a flock of startled birds. Twelve-year-old April—born as Crystal Cross in Los Angeles, California—had taken over.

"He'll just follow," Eddie said. "Someone else could get hurt. I'd rather take him here."

I was already on my feet, running in a low crouch toward the front of the living room, keeping clear of the picture window. Eddie moved behind the sofa, out of sight. For a big man, he moved with absolutely no sound.

I took in the window, trying to calculate my best position. I had to be where Haller wouldn't see me before it was too late. I had just tucked myself against the wall under the left corner, behind a side table, when a shadow moved across the window.

I only had a split second to think before a gunshot smashed the glass, and I ducked so I wouldn't get hit with the shards. The sound must have been heard through the entire neighborhood. Did he think he was going to walk away from this, whether Eddie and I died or not? *He's insane*, I thought. *He must be.*

"I reloaded," Haller's voice said. "Here I come."

I could hear sirens in the distance. Someone in the street was shouting. I pressed myself against the wall, going still as I heard the scrape of something on the windowsill. Then John Haller's legs swung over and his feet hit the ground. He had a rifle in his hand, and his gaze was on the sofa, where he'd caught sight of Eddie. He hadn't seen me. He raised the gun.

I pivoted and jammed the knife into the back of his thigh as hard as I could.

Haller roared and dropped to one knee. He kicked hard, catching me in the chin, and I dropped onto my ass, scrambling back against the wall. Haller turned to aim the gun at me.

But Eddie was already there. He knocked the rifle from Haller's grip and picked it up, aiming it at him. Haller barely paused. In one quick motion he drew a handgun from the shoulder holster he was wearing and aimed it at Eddie, thumbing off the safety.

The three of us froze, Eddie standing and aiming the rifle, Haller aiming the handgun back at him from his position on one knee, and me against the wall, my jaw throbbing.

Eddie and Haller locked gazes, both of them breathing hard. Grandfather and grandson.

"Don't move," Eddie said, and whether he meant me or Haller or both of us, it didn't matter. I stayed still. What if a movement from me made one of them pull the trigger?

The men didn't move with gazes locked. Both of them had steady hands, used to holding guns. There wasn't a tremble in either of them.

"Why did you do it?" Eddie's voice was hoarse, but his gaze didn't waver, and neither did his aim.

"It was an accident," Haller replied. "She called me to come get her because she'd run out of money, couldn't afford a bus ticket. When I got there, I found her hitching on Atticus Line. I pulled over and she told me to go home because she'd changed her mind."

"So you killed her?" Eddie's voice threatened to crack.

"Like I said, it was an accident. I tried to force her into the car. She fought me. I was goddamned mad. She'd been a problem her whole life, running wild, getting into trouble, just like her mother. She got high and got pregnant and stole my money. So what if she said she was turning her life around? She was probably lying. So I grabbed her, held her down, even though she was screaming. I was so goddamned mad. I'd had enough. Everything went wrong, and then she was dead. I took her things and I got out of there."

He'd left her—left his own daughter, dead by the side of the road. But first he'd taken off her jacket and thrown it away, then ripped the tag out of her shirt. I'd written my name on my clothing tags plenty of times as I traveled. When you used communal laundry facilities in hostels or split the cost of a laundromat with someone else, it was the easiest way to determine whose clothes were whose.

John Haller had stripped his daughter of her identity, then left her there. She hadn't been found for weeks.

"You're Jeremy, aren't you?" Haller said. Police lights flashed through the front window, and I could hear voices in the summer breeze blowing in. Someone was shouting that we should come out. "You're her boy. I can see it in your eyes, in your face. You look just like her. She sent you for me, because she never left. She was never gone, all these years. Part of me knew it. I've been waiting. I thought she'd come for me herself, but she sent you instead."

"I should shoot you," Eddie said in a voice so cold it made fear go up my spine.

"You could," Haller agreed, the gun never trembling in his grip. "But you might not kill me with one shot. And then I'd shoot *her.*" He meant me. "Are you going to take that risk? You think I care, Jeremy? I got terminal cancer. You shoot me now, you'll save me some hospital bills. That's all you'll do."

"Why?" Eddie said. "She was my mother. Why did you throw her away like she was trash?"

"Because she was trash," John Haller said. "So am I. What do you think that makes you?"

The front door banged open and Officer Kal Syed came in, his gun drawn. "Drop your weapons," he said calmly. "Both of you. Now."

Neither man moved. Their gazes never wavered.

"Your move, son," John Haller said softly.

Eddie's hands were steady on the rifle.

Then John Haller pulled the trigger.

CHAPTER FORTY-THREE

THREE MONTHS LATER

I rolled down the window as I drove, letting the cool autumn breeze blow into the car. Led Zeppelin played on the radio, coming from a classic rock station that had just come into range. I took a deep breath, letting the music relax me.

I moved to the right lane and eased off the gas. According to the map, the exit was close. Five minutes, maybe ten. Then I saw the sign.

COLDLAKE FALLS. 2 MILES.

I waited for something to bubble up through me at the sight of those words—fear, anger, anything. My hands tightened a little on the wheel, but that was all. I was going back to Coldlake Falls. I was ready.

After everything that had happened, it was time to go back.

I wasn't in Eddie's Pontiac this time. That car had too many memories, and the smell had never dissipated. Today, I was driving a Cutlass, and if I missed that Pontiac now and then, I never said it aloud.

I turned the radio down. "Wake up," I said.

Silence from the passenger seat, and then Eddie stretched. "Where are we?"

"About to take the exit."

He ran his good hand through his hair, rubbed it over the short beard he'd grown. "Jesus, did I sleep the whole way?"

"Most of it. You were tired."

He looked out the window, watching the scenery go by. He was wearing dark gray sweatpants and a matching sweatshirt, tennis shoes on his feet. He had lost weight in the last three months—most of it muscle. He hadn't been able to train with an arm broken in two places, the bone smashed by a bullet, and his running regime had been replaced by walks. Some of his walks lasted for hours.

Now, with his arm just out of its cast and sling, he wanted to train again, though the process would take time. It didn't matter to me that Eddie had lost his army bulk, that he was slimmer now, that he had let his beard grow in. To me, he was still beautiful.

"I don't feel anything," he said. "Do you?"

"No." I signaled and pulled into the turnoff. "Maybe soon."

Eddie shook his head. "We would have felt it by now. Felt something."

"I honestly don't know," I said.

We turned off the interstate. There was a four-lane road with a sign for Coldlake Falls—and just past the sign, another turnoff onto a narrow two-lane road with no sign. Atticus Line. This was where we'd taken a wrong turn that night in July.

Eddie and I said nothing as I sped past Atticus Line, leaving it behind us and taking the main road into Coldlake Falls.

Eddie took my hand and kissed the back of it, his beard scratching my skin.

"We should park somewhere," I said.

He laughed softly. "You're never going to stop suggesting that."

"One of these days, you'll give in."

The last three months had been hard. John Haller had shot Eddie, and Kal Syed had shot John Haller. They'd had to do surgery to put Eddie's arm back together. Haller had died within an hour without saying another word.

We didn't know why Haller had done anything he'd done—if it was true he'd killed his daughter by accident, if so why he'd left her body by the road, why he'd filed a missing person's report after so much time, why he'd come to Rose's place to kill us. We didn't know why he'd done something so obviously crazy, something he wouldn't get away with.

Haller had no criminal record and no history of strange behavior, though he'd had a decades-long drinking problem that all of his friends knew about. His autopsy had shown that what he told us was true—he was suffering from a form of brain cancer that had been diagnosed only weeks before he died, much too late, and as a result was going to kill him. His final act of shooting at us was ascribed to the cancer affecting his impulse control and causing violent tendencies.

Eddie had come out of surgery, and a few days later we'd gone home and the story was over.

I cared for Eddie the best I could in our little apartment while he recovered. I lost my job at the bowling alley, but I got a new job as a receptionist at an accountant's office, where the hours were better and all I had to do was look pretty and answer phones. I was good at both of those things. I was also good with numbers, as it turned out, so with my boss's help I had started a bookkeeping course at night school. When I finished a few months from now, my boss wanted to hire me.

Eddie wanted to go back to work. His boss loved him—we got our new car through the garage—but it was impossible to fix cars with one arm. So his boss had moved Eddie to a manager job, dealing with bills, suppliers, hiring, and advertising. Eddie was a novice, but he was smart and he was willing to learn. Lately, Paul had started talking about having Eddie take over the entire business when he retired in a few years.

Eddie hadn't had any nightmares for the last three months. But sometimes he had shadows behind his eyes. It haunted him that he had never known his mother, and it haunted him even more to know what she had become after she died. In life, she'd been troubled and trying to turn her life around—but in death, thwarted of her chance at life, she had become something else, an entity that wanted other young people to suffer the same fate she had. The smiling young woman in the photographs had taken so many lives, and she had tried to kill me. Eddie wrestled with that. There was no easy answer.

We drove into town, passing the hospital where Rhonda Jean had died, passing through downtown. Eddie read aloud the directions I had written down, and they took us to a spot just past the center of town where a small church stood. Behind the church was a cemetery, a peaceful stretch of green.

As I parked, we saw a familiar blue car in the parking lot. Two teenage girls were leaning on it.

"You're late," Beatrice Snell said.

"You said noon," I replied. I looked around. "Did we need all of the subterfuge? You really think someone might be following you?"

Gracie shrugged. "You can't be too careful. Let's take a walk. We have lots to tell you."

The trees were in full color at this point in October, wild yellows and flaming reds. It was a perfect day, with the smell of damp leaves beneath our feet as we took the first path into the cemetery. "All right, we're here," I said as Eddie walked beside me. "Go."

"First of all, Trish Cho," Beatrice said. "From everything we can tell, she's perfectly fine."

I felt something loosen in my chest. It hadn't taken long for the Snell sisters to find Trish, who was a dentist with a nice husband and a nine-year-old daughter. The sisters had taken turns watching her house for a while, noting as she left for work and came home again, seemingly innocent and unbothered by almost killing me. Either she was a psychopath who remembered that night and felt no guilt, or she had no memory of it at all.

None of us had ever given her name to the police, so Trish Cho could go back to her life, never the wiser.

"Okay, good," I said. "What else?"

The sisters looked at each other. "Um, John Haller," Gracie said. She glanced at Eddie. "Your grandfather."

"It's okay." Eddie flexed the wrist of his bad arm. "Go ahead."

"Did you find the adoption records?" Beatrice asked.

"It's a long process," Eddie replied. "I've talked to my parents— my adoptive parents—and they've put in a request to unseal the records. It has to go through a bunch of approvals, and even then, it might not happen."

"So you might not get to know," Beatrice said.

"I know," Eddie answered her. "Shannon was my mother. Records or no records, I know."

Beatrice nodded. "Okay, well. Gracie figured out how he found you guys that day, if it matters."

"I overheard a conversation at the police station," Gracie said. "I still volunteer there, even though I'm not in trouble with the tickets anymore. Anyway, I heard one of the officers saying that Kyle Petersen took a phone call that day from a man wanting information about the car parked in front of his house. Officer Syed had come to the guy's door, and this other car had been with him, parked behind the cruiser, so he thought the car was from Coldlake. He gave the license plate and Kyle looked it up."

"Our car," Eddie said. "We took Robbie's car that day."

"Right," Gracie said. "So Kyle told Haller the car was registered to Rose's address and gave it to him—just handed out the information, no questions asked. Haller said thanks and hung up. I think Kyle got in trouble for the whole thing, because he left the PD. There's a rumor he went to Indiana."

That filled in one of the blanks in the story. We hadn't known how John Haller had found Rose's address, and no one on the Coldlake Falls PD was willing to tell us. Now we knew why.

We were walking past the center of the cemetery. There were half a dozen people here, visiting their loved ones' graves on a sunny autumn Saturday. Beatrice and Gracie seemed to be walking with a destination in mind. "Where are we going?" I asked.

"Max Shandler," Gracie said, ignoring me. She flipped her hair off her shoulders. "It was super hard to get information, even though we both worked on it."

"I had to volunteer as a candy striper so I could try and access hospital records," Beatrice complained. "It *sucked*."

"No one wants to give out information," Gracie agreed. "His file wasn't kept in the records room like the others. I can't even get hold of a Post-it Note with Rhonda Jean's name on it. It's like the entire case has been locked in a vault."

"Still, we got a few things," Beatrice said. "One of the nurses at the hospital told me that Max Shandler had brain cancer."

I felt a chill at the back of my neck. "Like John Haller," I said.

"Exactly," Beatrice agreed. "Weird, right? Not diagnosed or anything, like he had no idea. But our hospital here is small, and we don't have a cancer center, so Max got sent to Grand Rapids. I think he's really sick."

"Officer Syed told me that he tried to visit Max Shandler and got turned away," Gracie said.

"Kal tried to visit?" I asked.

Gracie nodded. A flush stained her cheeks, and I realized it was at the mention of Kal. I couldn't blame her for having a crush, even though Kal was married. "He talks to me sometimes," Gracie said. "He's pretty cool. I think he has some idea that there's weird stuff happening in this town. Anyway, he had some questions for Max, so he drove to Grand Rapids one day. Max is under security because he's charged with murder, even though he's too sick to go to prison. But Officer Syed assumed he'd be let in, since he's police. He wasn't. He was turned away."

"He isn't in a normal hospital," Beatrice added. "He's in some kind of exclusive, private clinic, under lockdown. Which is weird, because I don't think the government is paying for that, and I didn't think the Shandlers had that kind of money."

"Maybe they came up with it short term," Gracie said. "Max might not last to the end of the year."

"Maybe," Beatrice said. The word hung in the air, unanswerable. None of it made any sense. Why was a man charged with murder being kept in a private hospital instead of in prison, no matter how sick he was? Who was paying the bill?

Detective Quentin would know the answers. Though I was sure if I waited a thousand years, he'd never tell.

"We're here," Beatrice said, and suddenly I knew where they had taken us.

We stood in front of a headstone, newly placed. SHANNON HALLER, it said, along with her date of birth and her approximate date of death—March 1976.

The dental records had proven it. The Coldlake Falls PD, led by Kal, had found Shannon Haller's dental records and matched them to the X-rays taken from the unidentified body. She was Shannon.

She'd been buried here in 1976, with a headstone stating only: JANE DOE, FOUND APRIL 1976. REST IN PEACE. Now they had her name.

We stood there for a long time, silent. Eddie rubbed a hand over his beard, his eyes tender and watery. Finally, he said, "Who paid for the new headstone?"

Beatrice smiled. "A local community organization. I raised some of the funds myself. It's called the Officer Robbie Jones Memorial Foundation. Want to guess who runs it?"

CHAPTER FORTY-FOUR

R ose's windows had been repaired, but I still felt a chill as we got out of the car and I looked at the front window. I could still see John Haller climbing through it, his gaze on Eddie as I lunged with the knife in my hand.

Rose opened the door with a look of surprise on her face. "Oh," she said, and I could have sworn she looked almost pleased. "It's you two."

"We came to thank you for the headstone," Eddie said.

She flushed, a full-on blush that went from her forehead to her chin. She turned away to hide it. "You want some Bits and Bites? I got a bowl of it here."

We stepped into the main room. It was strange to be here, where so much had happened. The carpet had been replaced—it had likely been too bloodstained to be cleaned. As Rose got the bowl from the kitchen, I walked to the bedroom door and looked in, noting that the plaster where the bullets had hit was fixed.

"You got rid of your picture," Eddie said in the main room.

I followed where he was pointing. The portrait of Charles and Diana was gone from the wall. There was new plaster there, but no new portrait.

"A bullet hit it," Rose said. "Hit Diana right in the middle of the forehead. It was upsetting. I'd have been happier if the bullet had hit Charles. I don't care if anything happens to him. I don't like the idea of anything happening to Diana, even just a picture of her."

"I guess you need a new one," I said.

"I don't know." Rose put the bowl on the counter. "Maybe I'll redecorate."

I walked to the counter, and Eddie took a seat on one of the kitchen chairs.

Rose's gaze followed him, sharp. "Are you okay?" she asked.

"Yeah, Mrs. Jones. I'm okay." He raised his left arm, flexed the fingers. "It aches a lot, but they say that will get better with time. And I can't do a push-up to save my life."

Rose sniffed. "Too bad. I need help raking leaves."

Eddie smiled at her, one of his real smiles. And Rose almost— almost—smiled back. "Let's go," he said.

So the three of us went outside. In the crisp air of afternoon, we raked leaves and put them in bags. We didn't talk, and yet we did. In our way, we thanked Rose, and she thanked us. We were even.

After an hour, Eddie went into the house to wash his hands, and I turned to Rose. "I have to tell you. I saw Robbie that day."

Rose didn't even flinch. "I know you did."

"He was in the bedroom. I saw him as clear as I'm seeing you now, except he was a little transparent. He pushed me to the floor right before the first shot. He saved my life."

Rose blinked behind her glasses, looking away. "That sounds like him."

"Eddie saw him rounding the house into the backyard once. I'd seen him before, too. Heard him. But it wasn't frightening. It was . . . warm, somehow. Really nice."

A tear rolled down Rose's cheek. "It's wonderful, isn't it?"

"You've seen him?" I asked.

She sighed. "He's sorry about how he left me. I know that much. I tell him it wasn't his fault, but he feels bad, so he stays." She dashed the tear away and looked at me again. "He'll be here until I go, too. And that's just fine with me."

CHAPTER FORTY-FIVE

Are we lost?" I asked.

Eddie had taken over the driving for the trip home, but we hadn't left Coldlake Falls yet. Instead of taking the turn for the road back to the interstate, we were driving through a neighborhood I didn't recognize.

"We're not lost," Eddie replied. "Not this time. There's something I want to see first."

The houses were larger on this street, newer, the lawns trim and green. This was a well-to-do neighborhood for Coldlake Falls, removed from the strip malls and corner hair salons of downtown. It wasn't far, I thought, from the Snell house. "What are we looking for?" I asked.

"An address I got. We won't go in. I just want to see it once before we go."

I frowned at him, but Eddie didn't look troubled. He looked

sure and confident as he drove, as if he knew exactly where he was going.

"All right, keep your mysteries," I said. "I'll follow along."

"You'll find it interesting. I promise."

I had no idea who we knew, besides the Snell sisters, who would live in one of these houses. Then I saw a man standing in his front yard, and I understood.

Detective Quentin had a Saturday off. He wore dark blue jeans and a white tee with a blue button-down over it, unbuttoned. He even wore sneakers, which were brand-new and blindingly clean. There was a line of tied-up leaf bags along the edge of his lawn, and he was unlooping a garden hose to start watering.

"I just wanted to see where he lived," Eddie said as we slowed the car. "I'm curious about him. Now I know."

Quentin caught sight of us almost instantly, his blue eyes fixing on Eddie and me. He put down the hose and motioned to us to pull the car in. We'd been busted. Eddie pulled up to the curb and rolled his window down, putting the car in park but not turning it off.

"Nice day, isn't it?" Quentin said as he walked toward us. Behind him, I saw children's toys lined up against the garage, a basketball and a bike. I had never pictured Detective Quentin with children.

"Very nice," Eddie said easily, as if he hadn't just been caught scoping out the man's house like a potential burglar.

"It's good to see you, Mr. Carter." Quentin also spoke like we were neighbors passing the time of day. "I trust your arm is healing nicely."

"It is, thanks," Eddie said.

"Have you satisfied your curiosity? My wife took the children grocery shopping. I'm to have the yard done by the time they get back. It's my assignment."

"You have a very nice home," I said politely, trying to smooth over the awkwardness.

Quentin blinked at me. "It's nice to see you, too, Mrs. Carter, and you needn't feel strange. I always thought you two would come back at least once. There's still unfinished business between us."

He was right. There were questions that had never been answered, things I still didn't understand about what had happened. I leaned toward Eddie's window and looked into those icy blue eyes, which were so much more relaxed than I'd ever seen them. Was it an act? Or was the chilly, heartless way he'd treated us before an act? Neither? Both?

"Are you ever going to tell us the truth?" I asked him.

"About what?" Quentin asked.

"About why you were so focused on us in your murder investigation, even after you knew we didn't kill anyone."

I expected the cold rudeness he'd shown us before, but Quentin stepped forward and leaned a forearm on Eddie's open window. "I'll tell you a story," he said.

My breath paused. Eddie went still.

"Once upon a time, a man was dying," Quentin said. "I won't tell you the year, the location, or the man's name. The man had brain cancer, and he was in hospice care. In the last hours of his life, he confessed to a murder."

We were silent, listening.

"The man told the attending nurse that he'd picked up a hitch-hiker outside of Coldlake Falls one night—a young man. The dying man had been to a family barbecue out of town, and he had a cooler in the back of his car that had had ice in it. It also had an ice pick in it, brought with him so that he could break up the ice at the barbecue. The man told the hitchhiker that he needed to pull over for a moment. Then he took the ice pick from the cooler. When the hitchhiker got out of the car and tried to run, the man killed him with it."

I fixated on Quentin's strangely handsome face, his words hitting me like bricks. "Tom Monahan," I breathed. "Killed in 1982."

"The dying man told the nurse that he had forgotten about the murder until that very moment, when he was dying," Quentin said, ignoring me. "As his life ended, he suddenly had a rush of memories. In my opinion, deathbed confessions are a gift to law enforcement—a case gets closed, there's no expense of a trial, and the guilty party leaves this world without our having to decide his punishment. The problem with this particular confession was that the dying man also spoke of a lot of memories he could not possibly have had—memories that simply could not be real, like recalling being pregnant and giving birth to a son. So the obvious lies colored the truth of the murder confession."

Somewhere down the street, a dog barked and a child laughed. It sounded like it was a world away.

"Still," Quentin continued, "lies or not, the nurse reported the confession to the police. The man was dead by then, of course, and his likely delirium meant the information was of low value. Still, the report wound its way through various law enforcement agencies, and eventually, it came to me. So I came to Coldlake Falls."

"Why you?" Eddie asked.

"You ask a lot of questions, both of you. I'm not going to tell you everything—you need to accept that. Suffice it to say that the report did come to me, and I came here. I found the murder the man was referring to. The dates matched up, as did the murder weapon, which was very specific. But this man couldn't have done any of the other murders that came after on Atticus Line, because he was dead. As I investigated, I began to see that something was at work that I didn't fully understand—that maybe I couldn't possibly understand. Still, it was at work here. So I stayed here, waiting for it to show itself in a way I could comprehend so I could stop it. I have a great deal of patience. I solved other cases and did my job. But always, I waited."

"You knew," I said. "About the Lost Girl. The entire time, you knew."

"What I knew, Mrs. Carter, was that there is more in heaven and earth than is dreamt of in my philosophy. When a single killer is ruled out in a series of murders, the only answer is that there are multiple killers. What would make multiple people in a small town commit murder and never get caught? What indeed? And then you two came along." He looked from me to Eddie. "You were the only ones to find a victim and speak to her before she died. You were almost witnesses—you probably missed the attack by mere minutes. When you weren't sure how you got here, Mr. Carter, going in the wrong direction from where you needed to be, then I knew you had been called here. For what purpose, I needed to understand."

Eddie bit his lip and looked away from Quentin.

"I looked at all of the possibilities," Quentin said. "It was possible, Mr. Carter, that you had killed Katharine O'Connor while on leave and had no memory of it. The dates lined up. It was also possible that you had been called back here, that both of you had killed Rhonda Jean Breckwith and had no memory of that, either. I had to work with what I'd been given, as crazy as it was, so I did. I looked into your medical records for brain cancer. Because I was looking for a pattern." He leveled his blue gaze back at me. "When I could find nothing about you, Mrs. Carter, I became even more concerned. Until I looked at the recent phone records from Mrs. Jones's phone line and saw an unusual long-distance call."

"Jesus," Eddie breathed.

"Then," Quentin said, "the two of you requested a meeting with me and you handed over the answer, complete with Shannon Haller's name and her photo. I knew then that she had never been willing to reveal herself to me, no matter how hard I tried. She was only willing to reveal herself to you. Because I'd kept you in Coldlake Falls, you'd followed her trail and done all of the work for me."

"You told us you didn't believe us," I said. "You said we had no evidence, that what we brought you was worthless. You told us to leave town."

"Because I was done with you," Quentin said. "I had no use for you anymore. I still have no use for you. I have moved on to other methods."

"Like what?"

"You've talked to the Snell sisters, I assume? They're likely part of the reason you came to town today."

Eddie and I both stared at him, shocked.

Quentin looked smug. "Of course I know about the Snell sisters. I knew from the first day Gracie Snell took photocopies from the file room at the local police station. They're not in trouble, at least from me. For a while, I hoped they'd come to a solution I couldn't see, but they didn't. They are just two teenage girls who are smart and difficult to predict. I should get the FBI to recruit them when they're old enough, though I have no idea if they'll say yes. I'd rather have them working for our government than against it."

Beatrice and Gracie as FBI agents. It was possible. It was also possible they'd laugh at the idea and never think about it again.

"The Snell sisters probably told you about Max Shandler," Quentin said. "He is in a private facility, guarded by security—dying, as it happens, of brain cancer. He has no memory of killing Rhonda Jean, a fact that he has repeated over and over again, and which I believe. I will be alerted when his final hours are near, and I will go to him. I will watch his memories come back. I will record every single one. And before Max Shandler dies, I believe I'll finally have the chance to interview Shannon Haller."

"Oh my God," I murmured.

Quentin was looking at Eddie. "I don't often break rules, Mr. Carter, but given the extraordinary circumstances, I could make an exception. It's possible I can get you to Max Shandler's bedside with me before he dies. I'll do it if you want, but if I'm being honest, I don't recommend it. I have a lot of questions for Shannon, and none of them will be pretty."

Eddie shook his head. "I don't want to be there. The killer—that isn't her. I don't want to meet that version of her. The Shannon that was my mother—I'll never get to see her again. I've come to terms with that."

Quentin's voice was gentle, almost sympathetic. "I understand. Is there anything you want me to ask her when I get the chance?"

What could Eddie ask her? *Did you love me? Did I matter to you? Would you have come back for me if you'd lived?* He already knew the answers. He shook his head. "Just tell her . . . tell her I'm okay, if you can. Tell her it worked out for me in the end. Tell her I'll be just fine."

"All right," Quentin said.

"And give her a message for me. Tell her to leave Trish alone."

Quentin's blue eyes lit with cold curiosity. "Who is Trish? What does that mean?"

"If you want to know, you can ask Shannon," Eddie said. "But it's important. She needs to leave Trish alone."

The detective wasn't going to drop it without questions. I wondered if he would figure out who Trish might be and why she mattered. But the thought of Trish dying like the others when she hadn't killed anyone made me sick. It was my fault, even though I hadn't intended it. Eddie was right. Shannon needed to leave Trish alone.

"Fine," Quentin said, his voice returning to its usual cold tone. "No one will ever believe this. If you repeat anything I've told you, no one will believe you, either. But I'll know. Before Max Shandler dies, I'll know everything. You can count on that." He tapped his fingers against the car doorframe. "As you leave town, Mr. and Mrs. Carter, you should drive down Atticus Line. I think you'll find it interesting."

"Is she gone?" Eddie's voice was hoarse. "I didn't feel anything as we came to town. I haven't felt anything, being here. Nothing at all. Is she gone?"

"I believe so," Quentin said. "Though of course, should I be wrong, I'll be here waiting. If for some reason she comes back, I'll be here. You won't see her on Atticus Line, but you'll see something else—the other, final part of my investigation."

"What do you mean?" I asked.

"There have to be more bodies. Don't you agree? I don't think we found them all. But soon, I'll know for sure." Quentin stood up. "My family will be home soon. Goodbye, Mr. and Mrs. Carter. Have a good life." He turned and walked into the house.

We didn't speak. Eddie put the car in gear. Detective Quentin didn't come back out of the house as we pulled away.

Twenty minutes later, we were parked on the shoulder of Atticus Line, looking at the sign that had been placed at the side of the road.

"I can't believe it," Eddie said. "This seems like a bad idea."

"Terrible," I agreed.

A car passed us, and then another. There was traffic here now. The breeze blew in the trees on an innocent weekend afternoon. Atticus Line was peaceful, bucolic. No longer haunted. There were no lights or strange winds, no sudden thunderstorms. In fact, it was beautiful.

Except for the sign.

It was ten feet high, at least six feet wide, overpowering the road. It had a drawing depicting a building of cream brick and glass, with gaudy brass-colored doors. In the drawing, the sprawling building was surrounded by a landscape of parking lot. The lettering across the top read: WATCH THIS SITE! FUTURE LOCATION OF THE COLDLAKE FALLS MALL!

"A mall," Eddie said, shocked. "They're building a mall."

I tried not to shudder. There was no money, no power on earth that would get me to walk through the fake-brass doors of the Coldlake Falls Mall. Not now, not ever.

"This is what Quentin was talking about," Eddie said.

"What do you mean?" I asked.

He pointed up and down Atticus Line. "In order to build this mall, they're going to dig. Everywhere."

There have to be more bodies. Don't you agree?

When they found them, Detective Quentin would be waiting. Whoever was out there, lost and forgotten—he'd find them and remember them again.

Eddie started the car and put it in gear. He took my hand in his. And we drove away.

ACKNOWLEDGMENTS

Thanks to the team at Berkley who put so much dedicated work into my books, especially Michelle Vega, Danielle Perez, Claire Zion, and Danielle Keir. Thanks to the marketing, sales, and PR staff who do such a stellar job. Thanks to the art department for the covers that hit it out of the park every time. Thanks to the copy editors and proofreaders who catch my embarrassing mistakes. Thanks to Orli Moscowitz and the amazing team at PRH Audio for bringing my books to life in audio. Thanks to my agent, Pam Hopkins, who believed in me from the very beginning, when she received my paper query letter in her slush pile.

Thanks to my husband, Adam, and thanks to my family, for being in my corner. Thanks to Molly and Stephanie for being my best friends.

Thanks to the booksellers and librarians who recommend my books. Thanks to the reviewers, Bookstagrammers, BookTokers, and other excited readers who pass my books around. Thanks to the readers who send me kind messages, fascinating insights, and encouragement. Thanks to anyone who took the time out of their day to come to one of my signings. I dedicated this book to readers, and I'm thanking them, too. Thank you, readers. Without you, books don't happen.

MURDER
ROAD

SIMONE ST. JAMES

READERS GUIDE

DISCUSSION QUESTIONS

1. Newlyweds April and Eddie find themselves under suspicion after trying to help a woman who was gravely injured. Have you attempted to help someone and it didn't turn out how you planned? Did the experience change how you react in those situations?

2. April and Eddie got married after knowing each other for five months. Have you ever made an impulsive decision? How did it turn out? If you haven't, do you ever wish you could?

3. After a difficult childhood, April has aimed to live an anonymous life, trying hard not to stand out or be noticed. What do you think of the choices she made prior to meeting Eddie? Would you have done anything differently in her situation?

4. Both April and Eddie are keeping secrets from each other.

How do these secrets affect their relationship? Do you think it is acceptable to have some secrets in a marriage or partnership?

5. The urban legend of the Lost Girl plays a significant role in the story. Do you know of any local urban legends? Are there any in particular that scare you?

6. Both April's relationship with her mother and Eddie's relationship with his shaped their lives. How do these relationships differ? How do they affect April and Eddie's relationships with each other?

7. After serving in the military, Eddie suffers from PTSD. Have you or anyone you know been affected by PTSD? Do you feel that it's an issue that has gotten enough attention/treatment?

8. The teenage Snell sisters are dedicated to finding out everything about the unsolved murders in Coldlake Falls. What do you think of their investigative prowess? Is there a topic you obsessed over as a teenager or an area of interest that you considered yourself an expert in?

9. Detective Quentin is extremely tough on both April and Eddie and uses some questionable tactics to get the answers he's looking for. Do you approve of his methods? Why or why not?

10. *Murder Road* is set in 1995. Do you have a decade you feel a particular nostalgia for? Or one that you distinctly didn't love? Does the music or fashion of the time influence your decision?

Keep reading for an excerpt from

THE SUN DOWN MOTEL

FELL, NEW YORK
NOVEMBER 1982
VIV

The night it all ended, Vivian was alone.

That was fine with her. She preferred it. It was something she'd discovered, working the night shift at this place in the middle of nowhere: Being with people was easy, but being alone was hard. Especially being alone in the dark. The person who could be truly alone, in the company of no one but oneself and one's own thoughts—that person was stronger than anyone else. More ready. More prepared.

Still, she pulled into the parking lot of the Sun Down Motel in Fell, New York, and paused, feeling the familiar beat of fear. She sat in her beat-up Cavalier, the key in the ignition, the heat and the radio on, her coat huddled around her shoulders. She looked at the glowing blue and yellow sign, the two stories of rooms in two long stripes in the shape of an L, and thought, *I don't want to go in there. But I will.* She was ready, but she was still afraid. It was 10:59 p.m.

She felt like crying. She felt like screaming. She felt sick.

I don't want to go in there.

But I will. Because I always do.

Outside, two drops of half-frozen rain hit the windshield. A truck droned by on the road in the rearview mirror. The clock ticked over to eleven o'clock, and the news came on the radio. Another minute and she'd be late, but she didn't care. No one would fire her. No one cared if she came to work. The Sun Down had few customers, none of whom would notice if the night girl was late. It was often so quiet that an observer would think that nothing ever happened here.

Viv Delaney knew better.

The Sun Down only looked empty. But it wasn't.

With cold fingers, she pulled down the driver's-side visor. She touched her hair, which she'd had cut short, a sharp style that ended below her earlobes and was sprayed out for volume. She checked her eye makeup—not the frosty kind, like some girls wore, but a soft lavender purple. It looked a little like bruises. You could streak it with yellow and orange to create a days-old-bruise effect, but she hadn't bothered with that tonight. Just the purple on the delicate skin of her lids, meeting the darker line of her eyeliner and lashes. Why had she put makeup on at all? She couldn't remember.

On the radio, they talked about a body. A girl found in a ditch off Melborn Road, ten miles from here. Not that *here* was anywhere— just a motel on the side of a two-lane highway leading out of Fell and into the nothingness of upstate New York and eventually Canada. But if you took the two-lane for a mile and made a right at the single light dangling from an overhead wire, and followed that road to another and another, you'd be where the girl's body was found. A girl named Tracy Waters, last seen leaving a friend's house in a neighboring town. Eighteen years old, stripped naked and dumped in a ditch. They'd found her body two days after her parents reported her missing.

As she sat in her car, twenty-year-old Viv Delaney's hands shook as she listened to the story. She thought about what it must be like to lie naked as the half-frozen rain pelted your helpless skin. How horribly cold that would be. How it was always girls who ended up stripped and dead like roadkill. How it didn't matter how afraid or how careful you were—it could always be you.

Especially here. It could always be you.

Her gaze went to the motel, to the reflection of the gaudy lit-up blue and yellow sign blinking endlessly in the darkness. VACANCY. CABLE TV! VACANCY. CABLE TV!

Even after three months in this place, she could still be scared. Awfully, perfectly scared, her thoughts skittering up the back of her neck and around her brain in panic. *I'm alone for the next eight hours, alone in the dark. Alone with her and the others.*

And despite herself, Viv turned the key so the heat and the radio—still talking about Tracy Waters—went off. Lifted her chin and pushed open the driver's-side door. Stepped out into the cold.

She hunched deeper into her nylon coat and started across the parking lot. She was wearing jeans and a pair of navy blue sneakers with white laces, the soles too thin for the cold and damp. The rain wet her hair, and the wind pushed it out of place. She walked across the lot toward the door that said OFFICE.

Inside the office, Johnny was standing behind the counter,

zipping up his coat over his big stomach. He'd probably seen her from the window in the door. "Are you late?" he asked, though there was a clock on the wall behind him.

"Five minutes," Viv argued back, unzipping her own coat. Her stomach felt tight, queasy now that she was inside. *I want to go home.*

But where was home? Fell wasn't home. Neither was Illinois, where she was born. When she left home for the last time, after the final screaming fight with her mother, she'd supposedly been headed to New York to become an actress. But that, like everything else in her life to that point, had been a part she was playing, a story. She had no idea how to become a New York actress—the story had enraged her mother, which had made it good enough. What Viv had wanted, more than anything, was to simply be in motion, to go.

So she'd gone. And she'd ended up here. Fell would have to be home for now.

"Mrs. Bailey is in room two-seventeen," Johnny said, running down the motel's few guests. "She already made a liquor run, so expect a phone call anytime."

"Great," Viv said. Mrs. Bailey came to the Sun Down to drink, probably because if she did it at home she'd get in some kind of trouble. She made drunken phone calls to the front desk to make demands she usually forgot about. "Anyone else?"

"The couple on their way to Florida checked out," Johnny said. "We've had two prank phone calls, both heavy breathing. Stupid teenagers. And I wrote a note to Janice about the door to number one-oh-three. There's something wrong with it. It keeps blowing open in the wind, even when I lock it."

"It always does that," Viv said. "You told Janice about it a week ago." Janice was the motel's owner, and Viv hadn't seen her in weeks. Months, maybe. She didn't come to the motel if she didn't have to, and she certainly didn't come at night. She left Vivian's paychecks in an envelope on the desk, and all communication was handled with notes. Even the motel's owner didn't spend time here if she could help it.

"Well, she should fix the door," Johnny said. "I mean, it's strange, right? I locked it."

"Sure," Viv said. "It's strange."

She was used to this. No one else who worked at the motel saw what she saw or experienced what she did. The things she saw only happened in the middle of the night. The day shift and the evening shift employees had no idea.

"Hopefully no one else will check in," Johnny said, pulling the hood of his jacket over his head. "Hopefully it'll be quiet."

It's never quiet, Viv thought, but she said, "Yes, hopefully."

Viv watched him walk out of the office, listened to his car start up and drive away. Johnny was thirty-six and lived with his mother. Viv pictured him going home, maybe watching TV before going to bed. A guy who had never made much of himself, living a relatively normal life, free of the kind of fear Viv was feeling. A life in which he never thought about Tracy Waters, except to vaguely recall her name from the radio.

Maybe it was just her who was going crazy.

The quiet settled in, broken only by the occasional sound of the traffic on Number Six Road and the wind in the trees behind the motel. It was now 11:12. The clock on the wall behind the desk ticked over to 11:13.

She hung her jacket on the hook in the corner. From another hook she took a navy blue polyester vest with the words *Sun Down Motel* embroidered on the left breast and shrugged it on over her white blouse. She pulled out the hard wooden chair behind the counter and sat in it. She surveyed the scarred, stained desktop quickly: jar of pens and pencils, the black square that made a clacking sound when you dragged the handle back and forth over a credit card to make a carbon impression, puke-colored rotary phone. In the middle of the desk was a large, flat book, where guests were to write their information and sign their names when checking in. The guest book was open to November 1982.

Pulling a notebook from her purse, Viv pulled a pen from between its pages, opened the notebook on the desk, and wrote.

Nov. 29

Door to number 103 has begun to open again. Prank calls. No one here. Tracy Waters is dead.

A sound came from outside, and she paused, her head half raised. A bang, and then another one. Rhythmic and wild. The door to number 103 blowing open and hitting the wall in the wind. Again.

For a second, Viv closed her eyes. The fear came over her in a wave, but she was too far in it now. She was already here. She had to be ready. The Sun Down had claimed her for the night.

She lowered the pen again.

What if everything I've seen, everything I think, is true? Because I think it is.

Her eyes glanced to the guest book, took in the names there. She paused as the clock on the wall behind her shoulder ticked on, then wrote again.

The ghosts are awake tonight. They're restless. I think this will be over soon. Her hand trembled, and she tried to keep it steady. *I'm so sorry, Tracy. I've failed.*

A small sound escaped the back of her throat, but she bit it down into silence. She put the pen down and rubbed her eyes, some of the pretty lavender eyeshadow coming off on her fingertips.

It was November 29, 1982, 11:24 p.m.

By three o'clock in the morning, Viv Delaney had vanished.

That was the beginning.

Photo by Perrywinkle Photography

Simone St. James is the *New York Times* bestselling and award-winning author of *Murder Road*, *The Book of Cold Cases*, *The Sun Down Motel*, and *The Broken Girls*. She wrote her first ghost story, about a haunted library, when she was in high school, and spent twenty years behind the scenes in the television business before leaving to write full-time.

VISIT THE AUTHOR ONLINE

SimoneStJames.com

 SimoneStJames

 SimoneStJames

 SimoneStJames

Learn more about this book
and other titles from
New York Times bestselling author

SIMONE
ST. JAMES

SCAN ME
or visit
prh.com/simonestjames